NILE GREEN

NILE

GREEN

David Jordan

THE JOHN DAY COMPANY
An Intext Publisher

NEW YORK

Library of Congress Cataloging in Publication Data

Jordan, David.
    Nile green.

    I.   Title.
PZ4.J8177Ni3 [PR6060.O624]   823'.9'14   73-16176
ISBN 0-381-98259-9

Second Impression, 1974

The John Day Company, 257 Park Avenue South
New York, N.Y. 10010.

Printed in the United States of America.

O this false soul of Egypt! this grave charm,
Whose eye beck'd forth my wars, and call'd
   them home,
Whose bosom was my crownet, my chief
   end,
Like a right gipsy hath at fast and loose
Beguil'd me, to the very heart of loss.

Antony and Cleopatra, Act IV, Scene xii

For D., who is not Sue

'You won't know Shahsavar,' she said, after the boy had brought the drinks out onto the terrace where the vines dappled the warm stone steps and the lizards flickered across the unshaded wall. 'It's a small village on the Caspian. A tiny place. The wind comes down from the north, across the Sea from Georgia. And when there's a wind...' She shivered, over-dramatising, in the hot sunlight, then reached across quickly and laid her hand on my arm for a second, laughing at herself before I had time to protest. There was a dish of pistachio nuts on the table in front of her and she had been going through them one by one, splitting the shell with her thumbnail, squeezing the kernel from the salted skin and dropping the fibre into the breeze.

She said, 'The road goes up from Teheran. It's fantastic —across the Elburz mountains. You go up over the skyline, then over the top, and the country's completely different. The Caspian forests. Rice paddies. Wooden villages.'

'Where's the Russian frontier?' I asked. I hadn't been listening carefully until then. 'It can't be all that far.'

'Just a few miles. You'd never know you were so near.'

'Any sign of the military?'

She shook her head. 'Not any more. Some people say there are still thousands of American troops there, hidden in the Shah's hunting estates. But I don't believe it.'

I didn't quarrel. It had been a quiet frontier for years. No one, not even the Pentagon, thought the Russians were now going to come over from Astrakhan. There was nothing sinister or romantic about the Caspian. I could have left it at that.

Three UN men were sitting across the terrace with empty beer bottles stacked on the table. They looked like Norwegians. Two of them had taken their shirts off and their chests were tanned golden against the Hammarskjöld blue of their foulards. Their jeep was standing on the road beneath us and the sea was down below, a cliff's drop away.

I said, 'You've been in Teheran pretty often lately,' and tried to make it a statement rather than a question. 'Is it still worth so much of your time?' I found I couldn't avoid the question mark.

She shook her head so the silver hair clasp glinted in the sunlight. 'Less and less,' she said. 'It used to be a goldmine, but the Iranians aren't selling their family collections as they used to.'

'So you go for the drive in the snow?'

'I went up just for the day. They told me there was an estate outside this place I was talking about—Shahsavar— where the old man had some carpets which were supposed to be very special. But he turned out to be in Europe and the house locked up and then there was a bad storm in the mountains which blocked the road so I had to spend the night in the village. They gave me a bed in a tiny room behind a sort of teahouse. They weren't sure what to do with me because I was a woman and in Persia only the men count—outside Teheran anyway—despite Farah Diba. It was a terrible waste of time. You were in New York and I kept wondering whether I'd get back to Beirut in time to catch you.'

'Catch?' I asked.

There was a moment's pause. 'Yes,' she said. 'Catch.'

She pretended to look shy. Her shoulders were bare, the flesh soft and brown against the pale cotton. I said quickly, 'Why are they still selling anything at all to dealers like you? They've got plenty of money these days.'

'That's what I mean. They're not selling any longer. It's partly the Shah's fault—he made it fashionable to hang on to everything they can call Persia's heritage. Whatever that means.'

She finished her drink, took a sip from my glass and made a face. The Cyprus dusk was coming down like a judgment. There was an abrupt burst of Greek argument from the back of the house which as suddenly hushed again as though a door had closed. The air was heavy with rosemary and cicadas. Her arm was lying next to mine; our hands touched, lazily held.

I hurried on. I knew what I had to do. I realised it in that moment.

'No trouble finding buyers?' I asked. Another statement framed as a question. I went on: 'You saw the Ambassador bidding at Sotheby's the other day. I meant to tell you, he was at the exhibition the day before I left London—the Sarvestan textiles. I think you just missed it.'

The words were coming more easily than I would have imagined. I pressed ahead: 'And wasn't there a big deal last year when the Shah bought those Qazwin-style miniatures for £200,000? We have a client who told me he would have liked them...'

I slowed down and tried to overhaul what I was saying. I said 'Yes—— you know! The Garkarian collection from Lisbon. It could never be worth a couple of hundred thousand.'

She moved away from me, twisting in her chair, looking for the boy waiter behind the trellis-work.

3

'It sounds a lot,' she said; she seemed casual, almost bored. 'But they were so wonderful. I suppose the Shah thought he had to seize them when he had the chance.' She flashed her smile, wide-mouthed, at the boy who had brought fresh glasses.

'He's got the money,' I said, and tried to echo her boredom. 'But I never liked the Qazwin school myself. In fact, the Indians leave me cold. Especially the Indian provincials. But of course, I don't know enough about them. And I don't see why the Shah should be interested in the Indian stuff.'

There was a long silence. The UN men paid, stared at us, put on their shirts and roared away. The sea had turned a cold steel blue and the silver of the olive trees shaded lower and out.

'Let's eat here,' she said.

But I was a mile away, trying to fight my fuddled brain into gear. I cursed the alcohol in my bloodstream. The sweat was prickling at my chest, which was all wrong because I was feeling distinctly chilly.

It had suddenly, horribly, been so easy. I was right, I was right after all, I knew it, and I wished I wasn't. I would have given half a lifetime to be wrong and I waited again for her to speak up and say it.

She sat there silent, relaxed, at ease. She took my hand again. I checked once more. The point was so simple: that there were no Sarvestan textiles and there never had been an exhibition in London. I had invented them two minutes before—conjured them out of my imagination. As for a mountain range north of Teheran, I could vouch for that, and there was certainly a Shah in his Summer Palace at Shemran, and there may well have been a village called Shahsavar, as she claimed. But no one had recently paid £200,000 for Qazwin miniatures and there was no Garkarian in Lisbon. And as for the Qazwin school of painting, it certainly existed, and was remarkably beautiful, but it had nothing to do with India or the Indian provinces nor with anywhere a thousand miles from India. Any Iranian schoolgirl could have corrected me on that, let alone a smooth, high-breasted career woman who travelled the Middle East with a Gucci holdall and claimed to be a dealer in Islamic art.

Which meant the bitch was lying, and how I wished she wasn't, because she was very beautiful and equally loving and she belonged to me, and the drink was strong and the tang of calamares came wafting from the kitchen and our room was down on the port and cool and the bed was ready and only a little while ago it had been so simple, but now it wasn't simple at all because if she was lying in this then she must be lying in everything, and I was the biggest fool who ever went out to make a fortune in the world.

ONE

When the Peruvian business had been signed and sealed I thought about getting back to London. There was a last lunch in New York with White, Weld at the Recess and a quick session with the lawyers, then an evening clear before me at East 81st with the first chance of a proper sleep for a week and a seat reserved on the morning plane.

But there's a useful BOAC flight which leaves JFK late in the evening and delivers you at Heathrow in time for an easy breakfast before the office, and at the last moment I switched my flight. Rosa was not in town and I'd had enough of New York to last me for another week or two. So I came home. Or rather, I went back to base.

They said they'd lost the key of the first-class lounge at the airport but the VC-10 was two-thirds empty and it was a good crew so they looked like making up for it. The stewardess was one of those tight-hipped double-barrelled English girls with the language flags on her sleeve which must never be taken seriously, and the sort of Roedean accent that I can still only take in short doses.

The airline is still serving a tired claret which must be laced with nembutal, it puts you off to sleep with such effect that they save a fortune on the brandy. So it was well past dawn BST and Cork was coming up to meet us when I woke with a mouth like a blanket and a faint kick of relief that the Peruvian loan was out of the way at last. We landed in the London rain and got through Customs just before the rush-hour influx from the tatty

6

old Commonwealth. I called a Hertz chauffeur car and went straight to the city.

As any financial journalist will tell you, Thorne Reinhard—known to all and sundry as TR and to the real insiders as my very own employer—is supposed to be the whizz kid of London's merchant banks. It has a reputation for pioneering floating rate issues and multiple-currency options, if you understand me, but there's a limit to everything and they don't expect one of their young men to arrive in the morning unshaven, wearing a crumpled tropical suit and humping a canvas grip, even when he brings one-half per cent of twenty million with him.

Inevitably, it was KK who found me shaving in the directors' bathroom, examining my stubble in the mirror and squinting at the Arp engravings on the wall.

'All well in New York or wherever you've been?' he asked, since he could hardly ignore me. I told him about the weather and said, 'Actually, it was Lima'—as though he didn't know. 'Never been there myself,' said KK. 'Nice place?'

I said, 'The police go in pairs: one to read and one to write.' He sniffed suspiciously. KK is one of our managing directors and reputed to be the most brilliant investment analyst in EC2. I wouldn't know. He spends too much time away from his p/e ratios and his indices for my liking, querying my airfares with the suspicion of a man whose highlight of the year is a weekend at the Karlsruhe conference on cash flow analysis. He said, 'I suppose you'll be reporting to the Chairman.' He knew perfectly well that I reported to no one else but Lord Magnus. He was banging on, 'I can never remember, Kane, whether you consider yourself British or American.'

With some people, I explain I'm genuine mid-Atlantic. But KK wouldn't appreciate that.

'Best of both,' I said. 'UK passport, US credit cards.' 'Ah!' said KK. 'Privilege without responsibility.'

I said ho-bloody-ho to myself. He is the City at its most insular, and a right royal pain in the arse. KK finished drying his hands, then paused. He might almost have been interested. He said, 'You must admit, Kane, that you are an American in most senses of the word. I often wonder what made you throw in your lot with our side.' It's something I often wonder too. 'I suppose I like it here,' I said, with careful respect.

Sometimes I'm not so sure.

Lord Magnus hadn't arrived. He was at the Bank of England, Miss Spielter told me, inspecting me with her tired brown eyes. She gave me my first smile of the morning. Miss Spielter is the Chairman's secretary and, I think, an ally, one of the spinster women who live in Finchley and get on with their knitting when they aren't telling their masters what to do next. But she's different because she isn't English. Nobody claims to know her exact age; she probably pushes sixty. She arrived as a refugee in 1938, looking down on the Nazis with the Prussian contempt of an Assistant Chief Actuary of the Germania Versicherungsgesellschaft, Königsberg. Like all the others she went to work as a domestic and Magnus discovered her in 1942 as the housekeeper organising one of those wartime country house conferences. He snatched her for his own staff, and she has been with him ever since, organising his life, protecting him from the unwanted, reminding him of the others.

Now she was saying, 'He's expecting you later. There's a note on your desk.'

I must have winced because she added, 'It's all right.

8

You're popular. But better not to unpack.' I knew all about that.

My own secretary was not happy to see me. She never bloody is. A stack of letters was open on my desk including one that should have been locked away from the cleaners and two which must have been marked 'Personal' on the envelope. An old habit of Monica's and time it was stopped. On top of the pile there was the usual monogrammed sheet of paper and a short scrawl in green ink 'Need you for foursome Thursday a.m. 10 sharp at Wentworth.' No signature.

I collected the *Financial Times*, *Le Monde* and the *Daily Express* and went across to the Poulbot, where they serve the only real French coffee for miles and will let you sample it if you tap on the door and ask nicely. It took me less than an hour to reassure myself that the Prime Rate still hadn't gone up, that the copper slide was checked, that the Eurodollar new issue queue was lengthening and that the Peruvian government hadn't fallen overnight. It's the one part of my job I can't afford to skip—knowing what's going on.

There is no such thing as the City. There is certainly nothing like the 'City opinion' which the BBC likes to talk about. There are simply a lot of people trying to make money, swarming round the streets crowded between Temple Bar and the Tower. Banks, insurance firms, stockbrokers, shipping companies, the discount houses, commodity traders, all of them with their place in the system. Overgrown village, rumour mill, with the atmosphere of a regimental mess and the sense of humour of an Edwardian boys' paper, full of private language, secret rituals and enough games to last a working lifetime. And crouching at the centre of the City web, the merchant banks, still cultivating the traditional mystery but all competing for business, leaping from one possibility to another, constructing combinations, turning over stones, bringing together those who have and those who merely want.

TR itself is a classic City hybrid, an amalgamation of the old house of Thorne, Jakes, which had declined into fat immobility after the First World War, and Reinhard, Guth & Co., originally a Frankfurt firm, with London and New York offices since the 1890s. The merger took place in 1924, and the last of the Reinhards still comes occasionally to Board meetings—old Sir Felix Reinhard Rendon, born in Germany but formed by English nannies, Winchester and the First World War anti-Hun hatred which compelled him to change his name.

I suppose we are his heirs, though it gives him no joy to see us—professionals like myself, and like Condon too, who joined me briefly in the Poulbot, on his way to a meeting with the lawyers, judging by his briefcase and a tightness in the jaw. But Condon comes from a traditional mould, I don't, and the difference would be obvious even if our accents didn't betray us. A lot of people are surprised that we get on so well. Not that I'd say we are exactly soul-brothers.

Thorne Reinhard lives in one of those discreet vaguely Georgian buildings off Old Jewry: Fredericks Place, No. 6A, four storeys, porticoed entrance, window boxes—could have been home to a law or accounting firm. Americans always have to be led there by hand, it's so carefully tucked out of sight. Quieter still inside: a marble hall, then carpeted corridors, standing clocks, dark mahogany furniture. Blue-coated porter at the door, a shaky grillework lift. Offices scattered on several levels; here and there a leather-topped desk. But no coal fires now in the corner fireplaces, and a certain no-nonsense air about us. TR New York, Transworld Corp.—well, that's something else, all glass and chrome and twenty-first century, they seem to lap up that sort of thing in New York, even in Wall Street. But as I said earlier, I prefer it here.

As I arrived on the fourth floor Lord Magnus was getting ready to rush off again. 'No time to talk,' he said, his voice surprisingly crisp for so shaggy a man. There was greeting in his tone but not too much. They never overdo the welcome in TR, I'd discovered. 'Thank God the Peru thing is over at last. Don't go off on holiday though.'

I let him play it his way. He was my boss after all. Physically a big man, thin grey hair brushed loosely back from a broad forehead, tangled eyebrows over blue eyes, large mouth. Very much in command, always.

'Talk tomorrow,' he said. 'Make it first thing after lunch, with Condon. There's work to be done and precious little time to spare. You'll have to put your skates on. And don't forget Wentworth. Couple of Japs. Better let them win—pretend you play off four.'

'They're not stupid,' I said. 'They'll see at once I'm not a single figure man.'

'Thomas, I've told you before——' he began, and paused to shout through the wall for Miss Spielter '——Golf is your only gentlemanly pursuit and you must make the best of it.' He paused and reconsidered. 'Except that it's not really a game for gentlemen.' He decided he needed the chauffeur after all and a commotion began to spread through the building.

'Miss Spielter said something,' I hazarded, 'about not unpacking. You're not sending me to Tokyo?' I had a fleeting image of wet grey streets and an impossible language and scurrying crowds wearing white masks over their faces to combat the common cold. A grim prospect.

'No, no! Wouldn't dare!' cried my master and departed. 'Something more interesting. Nearer home too.'

'If you call this home,' I muttered, which of course he did. I went to telephone Sue. Praise God it wasn't Tokyo. Not this time.

TWO

Susannah Patricia Carew has a flat above an antique shop in Camden Passage, which embarrasses her now the address is so damned trendy. I got there early, dodging through the petrol fumes, and counted three more antique shops since my last visit. But the big African mask in the corner of the arcade hadn't been sold, the menus in the window of Carrier's were as exorbitant as ever, and the joss sticks were still burning in the hippy bazaar just opposite the flat. I let myself in with my key. Sue's place was as untidy as the morning I left for New York. It's one of the curses of the English public school girl that she never believes in making the bed first thing in the morning. Sometimes they make up for it in other ways; more often they don't. Which is one of the reasons—and I'm looking for them more and more often these days—why I don't marry her.

I rehearsed a grunt of disapproval, but then I saw the kitchen table stacked with food, a crate of cut-price Valpolicella on the floor and a new bottle of Scotch ready on the coffee table, and forgave her. I threw the flowers out of the window. She always forgets that most of us have hay fever and the pollen index was high enough to have no need of commercial support.

The flat would tell any half-assed burglar what sort of girl she is. Airmail letters behind the carriage clock on the mantelpiece and a clasp of family photographs taken in high sunlight; a fine old walnut desk, honeycombed with drawers, two surprisingly good rugs on the floor, and a heavily embroidered Baluchi cloth covering the old kitchen table which was bought for £4 downstairs in the Passage. There is the usual flotsam which washes up from SW7 to W14, to NW3 and now into N1. It all means the family were in foreign parts and that Daddy had originally been ICS. Daddy is currently Ambassador in Ouagadougou, which his daughter says is pretty good going for someone who doesn't speak French. I never know whether Sue owes her job in the Foreign Secretary's private office to Daddy, or Daddy his eminence to Sue.

And the rest? She is dark, almost petite, and has wide shoulders and green eyes, and when she came through the door that evening I was surprised to find how glad I was to see her. She came over and kissed me carefully.

'How was Lima?' she asked.

'I'm getting fed up with all this interest in Peru. Anyhow, it was New York.' Then the penny dropped. I said, 'Damn! No postcard. Sorry.'

'No postcard.'

'But I cabled from New York.'

'No postcard from Peru?' she said. 'And what happened to my flowers?'

She has one of those tentative, clear, English voices which sometimes make a girl sound slightly breathless, as though she's just recovering from a rousing game of lacrosse. On the telephone it could drive me up the wall.

'How's Daddy?' I asked, to be nasty.

She wrinkled her nose. 'Peace,' she said. 'I missed you.'

'Missed you too.'

'Truly?'

'Yours very truly.'

'Even in New York?'

'Particularly in New York.'

Sue knew about Rosa in Greenwich Village but some feminine intuition told her that she had no need to worry. Sue poured me some Scotch and took a long gulp at it before passing the glass to me. She swallowed hard and made a face. 'I've acquired the taste,' she said, 'but I still don't really like the stuff.' 'So stick to your sherry,' I said, and patted her on the behind to show I didn't mean it. I put my feet up. I was in no hurry to get back to my own place in Pimlico.

She put her head round the kitchen door. '*The Times* had something about you yesterday. There's the cutting, under the ashtray. It makes the Peruvian loan sound rather small.'

I said, 'It's what comes after it that matters. So you'd better reassure your Latin American desk.' I didn't want them thinking I was playing footy-footy with the State Department.

It was not yet dark outside. We ate a salad and Pasta con le Sarde, which turned out to mean hot tomato sauce, sardines, pine nuts, fennel, and, God help us, sultanas, and washed it down with the cheap Italian red from Parmigiani's. Afterwards I got out the duty-free cognac and then other things intervened and we discovered it was good that I was back and the flat looked untidier than ever with dirty plates and glasses all over the living-room and sticky non-stick frying pans in the sink and the bedroom curtains wide open to anyone bored enough to look in.

THREE

I took my time over the newspapers the next morning, after Sue had rushed off to do the Minister's bidding managing to look demure in a twinset from the Scotch House matched with her grandmother's agates. When the rush hour had eased a little so that the bus drivers were getting through Islington High Street in less than half an hour, I put on a dark suit that obviously came from within a half-volley of the Royal Exchange, lightened it with a tie from Beale & Inman and went out to forage for a taxi.

Thorne Reinhard really begins to move about ten every morning, after the markets open and early enough to have an interval for paperwork and conferences before getting down to other work at lunch. The messengers had discovered my return and my desk was weighed down with the foreign press and the new number of *Barron's* which I'd caught in the Harvard Club two days before.

I sat and stared at the wall and wished I could change my secretary. Then I did an hour's hard work, letters, appointments, apologies, the lot, and wondered why I felt like a cigarette butt in a pool of seawater. It might have been the food last night, but it was probably the delayed after-effect of a night short of five hours at 35,000 feet.

Outside the girls were moving up Cheapside in waves of shock troops from the direction of Bank, intent on Woolworths and the crumby shoe-shops and a luncheon voucher doughnut in the Kardomah. I'd been back in London for two days and I was fed up with the City already. I wondered what the hell Lord Magnus was hatching.

I tried three bars in turn for a Fernet Branca, gave up and settled for a pub lunch: two sausages, French bread, cheddar which set my teeth on edge, and a pint of cider. I went back to Fredericks Place to contemplate the pile of papers on my desk. After a while I felt better and began to tackle the backlog. By mid-afternoon I was deep in the files of the Helsinki DM issue when Miss Spielter called me.

Lord Magnus was slumped at his desk chewing a Monte Cristo and toying with a jagged lump of dirt, a souvenir from his latest Australian copper venture, which he used as a paperweight and an object of sentiment. KK was sitting in the window seat, gazing out at the comings and goings of Price, Waterhouse in the building opposite and looking as if Gilts had touched fifty. Condon was there too, British as ever, tall with dark brown hair, deep-set grey eyes, cool stare, correct, ageless clothes made by some naval tailors. He was giving me his careful Harrow-Balliol smile. A full-dress meeting, was the signal.

'Won't waste time congratulating you on Lima,' said Lord Magnus, which was a nice way of doing so in the briefest acceptable manner. 'There's something else on our mind.'

'The Middle East?' I asked.

Lord Magnus snapped, 'Who on God's earth told you that?'

I said, 'Griegson's appear to know it. Or guess it. They're treating it as a joke. At least they're pretending to.' I'd had that from the Poulbot net.

I went on: 'I don't know what all this is about, but if everyone assumes we're involved, isn't it some reason for going ahead? We don't want to give the impression that we've got cold feet.'

'Why not?' asked KK. 'I'll tell you why not. Because second thoughts are our prerogative.' He gave me one of his heavy market-slump sighs. He was brushed aside by Lord Magnus, who erupted out of his chair and began to to stride up and down, scattering cigar ash with the abandon of the man who has always known that someone will clear the mess away.

'Thomas is right,' said my Chairman. 'I'm not going to be rogered by those asses down the road. The idea is fine. At worst, it's worth investigating. And that's what Thomas is here for. Guy can't hope to do it all by himself. Someone has to go out East while Guy concentrates on the European underwriters. And there's a pile of work in New York and Washington. Above all, we have to move fast—say, three months to tie everything together. If we give ourselves any longer, we'll be scuppered.'

Magnus must have been a difficult man to control in Cabinet. Perhaps that was why he'd quit politics and come back to his first love. Politics and banking, they both had to do with power. I used to reckon that Magnus had moved back east from Westminster to the City because he had discovered it was here, not there, that the real thing was to be found.

'What would you say,' asked Lord Magnus, and the question was directed at me, not the other two, and wasn't rhetorical, 'what would you say if I told you I have been talking with the Egyptians?' He waited for the reply, the grey eyebrows standing up like ancient shaving brushes in interrogation.

I said, 'I'd be considerably surprised.'

'Why?'

I went on, slowly, 'Because it's years since Cairo has been a suitable field of operation for any Western merchant bank.' I omitted to add that Lord Magnus bore some personal responsibility for this sad state of affairs, having been a Cabinet Minister in 1956.

'You agree with that supposition?' demanded Lord Magnus. 'You? Personally?'

I said, 'In the absence of any evidence to the contrary, I'm afraid I do.'

Condon began to say, 'What if there were good evidence ...' but Lord Magnus had pounced on me.

'Afraid? Why "afraid"? Tell me.'

I began to improvise. 'Because it is—it is unfortunate that a country as large as Egypt, and as important, with enormous development needs ...' I heard my voice trailing off. 'Because of the political obstacles, of all sorts ...' 'Very nicely said,' murmured KK, with malice unconcealed. Condon added, 'You sound as if you mean they wouldn't let us touch them with a bargepole.' I said, 'Right.'

Lord Magnus marched across the room and struck a pose in front of the varnished Victorian globe that he had insisted on bringing with him from King Charles Street. He usually had his way.

'KK and I have had this out before. We disagree. We agree to disagree. As Guy knows'—he glanced at Condon —'we have undertaken that an investigation be launched. By you, Thomas! Remember, the directors don't want you to spend too much money for the time being. You will start by clarifying the view from Cairo—details of the project, that sort of thing. Guy will be needed here and on the European circuit.'

'Investigation where? Of what?'

'Of the Egyptian situation, of course. What else have we been talking about?'

'I beg your pardon,' I said, and threw in the courtesy 'Sir' of the English Establishment. 'I beg your pardon, Sir, but you must have something more specific in mind.'

'Yes, of course,' said Lord Magnus shortly and sketched another gesture in the air. 'We plan to take up once more the ties between Egypt and the West! I have decided that it is time that we here in the City went back into Cairo.'

He paused again and this time surveyed us as though daring us to argue. Lord Magnus always went down a treat at the Primrose League but if all this meant that I was supposed to pick up the pieces from the débâcle which he voted for in Cabinet back in 1956, then he must be getting out of touch.

'Do I make myself clear?' Lord Magnus demanded. Really, he was overdoing it this time.

I said, 'It will take many years before we are going to be welcome in Cairo. Any of us. You know that, Sir, you know it better than I do.' Condon was scowling at me, but to hell with that. 'They're not going to forgive us in less than a generation, and how on earth can we blame them for that? Anyway, the Russians are swarming all over Egypt at this moment and intend to stay.'

'I voted against Eden, I'll have you know,' said Lord Magnus quietly but beginning to bristle. He encouraged his staff to argue with him but only up to a certain ill-defined point which I'd apparently passed. 'I left the Government shortly afterwards. But that's neither here nor there.' He swung away from the fireplace and thumped into a chair. His skin, I noticed, was beginning to lose its Guards ruddiness.

'Don't underestimate me, Thomas—and the rest of you —just because I'm old enough to be your father. I wouldn't have had this idea if I had nothing to go on. And I have. A lot! There—you see, KK is looking sceptical again. But I still have my contacts—and he can't deny it. They keep me posted. And I've just had a certain visitor from Cairo. Very discreetly done, but no nonsense about it. He came when you were away, Thomas. Guy and I saw him.'

Condon nodded and uncrossed his legs. I noticed he didn't look particularly happy.

'What do they want?' I asked.

'Advice.'

'They don't want money to go with it?'

'Of course they do. A great deal.'

'Then they must be crazy,' I said.

'Why?'

'Because no Western financial institution would touch Egyptian paper, and probably no one else either. Look at their record. They started by grabbing the whole Canal, pure and simple, and they've gone on from there like a kid in a toy store. What about the Israelis? And the war? It's hopeless! No investor would risk even a blocked piastre now.'

'How are you so sure?' Condon put in, quietly, from the direction of the bookcase. He was the Chairman's man. He still wasn't looking happy. But his question seemed to be meant seriously.

I shrugged. I didn't really know. I'd made my protest. But true, I'd been out of touch.

So I began to think.

And that, for me, was the start of the Nile affair.

▩▩▩▩▩▩▩▩▩▩ FOUR ▩▩▩▩▩▩▩▩▩▩▩

We got serious. Magnus threw away his cigar and we sat down at the great polished desk with the clean morocco-edged blotter and the *Economist* diary.

'What if we had guarantees?' Magnus was saying.

'Worthless!' I replied at once. 'The streets of Cairo are littered with torn-up guarantees.'

'Government to government?'

'Which government?'

'British? American? French?'

'And the Russians?' I asked sourly. 'Where do they fit into this scheme?'

'You mustn't be naïve, Thomas. The Russians aren't the masters yet, whatever you might be told. And you don't think the Egyptians *enjoy* being in Moscow's pocket? The most important element in Egypt is this nationalism business. Which simply means they don't like their colonial masters—any of them. We learned that when I was in Government. It wasn't just the English accent they couldn't abide, they don't like the Russians either, even when Ivan is trying to speak Arabic and giving them more MiGs than they know how to fly.'

'And even when they are utterly dependent on Moscow for their arms supplies?' It was Condon who asked the question. Whose side was he on?

'They've got all they want,' said Lord Magnus, with the unshakable assurance that comes from a high-level intelligence briefing. He went on, 'At least, they've had all they're going to get. And they know it. So now is the time for our government to try to correct the balance. Don't ever forget Bandung. The Egyptians were the loudest of all for non-alignment and they weren't doing it only for propaganda value. They believe it. Still! And they want to keep their options open. So does any government which isn't blinded by principle.'

KK said, 'Precisely. Their principle is to do dirt on the West.'

'That's the *Telegraph* view,' said Lord Magnus dismissively. 'Thomas?'

I said, 'The only principle is to get even with Israel. They know they can't do it for years, if ever. Unless they achieve a technological breakthrough ...'

'But in the meantime they throw everything they have into economic development,' said Lord Magnus triumphantly. 'Building up their industry. Exploiting the new oil discoveries.'

'They can't do it themselves,' I said. 'It's too much for them.'

'Obviously they need help. And they don't want to turn to the Russians for everything, or one day they'll wake up to find guards on the door and their oil and cotton streaming north at even more ridiculous prices. *That's* what they fear.'

'What did your visitor actually say?' I asked. I began to read the writing on the wall; I tried a quick calculation on whether to stay in the Semiramis or at Shepheards.

'He said they wanted help with their new development scheme.'

'Yes, but which one?'

'The one that follows the Aswan Dam.'

'The Nile Cascade?' I asked.

'That's right,' cried Lord Magnus, and allowed himself the beginnings of his excited look, like a member of the hunt when the hounds start yelping. 'You're getting warm! You know about this project?'

'It's the next stage after the High Dam,' I said. 'Eight or ten barrages downstream—I forget the exact number. Irrigation and further power supply. But surely the Russians will want to do it, as they did the High Dam.' I went on silently with the recital: the Russians did Aswan because the Americans pulled out. Nasser nationalised the Canal to pay for the Dam. Which led to Lord Magnus and the Anglo-French-Israeli invasion. And utter defeat.

'I tell you, they don't want the Russians to do it,' Lord Magnus argued. 'Not if they can help it.'

I asked, 'Why don't they go to the World Bank?'

'They have,' Condon replied. 'No joy out of 1818 H Street on the full financing—there's this debt rescheduling problem still unsolved, as you know. But there's a strong chance we could talk with the Bank and do a joint deal. We'll have to see them in Washington about that. Then there's another possibility, that we might work out some sort of guarantee based on the projected offtake of their new oil discoveries in the Western Desert.'

KK squinted at his watch and got up to leave. He said, 'I fail to understand how you can hope to persuade any reputable bank in the world to go along with it. Even if you gave them a fifteen per cent coupon at a fat discount. Except the Kuwaitis, if Kane holds a gun at the head of the Sheikh.'

I said, 'The Ruler of Kuwait is an Emir, not an ordinary Sheikh'—but KK had left, angry, intent on his portfolios.

Lord Magnus was gazing at me from his desk. 'Never mind KK,' he said. 'He wants to move you into the investment side. I vetoed it.' I bowed my thanks. 'But he has got a point. You may be able to offer investors the juiciest terms since the War.' He said it as though to encourage me. 'But remember, Thomas, you'll have to move fast. No sitting on your backside. And you'll get official backing from London and Washington, I promise you. I've already fixed for you to go along to the Foreign Office.'

I still wasn't quite sure why I should be going off on this forlorn paperchase. Then I began to understand.

'That's the real point, isn't it?' I said slowly. 'The Foreign Office is the clue. You're going for the diplomatic coup, sir, aren't you, not the business? Thorne Reinhard with a chapter in the history-books. The comeback of the West in the Arab heartland! The return of the prodigal.' A very Middle Eastern concept, I realised. The tragedy of Lord Magnus was that his political career—no mean one—had already been forgotten. It had been a mistake to take a peerage. No one today connected Lord Magnus of Thorne Reinhard with Ted Crichton, the odd-man-out in Eden's last Cabinet, and he could hardly hire a PR man to make the point for him.

He was saying, 'They *do* want us! I tell you both, I know it. They *want* us, despite poor Anthony. They want us back where we belong, in a whole variety of ways. They want us to be with them, at their side.'

'And they want our money,' said Condon, flatly.

'How much?'

'$125 million,' said Lord Magnus. 'First stage.'

'God,' I said.

꧁꧁꧁꧁꧁꧁꧁꧁꧁꧁꧁꧁ FIVE ꧂꧂꧂꧂꧂꧂꧂꧂꧂꧂꧂꧂

'You wanted me,' my secretary Monica was muttering.

Heaven forbid, I thought, and threw the pink newspaper on the floor and started work.

There was a mass of correspondence. Tiresome letters from a Zürich bank, complaining in that veiled-threat Swiss-banker's way about their small allocation in the last underwriting but one. The dregs of Peru—fiscal agency arrangements, termination of the Selling Group Agreement, that sort of thing. And other letters, some enquiring, some fawning, too damned many of them. I dictated and swore, and then slashed and swore again through Monica's drafts.

It took a couple of hours before I could start on the

confidential digest of the High Dam Authority's sup-
posedly secret nine-volume report on Aswan. I had it by
courtesy of a British consultant engineer, one of our
clients, who had paid someone £2,500 (Egyptian) for a
copy. It was unrelieved gibberish to me, even in an English
translation. I wondered again whether or not to try to
learn some serious Arabic. Monica buzzed. She said,
'Don't forget your Foreign Office appointment.' I slammed
down the receiver and ran.

The best thing about going to the FO is the stir you
cause among the tourists as your taxi pulls towards No.
10. There's much staring and muttering in assorted
languages—'Is he the Chancellor?' and *'Er ist aber so
jung!'*—and a Kodak Instamatic pushed at the window
while you lean back and study the *Standard* and practise
the man-of-destiny-wears-a-Rolex expression. Then you turn
abruptly left through the archway into the Gilbert Scott
quadrangle and all is anticlimax and badly-parked Hill-
mans.

Only in Jerusalem is the External Affairs Ministry less
imposing. The Israelis live in prefabs straggled through a
garden, as you'd expect if you thought about it; the Brits
rule the world from a cross between a palace and a slum—
which again, I suppose, is appropriate. The lady receptionists are genteel and monoglot, the messengers Chelsea
Pensioners without the uniform. The lifts are the slowest
in London. The passages are cream or green, chipped,
smeared and sordid, lined with rows of yellow cupboards
stacked with old files: 'Tanganyika to Tonga, 1932', and
miles of others, a crumbling Empire of nostalgia.

'This is nothing to do with us, of course,' said my
distinguished diplomat, waistcoat splashed with Travellers
Club claret, his down-at-heel black Oxfords dusted by his
daily stroll across the Park. 'But let's say we're taking a

25

sympathetic stance on the touch-line.'

'I'd like to know who else is on my side out in the mud,' I said, and thought black memories of the last time I'd asked a Counsellor (Commercial) to bail me out of a tight spot.

'The Embassy will give you the details,' he murmured and tried to sit on the desk when he saw me squinting at his 'Confidential' files. All of us at Fredericks Place had learned to read cables upside down at fifty paces. I pulled myself back.

He was saying, 'HMG are very keen, very anxious ...' and it tailed away like an empty aerosol.

'So you think it's on?' I demanded.

'I beg your pardon?'

I explained.

'Yes, of course. Good gracious me yes, we hope so. Why not?'

'You don't appreciate how hard it's going to be to explain your optimism to the men with the money,' I said.

'But surely the project is very sound,' he said plaintively and his fleshy, elegant face drooped slightly at the edges. 'Very sound indeed, I was led to believe. And we are particularly interested in the exports that could flow from this sort of loan.' I had been expecting to hear that one. Even at the top levels of the Foreign Office it is now respectable to admit concern for the country's balance of payments.

'Go and ask the Board of Trade,' I said. 'See what a short rein ECGD are holding on the Egyptians. It isn't a simple matter of thirty million on the trade figures.' He looked unhappy at the mention of those commercial wallahs in Victoria Street.

'Oh really!' he murmured. 'How short-sighted of them.'

'Correct me if I'm wrong,' I said, and bared my teeth in a gesture of chumminess, 'but this thing about being pals with the Egyptians is pretty new, isn't it?'

He didn't like the way I said it.

'Not at all,' he countered and summoned the manner in which he would have addressed a stroppy Latin American third secretary. 'We have our ups and downs, of course, but relations have rarely been so cordial.'

'And would be a lot more cordial if this issue could be arranged?'

'You take my meaning precisely, Mr Kane.'

'And the Russians?'

'Now really, it's far better if I leave this sort of thing to the Ambassador when you get out there.' He fumbled at a fob watch and frowned, making sure that I saw him. 'I suppose you'll be going out there immediately.'

'I don't know,' I said. 'We've got to know if it's feasible first.' Damn it, I wasn't working for War on Want.

He was beginning to chafe at the bit. 'I'll send a cable to HE,' he conceded. 'Splendid fellow, Wilfred. Sure to tell you everything you need to know. Anything else I can do for you?' It was a question expecting the answer No.

I shot back quickly, 'Yes, a couple of documents.' There was no harm in asking.

He looked politely surprised.

I said, 'I need the annexes to the reports of the last three World Bank missions.'

'They're confidential, you know,' he said primly.

'That's right.' I reckoned I could always get them from friends in Washington if he wanted to play percy.

'Try the Board of Trade,' he said, and chortled abruptly. The bastard.

I worked at it for three days. The weather turned warm, or at least less cold, and the British went mad, taking off their clothes and lying down on wet grass wherever it could be found. There was another strike at Fords. The FT Index gained twelve points and share quotations were suspended for two dodgy finance companies. Coffee was still weak. Tin rallied. KK went on holiday in Portmeirion. Sue cooked Sicilian again and this time we threw it into the Portofino dustbin. The Israelis and the Egyptians fought an air battle and I sent the cutting from *The Times* to Lord Magnus with a note saying 'Sir, get me out of this. Call it off!' The reply said, 'Faint heart never won fair lady,' which was Magnus all over.

In the middle of all this the South Africans tried to rewrite a clause in the West Rand merger and, as Condon said glumly, seemed to be talking Afrikaans on the telephone in the brief intervals when sun-spots allowed us to get through. Sorting that out took my next three days, 12,000 miles, two and a half hotel beds, a brief bout of dysentery and a very unpleasant confrontation with a man called Labuschagne.

When I got back to Fredericks Place Miss Spielter announced, 'You're to go to Cairo the day after tomorrow. The Egyptians have been asking for you.'

The laundry still hadn't found my blue lightweight suit. Sue said, 'I've run out of Ma Griffe, darling, if you can remember.'

Lord Magnus sent his driver and the big old Armstrong Siddeley to take me to the airport. No one told KK.

SIX

Cairo was early June and the heat bounced off the tarmac. It was the real, authentic heat of the sun, slamming down like a hammer at the back of the skull. The Mediterranean seemed far away in the frozen north. I felt the sweat drying on my neck like spilled milk sizzling on a hot plate and the airplane gin evaporated in my veins. There was the familiar sour stale stink of the old Middle East. A welcome to poverty, choking dust and open sewers, diesel fumes and Stella beer, fires of camel dung, and gobbets of phlegm lying thick in the gutters.

Cairo is too old, too big, the colour of mud—not biscuit, not khaki, but a range of greyish browns. It is a place of immense civilisation. Of 600 mosques and 100 ravishingly beautiful women. Of ramshackle, blaring taxis, weaving round the squares with the recklessness of stock-car drivers. It is green, too, crowded with dusty heavy old trees, and at night the foliage stands massive behind the lights of the Gezira and the Nile is as dark as the Thames. It is the shabbiest city in the world.

I was met, to my surprise, by a long, low, scarlet E-type, an offence to all Arabs. The driver was an Englishman, young, blond and nervous as hell behind the lackadaisy.

He said, 'I'm from the Embassy. London said you'd be on this flight, so I thought I'd come and see you through Customs in one piece.'

I began, 'This is very kind. You shouldn't ...'

'Not a word of it.' He tossed coins at the porter. 'Nothing else to do with my time. Don't tell HE.'

I said, with careful enthusiasm, 'Do I gather you'll be having something to do with the job I'm doing?'

'That's right. HE said to chuck everything and give you a helping hand.'

I said, 'You? Give me a hand?' and looked at him. He smiled back. Jesus.

'We're all very anxious to see something emerge. There was even a cable about you from the Secretary of State's office.' I wished Sue would mind her own bloody business.

He was tall, like all Englishmen of the type, and slim-to-bony. Pink skin, beard invisible. His teeth were strong but uneven, the nose a shade too sharp, hair carefully kept long but not too long. He wore a featherweight white jacket and a heavy cream shirt, old school tie. His hands were a surprise, big and blunt fingered; it suggested a cruel man on a horse. He replied once to a taxi-driver's insults and spoke in a harsh accented Arabic.

Toby Underwood, he called himself. Amiable, rather nice, somehow depressing: when a born failure starts with a silver spoon in his mouth he finishes with problems—a slight stammer, a job as Commercial Secretary, and a Jaguar at Cairo airport.

I said, 'I'm hoping one of you will be able to brief me.'

'Good God,' he said, and sounded panic-stricken. 'Haven't they done that at the Office?'

'They said you would.'

'But we don't know anything.'

'Nothing at all?'

'Only that you would come out and set up the whole deal. Something to do with your boss—nice old fellow who used to be something in Smith Square.'

'Do you mean the Egyptians are keen on a deal, whatever it may be?'

'They're keen on the money.'

30

'And not so keen on roubles?'

'Dollars still best of all.'

'So they all say,' I murmured. The car pushed through the heat, splattering us with almost visible waves of shimmering air.

'Eurodollars, hey?' he shouted above the din of brakes and horns.

'What's that?'

'Eurodollars. Read the other day there are millions of them floating around. HE said you're one of those blokes who shovel them up and distribute them to the needy.'

I said, 'They're not exactly *tangible*, you know.'

'All Dutch to me,' he said half-apologetic, but then complacent. 'My job is to sell British exports. Trouble is, none of the chaps back home are very keen on selling out here. Don't seem to trust the locals.'

'Should they?'

'My dear chap, of course. You probably knew them years ago when there was a lot of nonsense going around. They've changed, you know. You'll see it at once.'

'But if you think you have problems with the Sheffield exporter who wants to sell widgets and needs reassuring that he's going to get his money, do you realise what it's going to be like trying to flog bonds with this government's name on them?' Egyptian bonds, I thought! It was a bad music-hall joke.

He looked puzzled. 'You've got guarantees?' he asked. 'Can't you make the terms so attractive no one can afford not to take up a block?'

'Guarantees that iron-clad are the best way to convince everyone the bonds are phoney.'

'But it isn't a phoney project. It all makes sense. Everyone here agrees on that.' Now he was sounding querulous and I hadn't even begun my briefing.

'Go on! Encourage me,' I urged. Sweat was trickling down my chest.

We were swinging behind the City of the Dead, past Mohammed Ali Mosque. The Old City was strewn before us, Ibn Tuluun held the eye to the left, Al Azhar topped the straggle of Khan-Khalil to the right. Modern Cairo lay straight ahead, the Nile greenback-green in the distance. There were new skyscrapers since my last visit. I suppose I know Cairo better than Cardiff. Which doesn't make me an Arab. Or glad to be back.

SEVEN

Cairo was still a city at war, in a bilharzia-ridden way. It was easy not to notice it any longer, the war had gone on too long and had become a way of life. The newspapers still screamed abuse at the Zionists but the journalists had become parrots, their minds were on other things—poetry or arak or the sand in their coffee, the waiting list for a new car. But the Egyptian Army was still everywhere, slumped on the sidewalks under the Nile bridges in their World War Two uniforms. They were all old-young with eyes the colour of the Nile in flood, and hardly seemed to have the strength to lift their boots, let alone their rifles. 'L'Abri Dessous' said the signs pointing to blast walls across the doorways. The paint had faded, the walls were covered with posters, and the sand was spilling like snail smears out of the rotting jute of the sandbags. I was on the wrong side of the Canal, I reckoned—I ought to be selling Israel Defence Bonds.

I got to the Minister in two days seven hours and twenty-three minutes, which was a record for the course and adequate proof that the Egyptians were happy to see me. The Department was over across on the third island, beyond the new Sheraton, and there was none of the usual rubble and incomprehension in the foyer. Smooth young men, shaved, laundered and multilingual, emerged from out of a dozen doorways to shake my hand and comment on the weather. The lift actually worked. There was polished parquet in the corridors, a hum of air-conditioning, and two elegant young ladies in tortoise-shell spectacles joined the party and asked about their Somerville friends. It was all extraordinarily un-Egyptian.

The Minister wore the heavy dark-grey worsted, immaculately pressed, which is the uniform of all Ministers south of Belgrade. He was waiting for me with hand out-stretched and we carried through a brisk negotiation as to whether to speak French or English. French lost out, as always happens these days. I proffered greetings from Lord Magnus, and was assured that the President greatly hoped to meet me. We sank into sofas as deep as my grandmother's featherbed and I hauled myself back into a seated-crouch, my knees barking against the gold-filigree table, refused cigarettes, accepted coffee, decided it was probably safe to drink the water that came with it.

The Minister said, 'Mr Kane, it is *very* good to see you.' He said it several more times, with embellishments, so that I began to think he meant it, and the phalanx of officials who were still standing around us nodded and grimaced their agreement. I reckoned it was their way of reminding me that some of his colleagues would not be so kind in their welcome.

'Forgive me, Minister,' I murmured, and tried to look the picture of innocence. 'I imagine that not everyone in this city agrees that a Eurodollar issue—through Western banks—is the best way of financing this project.'

The Minister looked genuinely astonished. 'But it *is* the best way, is it not? In the circumstances?'

I said, 'We don't yet know.' The Minister looked perplexed. I added, 'It depends on the circumstances.'

'But there is a much-improved relationship with our Western friends in the last two or three years. There are American companies which have been working here for years and are, they assure me, entirely happy with the cooperation they receive. As we explained to your people in London, they must please not doubt our desire for your friendship.'

And our money, I thought to myself.

'And your money,' said the Minister, abruptly, and threw back his head and roared with laughter when he saw the expression on my face.

I left it alone for the moment and gave him the spiel I reserve strictly for distinguished laymen before they give me their blessing and pass me on to the officials with whom the real work always has to be done. Time enough for a project breakdown later, which would be where the smooth young men probably came in, and with a bit of luck the Somerville girls too. But first I had to get the preliminaries clear beyond all shadow of doubt. Bankers can't risk skipping first principles.

He let me burble on like the doyen of the Diplomatic Corps on the imperial birthday.

'Mr Kane,' he said simply, and I liked the way he said it, 'you can tell your colleagues, and your Chairman —and all your other banks, and the Americans too— that I fully understand that they might hesitate. There are certain circles overseas where my country's reputation is not, I fear, what it should rightly be. I know that the only way to improve that image and that reputation is to demonstrate, by trading and borrowing with the West,

34

that we deserve a higher reputation for credit-worthiness. That is the best security I can offer you for your loan—that we shall want to look to the West again, and for more funds.'

He had leaned back in the cushions and was talking quietly now, intensely, privately.

'Sometimes we seem to be slipping backwards, for all our efforts and all our struggles. Sometimes I wonder whether our people are even poorer, more desperate, than when we came to power ... so you see, Mr Kane, I realise this is bound to be just one task out of many for you—a technical exercise perhaps, which you will study with my staff here. I do not blame you for that. But let me promise you, to us this Nile Cascade could be a turning point in Egypt's history. At last we may be able to say that we have mastered the river which is our life, first with the High Dam and now—equally important—with the barrages. Do not forget this in all your travels these next weeks ...'

I said, 'Weeks? It's going to take months, Minister.'

The Minister shook his head. There was a sudden stillness in the room. I remembered that everything in the end is politics, and that $125m is more politics than most.

'I must have time,' I said weakly. 'There is a lot of mistrust that must be dispelled. You mentioned it just now.'

The Minister shook his head again. 'You are assured I am with you, and I understand your difficulty. My Ministry will all do their utmost to help. But I must caution you—privately, in this room—that I have some friends who ...' He shrugged, his face creasing around the moustache like an ageing French film star. It was all he could allow himself to do to suggest that there were Ministers in town who, whether because of their Soviet friendships or simply their ideological bent, would cheerfully send me packing and might only be biding their time waiting for the best moment to do precisely that. 'There has been another offer, you must know ...' he added, so deliberately, his voice so empty of comment, that it was almost staccato. 'I need not tell you from which government. I personally do not believe the offer to be a serious one.'

'How long do you need?' asked a diplomat with tired eyes.

I tried to tot it up. 'First, we have to put together a group of underwriters—other bankers who join the syndicate and each take a proportion of the issue according to their status and placing power. In this case, in the special circumstances, that will need most of two months because we have to talk to as wide a group as we possibly can. They, the underwriters, then take a couple of weeks but again for this they would certainly need more to line up potential buyers of the issue. We call it "taking soundings". It can't be rushed because at the end of that we shall have a pretty good idea of what we call the "book" —the total amount of potential buying interest. At *that* stage we can pitch the terms of the issue according to the "book". This means we will need say four months before we can have the official signing of the underwriting agreements.'

'Where? In London?'

'No. In New York because we feel it would be useful to register this with the SEC. The Europeans can all delegate signing powers to agents in New York. On the actual offering date the underwriters proceed to sell the bonds to the buyers who ought to be waiting. They hope to get rid of their bonds by a date we call the "closing", which is usually a sort of ritual meeting, also in New

York, with everyone signing and telexing and celebrating, and so on.'

'And the money?'

'You would get it via a Luxembourg bank at the closing. About ten days after the offering day. The total you get represents the offering price of the bonds less the spread.'

'But of course,' said the Minister, who still looked unhappy, 'we should be happy for you to offer the most attractive of terms, at your discretion, if the funds were available—rapidly——'

I said, 'However large a discount you put on the coupon, for this operation we still need *time*. Even without snags.' And there are always snags, I reminded myself. Especially in view of the problems Condon and I were going to have with the New York end. Not to speak of the difficulty of tying in with the World Bank.

'How long do you need?'

'Fifteen weeks minimum.'

'That's too long.'

'Then it's impossible.'

'Mr Kane, I promise you that I am being very serious. You *must* make this shorter.'

I said, 'Look, I'll try. From our point of view, too, we can't waste a moment because once the news gets out we'll be vulnerable to rumour and any sort of sabotage in the market.'

The Minister nodded, as though sabotage made sense. 'Then let us aim for ten weeks,' he said. 'Remember, I cannot promise to protect the issue—*here in this city*—if you cannot keep that deadline.'

It was as simple as that.

EIGHT

At 1045 BST on Wednesday, June 9, Sue was taking the Minister of State his first ambassador of the morning and wearing a sedate skirt from Fenwick and a Galeries Lafayette blouse which made her look sallow. Lord Magnus was reading a Christie's catalogue with the attention a Welshman gives to his Bible and planning to get a quick glance at the new *Apollo* before his first appointment. KK was playing with one of those 'Call-master' telephones which dial automatically any of fifty numbers at the touch of a button—everyone from our Frankfurt dealer to his mother-in-law. Condon was sitting in the Euler in Basle drinking coffee and working out the fastest way to get to Milan. Across in Cairo it was two hours later and bloody hot. The British Ambassador was in a huddle with his Head of Chancery, talking about me and various other matters of high policy and hoping to get away for lunch.

And I was sitting in the Gezira Sporting Club, waiting for my host from the High Dam Authority. This was the land of *malesh*; easy to fall into every vice, including unpunctuality. The Egyptians seemed for ever as unready as Ethelred. My first week had been a sin; the actual work would have been squeezed by any Wall Street operator into a single morning session before the markets opened. But I was getting into the local stride. The Minister's deadline must have been a jest. I just couldn't give a damn. *Malesh!*

The sun beat down like the Israeli Air Force and I felt as tired as the great lawns that surrounded the Club. This was now the EAR, I reminded myself; the Revolution was accomplished and the Nile flowed on either side of our island, but over towards the racecourse they were still playing cricket in white flannels. The croquet lawns were grey and deserted. And there was the midday sun.

I sat on the first floor terrace of the shabbiest gracious building in Cairo, drinking lemonade with a chaser of Stella beer. Egyptian lemonade is the best in the world, sweet and also tart, cool yet not cold, soft and still sharp. The lunch-hour comes late in Cairo and I was casting around for an *Egyptian Gazette* when a group of new arrivals caught my eye. As they came up the stairs they seemed to be together but then they split into pairs and trios. Four of them were officers, plump and amiable, a safe hundred kilometres from the front-line. Three were women. One looked like a Copt, vivacious, cautious, with surprised-looking eyebrows. One, older, was the Egyptian middle-class wife, silent as the sands. The third was different. I couldn't place her. She was young and taut, and when she turned in my direction I saw that she was extravagantly beautiful.

Her dress was white and simple, so slight it was nothing, yet every man in the room had turned to look at her. She moved like a mannequin in a hurry, and her skin was browner than the Copt girl's, glowing rich, gold. Her hair was dark, not quite black, casually pulled back in the clasp of a comb that glinted in the sunlight.

And when she turned and looked directly at me, I held her gaze for five seconds before I was the first to drop my eyes.

But I knew that she recognised me; I knew that she somehow expected me.

Then her escort moved across the room behind her and I saw he was Toby Underhill.

I rallied myself. I said, 'It's a one-horse town.'

'Do you know Miss Tal?' he responded and introduced us. Her eyes were black as the shadows on the moon.

She asked, 'Are you a diplomat too?' and the way she said it made it clear she knew I wasn't.

I said No.

She persisted, 'What do you do, then?' Determined. Bold.

I said, 'I work in a bank.'

Usually they're surprised. Sometimes disappointed. She just smiled, wide-mouth, white teeth, and said, 'A special sort of bank.'

I said, 'You seem to know the answers.'

She smiled: 'It's self-evident.' I couldn't place her accent.

Toby pushed in. 'He's what they call an investment banker. Merchant bank. Very high-powered. He's out here to finance the big new development project.'

For a diplomat, I thought, that was a bloody stupid thing to say.

She said, 'Toby, dear, I'm sure you shouldn't have said that.'

Then my host arrived, without apology, and I settled down to work. I was a bit baffled by that 'Toby, dear.' It didn't tally.

NINE

He was still bloody smiling the next day when I saw them both again. I was sitting in Groppi, drinking coffee and struggling with airline timetables, when I saw them come in through the door and stand hesitating for a moment. She was dressed in pale green, drawn tight at the waist, and I made waving motions like an officious car-park attendant. I had the fleeting impression as they came towards my table that she was leading, pulling him behind her like some reluctant puppy not yet trained to heel.

'You're looking very cool,' I said. 'In all this swelter.'

There are very few people who can look you straight in the eye. She was one of them, she came right through the retina so you almost had to duck.

'But I'm boiling!' she exclaimed. She certainly didn't look it. 'We went up to Hatoun, in Mousky Street, and I wanted to walk back.'

'Bloody stupid,' said Toby, who was wearing a canary shirt open to the fourth button, exposing a pink hairless chest. It was presumably his version of mufti.

'Drink!' she cried. 'Please.'

'What will you have?'

'I'd love a grenadine.'

'A *what*?'

'Then a ginger beer.'

'It's as scarce as the United Arab timetable,' I said. Toby said, 'He means it doesn't exist.'

'Then I'll just have a *caffè freddo*.'

I said, 'You're trying to tell me you come from Rome,' and she flashed me an apology of a grin.

'Not really,' she said. 'I base myself there. But I do a lot of travelling.'

Toby butted in. He had been parleying in Arabic with the waiter and discovered that French was easier for both of them. 'Mara's a dealer,' he said. 'Antiques, you know. I mean, antiquities. Buys and sells. Very sordid. Very profitable!' He laughed, too loudly. Nervous, I thought. Good.

She said, 'It's because he doesn't understand. He resents me because I'm a liberated woman who can support her-

41

self.' She was talking to me across the table as though we were alone. She probably gave that impression to everyone she met; some girls make a ploy of it. 'He's right, but it's not really all antiquities. I usually specialise in Islamic art—the more obscure pieces, in a field which isn't so hopelessly crowded.' She frowned as though she was wondering whether I was interested.

'Go on.'

'So I go to and fro between Europe and places like Iran and Pakistan. And here of course. It just about pays for the plane ticket, which is what matters.'

It also paid, I noticed, for a Hermes scarf, a Gucci sling bag and a dress that looked like the Cardin Boutique. And shoes by someone Italian and very special. The Islamic art business definitely seemed to be booming.

I looked at her more carefully, lingered over it, then started all over again. She had a full tan, a skin with a hint of olive but now so browned by the sun that she could have had trouble in Texas. She held her head high, the charcoal hair drawn tightly back and clasped in a filigree comb of old silver. She was medium height, her dress cut to accentuate the firmness of her breasts, the silk clasped tight in a wide leather thong. She was slim and graceful; full of grace. Her mouth was sculpted, wide, it was her triumph, you decided, until you passed on to the high flat cheekbones. There was something Asian about her, something from beyond the Caucasus, and the eyes were so dark that their colour was almost lost and they had a trick about them, they were timid at first, melting, lost and frightened, and then you looked again, stirred to her defence, and they had changed, they gazed out at you firm and clear, unflinching, adult, old.

She knew I was looking at her; she let me look. Then she broke away from my gaze and, obeying, I said, 'That's interesting. I know something about Islamic art,' and she said, quickly, 'Do you? Are you an expert?' with something close to hostility.

I said, 'Not at all. My Chairman collects from time to time and drags me around with him. I've got a couple of miniatures, that's all. You could take me for a ride any day you chose.'

Toby grabbed his chance to crawl back into the conversation. 'Mara's here to talk to the Museum people. You've heard how the Egyptian Museum is selling off all those tons of Pharaonic stuff they've had stacked in the basement for years. Worth a fortune and they don't have any use for it. Well, they're also talking of clearing out the Islamic Museum.'

'The place across on Ahmed Maher Square?'

'That's it. The one the tourists steer clear of.'

'I was on my way back from Teheran so I thought I'd call in,' said Mara. 'I've stayed longer than I intended.' She seemed suddenly bored with the subject.

'Tell me about banking,' she commanded.

'Another time. When I get back to Cairo.'

'When will that be?'

'A couple of weeks, I suppose.'

We left it at that. A sort of date, though Toby didn't realise it.

　　　　　　　　　TEN

Two days later I was back in London. Sue was in Rumania with the Foreign Secretary and Monica was in her usual filthy temper. Camden Passage was dead and I retreated to my own flat in Pimlico. It doesn't see enough

43

of me, which is a pity because it's on St George's Square, high on the top storey under chimney stacks made unnecessary by smokeless zones and central heating. It looks down on the Thames and turns a stony wall to Dolphin Square and once-swinging Chelsea. The boats go past with satisfying regularity, making nautical noises in the night, and the seagulls come wheeling and mewing over the rooftops to remind you that London is still one of the great ports.

The flat is just right for a bachelor who tends to sleep out, a bit on the cold side somehow. There is the Breuer chair in chrome and leather, and an enormous Knoll International sofa all along one wall, too expensive for my Puritan soul, a stone-coloured carpet with a tread two centimetres deep, a Scandinavian bookstand, an Albrizzi lamp and my collection of old Baedekers. The bedroom is small and would not have offended St Jerome so long as he didn't look too closely at a couple of miniatures on the wall. The kitchen is just a kitchen, complete with Italian earthenware and a waste-disposal unit that never works.

It's fine so long as I don't have to stay there too long at a stretch. I don't. The House has paid its share, as well it might since Lord Magnus has got into the habit of saying to stray visitors from New York, 'Never mind a hotel—we'll get Thomas to put you up.' I suppose it's more comfortable than the Savoy and a hell of a sight less pricey. It's the only thing about me that KK approves of.

But it was a change after Shepheards and the IATA-regulated first-class cabin which assumes you have the posture of a toad. I slept the clock round, drank a pint of orange juice, took a small black coffee and found a cab first go.

Monica has a temper like a gorilla with toothache. She looks butch to me but probably isn't, though I've never cared enough to find out. We have a relationship of bare tolerance touched with dislike. I suspect her of broadcasting my little weaknesses throughout Fredericks Place —the rows with KK, the strange females on the phone, the alcoholic dictaphone tapes off the New York flight. I sat in my office thinking about the bitch and my problems for ten minutes, the morning cables in a jumble on my desk. A man needs someone to pluck the knives out of his back and all I had in the House was Condon, perhaps Miss Spielter and—I hoped—Lord Magnus. It wasn't enough. The others, with their brazen voices and impeccable suits with floppy ties, had no time for strange transatlantic chaps with the wrong accent who were always gadding off to the Andes or the Pyramids.

'Egyptian bonds,' I said out loud. 'We'll have to change the name.' Or, I reckoned, we were all losers from Endsville. Or Endsgrad, more likely. 'Nile greenbacks, Nile greens for short.' Much better.

Monica heard my laugh on the buzzer and came through to announce, 'Miss Spielter rang to say the Chairman is driving up from the country and wants to see you.' She paused for effect, or perhaps to read her shorthand. 'He wants you to report on progress.' She said it as though she thought I'd have my work cut out. To get my own back I sent her to Xerox the *Bank of Egypt Bulletin* for the last five years.

I saw Magnus. He listened and said nothing. Except to suggest I might go on to New York next. I agreed. Fairly soon, he said. I was already behind schedule, he added.

So I left at once.

ELEVEN

New York was throbbing and humming as it always seems to do in summer; I could hear it even before my yellow cab had reached the Triborough Bridge. A minor key but a distinct hum like the burning of too many cathode tubes somewhere down in the bowels of Manhattan. It wasn't any hotter than Cairo but it felt worse. The heat gets trapped in the asphalt streets and bounces back in blasts from the pavements and the buildings, not cooled at all by the gritty breezes off the Hudson. I had a wretched night in the bank's apartment on East 81st.

The next morning—it would be past lunchtime in London—I headed down Park, where the sun was already burning through layers of yellow smog. I found a cab and cut east, pushing into the downtown traffic on the East Side Drive. There was the usual jam-up near the UN as the sun beat down off the East River and the auto horns blared in frustration, then free again we sweated past the huddle of old brick warehouses, the great spider-web of the Brooklyn Bridge and on towards the sudden mass of towers that Wall Street presents to the River. That, briefly, was worth the horrors of New York City— thousands of windows dull orange and gold in the morning sun, the towers themselves like so many ant-hills crazily crowded on the edge of this island. Welcome home, I said to myself, but it didn't sound right here either.

Wall Street was already black with people hurrying to their offices in that head-down don't-give-a-damn rush-hour way. Our New York office—Transworld Corporation —has two floors in 29 Wall Street, a 35-storey building

46

put up in the late 1920s and still boasting cream-coloured marble in the lobby and lift doors with bas reliefs in sculptured steel. Our own lift, one of the ultimate status symbols in Wall Street, goes direct to the back office on the 19th and, on this morning, to the executive floor, the 20th.

In London we like to be offhand about Transworld, even though Lord Magnus is chairman here too and there are six London directors on the Board. A lot of our bread-and-butter brokerage business comes through Transworld's membership on the New York Stock Exchange. But for all their shoals of bright-eyed Harvard Business School whizz-kids, I suppose we in London reckon ourselves that bit brighter, faster, more imaginative. Magnus, of course, isn't above encouraging a bit of rivalry between his two empires—he thinks it keeps us all on our toes. But it doesn't make for friendly feelings.

The only welcome I got was from Carmen. She is small, dark, and packs a dense Brooklyn accent but her shorthand is just what Sir Isaac Pitman dreamed about, far faster than anyone's at Fredericks Place; she's the secretary New York lays on for London visitors.

'Mr Condon's flying in from Brussels later today,' she told me, and I wondered why. The air-conditioning made the office very cold, like a high-class funeral. But Carmen is a good thing, we work well together and this time she was laughing a lot; she almost made up for the hours I had to spend that afternoon with the statistical boys who had worked out all the flaws in the World Bank report. It was probably the homework I needed. Guy turned up in the early evening, listened to me for two hours over dinner at Sayat Nova, nodded assent, pushed aside his patlijan moussaka half-eaten, and announced we would go straight down to Washington in the morning. 'They're

47

expecting us,' he said. 'That's why I had to skip Amsterdam.'

So it was the Eastern shuttle from La Guardia to National, a taxi, and on to 1818 H Street, the undistinguished pile housing the World Bank and IFC.

Cool anonymous corridors; regulation international civil servant furniture; expertise and no nonsense from crisp European receptionists; hordes of statisticians. I met a Swede, a Canadian and a German from the Egyptian desk and we went over the project, worrying again and again at the essential problems: where were the Egyptians to get enough foreign exchange to service an international dollar issue, and who would even buy it in the first place? Well, yes, of course, Government guarantees and probably simultaneous World Bank financing, that was the assumption on which we were working. But what of the Middle East war?

And then how about the technical feasibility of the Nile barrages? That seemed to be the least of it. The barrage scheme was designed to overcome the biggest adverse effect of the Aswan High Dam: the Dam was trapping the silt which had always been washed down from Africa into the Mediterranean, and thereby was removing much of the enrichment of the annual flood. This could be matched by inputs of fertiliser, as the experts insisted, but the secondary consequence was disturbing—the water, without the silt, was moving faster, dangerously faster.

This greater velocity of water was tending to erode the Nile banks and alter the river's course. Somehow the water had to be slowed back, and Soviet and Egyptian engineers had reached the obvious and simple solution: to design ten or so barrages to span the Nile downstream from the Dam. The charm of this idea was that the barrages would also permit enormous gains to Egypt's economy from improved irrigation and the generation of yet more hydro-electric power at various chosen points downstream.

Yes, I had been over it a dozen times and agreed, it all could work, I saw their point—given the money to finance construction. Which was our cue. Which was why I was Egypt's favourite banker right now. And why I was growing old before my time.

Joe Larochelle was the man who mattered to us so far as the Bank was concerned. French-Canadian, middle-aged, paunchy, amiable, shrewd, tough—you name it—he'd been appointed loan officer in charge of the Nile barrage operation. We'd all done our homework and in case we'd forgotten the small print he had the members of the study mission just back from Cairo waiting to lunch with us. The World Bank goes in for reduced-calorie affairs, taken at a fast gallop with lots of iced water. I've always told them they go to excessive lengths to parade their consciences before the rest of us. But they persist with the water.

'The problem,' Condon said, when Joe was ready for the skull session, 'is terribly simple really.' Guy always plays up the limey accent when he's in the States, so when the crasser natives laugh at it they don't realise the laugh is on them. 'The Egyptians have a bloody awful image, or so our European colleagues insist. True or false?'

'True,' replied Joe, 'but not-so-true any longer. Or at least not-so-justified. Remember, we went in the other day with an IDA soft loan of $26m for a drainage project in the Delta. The first time we've been in Egypt since '59 when the Canal was being enlarged.'

'And if the drainage project makes good sense, the Cascade is a must.'

'The drainage project makes good sense,' muttered one of the economists.

Condon said, 'The point I'm getting at is that the more

49

unmistakably you people get involved in Egypt, the more respectability you give it. And our friends in the commercial sector will slowly draw the moral.'

'Which is a good discount?'

'Precisely.'

'So how much are you looking to us for?'

I said, 'I reckon we wouldn't want to go beyond an issue of $50m for the time being. First-stage foreign exchange project costs look like being $125m—you may want to query me on that—so I think we'd welcome at least a $30m loan from you here, simultaneous with our $50m...'

Condon cut in quickly: 'And then we'd have to have some sort of standby agreement for the remaining $45m.'

'Surprise, surprise!' said the Canadian. 'That's almost exactly what your titled chairman mentioned. And he said he was talking off the top of his head.'

'Now why,' I asked patiently, 'should you expect us to disagree with the top of our master's head?'

Joe grinned. 'I told him that was impossible. So he said, "The impossible, my dear Larochelle, just takes a little longer."'

I groaned. 'It's his favourite Israeli proverb.'

It was sounding too flip, too easy. We were leaving out all the banshees. The enemies of the Minister. The stupidity of European bankers. The caution of the market. The inefficiency of the Egyptians. The constant threat of a bust-up at the Canal. This wasn't the impossible, as Magnus liked to see it: it was the fantastic.

Condon was saying, 'We're all going too fast. Now let me tell you the *real* problems...'

We worked late, then went back to New York. By then those few rooms in East 81st looked like home.

TWELVE

London had changed in the space of four days. There were more dustbins on the streets, more tourists underfoot, and the Queen had left town. KK was back from Portmeirion and Sue had left Bucharest for Sofia and was due back the next day. There were two postcards from her. Condon had come back on an earlier flight and was being stroppy, no one knew why. Kaffirs had taken a tumble and interest rates were edging higher again. Bradford wooltops were strong, they told me, which was nice to know. I used to be happy for Bradford when I heard that sort of news.

Condon came into my office in mid-morning and slid into a chair. He was wearing his over-the-top-now-lads expression. I didn't like it and told him so. He shrugged. This was business.

'You know the form,' he said, from some cool height. 'You've got to go out and do the rounds as soon as possible. Which means at once.'

I said I was tired. And so, I suggested, was he.

He wasn't having any. 'We want to know where we stand before we start burning up the telex or sending you back out to Cairo—we've got to know fast whether this is a total non-starter as far as the potential underwriters are concerned. We simply haven't got any time to spare.'

'So I talk to the Swiss.' Of course, he was right. He knew I knew.

'Yes, and more than that. You'll have to start in Zürich. But we either get a *Cassa per il Mezzogiorno* type of syndicate—everyone and his brother, and the Kuwaitis, too— or the operation just is not on.'

I said, 'From what the World Bank people say, it's technically feasible. And I presume Magnus has worried through the political angles.'

'Then we've got to find out whether the "Free World Investment Community", as Washington stills calls it'—I winced—'is having any Egyptian paper today, thank you.'

Condon wasn't smiling. Neither was I. We both of us knew too much about our job. And I for one was feeling the old familiar jet-travel syndrome pounding at the back of my skull. Sometimes, I reckoned, we earned our money. Sometimes, I agreed, it was a mug's game.

Condon said, 'I've been checking the calendar. You can't afford to give yourself more than a fortnight in Europe because you'll have to be back in Cairo by the end of the month to get those technical points cleared up by the High Dam people. I shall have to fit in some overnight trips from here, and then we're due back in the States in the third week of July. That will just give you time to get to the Gulf if the Board decides you ought to go. And you're still pushing up against the Minister's deadline.'

I went back to Pimlico and slept twelve hours.

The next day I worked on my schedule with Monica. Zürich, Geneva, Amsterdam, Brussels, Paris, Frankfurt— to take soundings—and then straight to Cairo.

She asked, 'Hotels?' and I groaned for effect and said, 'The Amstel, I suppose, and of course the Westbury because of their concierge: and why not the Crillon? And it's summer so make it the Dolder in Zürich and finish up with the Frankfurt Intercontinental.' It was moments like these when I supposed I was turning my life into parody.

Later, Sue came home. I moved back to Camden Passage.

THIRTEEN

'Good to see you back with us,' said KK when I reached
the directors' dining room for lunch the next day, as
though I had been off for six months with a dangerous
disease. I said, 'Thank you, KK.' I wished I knew what had
been going on while I was away.

'Thomas won't be here for long,' said Condon, who
liked to come out with ambiguous remarks. I knew he had
spent half the morning talking to Frankfurt. He saw me
look askance and smiled dryly. 'Believe it or not,' he said
quietly, 'but this thing might be getting off the ground.
Our friends over there are rather intrigued.'

'But we don't print a circular yet.'

'No, but it may be an interesting clue. Watch how they're
interested here as well,' he added, nodding towards the
long oval of mahogany which was set up for what Condon's
friends in Frankfurt call a *Chefbesprechung*.

I needed to know more but it was too late, we were sitting
down and I hadn't had time to spy out the land. But Sir
Felix was here, I could see—Sir Felix Reinhard Rendon,
one of our founding fathers, eighty-seven if he was a day
and put out to lush pasture by Magnus years ago, but still
able to come up with a shrewd question when he wasn't
sound asleep in his chair.

'Any chance of a change of government in Cairo?'
asked one of the directors who rarely bothered to greet me.
He was probably thinking of cotton futures.

Lord Magnus said, 'Not unless we say so. Eh, Thomas?'

'Just what was decided in '56,' I said thinly. I was fed up
with that kind of remark. I sometimes wondered whether
I was working for the wrong side. Not that I'd have jumped

at a job in the Egyptian Finance Ministry, but perhaps something in the World Bank? God, Mammon and Third World uplift too.

The House has an obsession with security so it provides paper shredders on every floor and princely salaries for the telephonists. The directors serve their own lunch through a hatch-affair which occasionally shows a pair of disembodied hands doling out the silver salvers. Condon claims the hands belong to a deaf-mute.

But the food is good, verging on the simple—smoked salmon, steak, a ripe Brie, fruit. Not much of any of these. Almost Spartan if you know what some of the other banks go in for. KK had cut back on the lunches, banning the sweet course to Lord Magnus's secret fury. He's probably right. Most of us are more concerned about the claret ration; it's a small château which we've apparently had an investment in for years, but KK keeps us to a modest two glasses each. Lord Magnus doesn't object; he only drinks Malvern water at lunch.

We got through lunch faster than the junior staff could have imagined. Too fast for my liking. Lord Magnus said abruptly, 'Thomas! Speak up!' and the others scowled at their coffee. Sir Felix was snoring sweetly at Magnus's right-hand.

I said, 'Do you want all the details? Sir?'

'Of course not. The essence. The naked essence!'

'That's simple. We might—we just might—be on.' I took a Perfectos from the silver box and tried to light a match on my thumbnail. Condon hastily threw across a gas lighter.

'I won't know till I've gone back to New York and seen the Washington people again. With your permission. And Guy will probably want to do the European circuit once more before we try to form a group.'

Condon nodded. I went on, 'I'll go back myself to Cairo in a week or two, after I've done a flip through the European banks—I'll co-ordinate with Guy. But we have to move fast—that's why both of us will have to keep travelling—because I'm worried that Cairo may go cool on us. The Minister is adamant that we must bring forward our deadline if we are to avoid trouble there. Or the Israelis could blow up the Aswan Dam and that will be that.' No one reacted. Condon was studying the sediment in his glass, but he was nodding very slightly, imperceptibly to anyone else. So I pressed on.

'The market is favourable at the moment. There are not too many issues in the pipeline and everyone's hungry for a fat yield. The chief problem of course is guarantees, but the World Bank people are working on that aspect and are very keen on timing their loan to coincide with our issue. Preliminary soundings seem to indicate that the market could absorb an initial tranche of, say $35 million of fifteen-year bonds with another $15 million of three to five year notes placed at the same time with a commercial bank consortium. Further issues could be planned to coincide with completion dates in the various stages of the project.'

I paused. Lord Magnus, I saw, was squinting around the table, totting up the balance.

Sir Felix had woken up and was listening. KK was gazing at me the way an auditor looks at faked accounts.

Someone said, 'Shouldn't we try to get some idea of Israeli intentions? It's obviously one of the important factors in any equation...'

'That aspect is under control,' Lord Magnus declared. 'As you all know, we have remarkably good contacts in Tel Aviv.' It was the nearest any of us would get to commenting on the irony of a bank with what used to be a

55

Jewish name managing a bond issue for an Arab government.

Condon said, 'Speaking of Tel Aviv, someone might perhaps go to Israel. Thomas on his next trip? It's possible we might get some quiet help. There's no question of an appearance, of course, but one of the Swiss Israeli banks might just come in on the selling group. They do have some surprising placing power.'

An elderly bill-broker spoke up wearily for the cause of scepticism and Little England. 'Let's be more realistic on where we stand. It all sounds very pie in the sky ...'

The others looked more interested, though one of them murmured and slipped away, closing the door quietly like a mourner at a funeral. I said, 'The Egyptians have to have the money, and admit they'd rather get it from the the West; though they claim the Russians have made a firm offer. When I saw the Minister the other day in Cairo, he told me they'd be prepared to have a coupon at a substantial discount so long as we tap big funds.'

I hesitated, wondering how Lord Magnus wanted to play this. 'The Minister spoke at length about the restoration of Egyptian-Western relations—that sort of thing. It was all a little vague at this early stage, you understand.'

Sir Felix stirred himself and warbled faintly so that we strained to hear him. 'I cannot claim to have studied all the papers,' he confessed, and smiled his usual old-man's smile at all of us. 'But the sentiments, if that is the right word, seem perfectly acceptable. I wonder, though, about one detail in the project estimates. There is $25m for "ancillary engineering", I observe ...'

He tailed off into silence and acquiescence. Lord Magnus glared at me and I said, 'I'll look into it, Sir Felix,' very firmly and loudly.

Condon took over. 'Thomas has left out the most powerful of all our arguments here in London. This will be the biggest boost to our export figures since Rolls-Royce sold those engines to Lockheed—and this time there won't be any disaster to follow. We all know that most of the bonds will be placed in Switzerland. But if the Egyptians finance this part of the project through the City, there will be dozens of contracts for equipment and services let to British firms. Surely that's worth battling for too?'

Lord Magnus was grunting his agreement.

'What guarantees?' insisted the broker, and fought a battle with his cigar.

'Well,' said Condon carefully, 'the days of a charge on Customs revenues may be over. But the World Bank are willing to subordinate their financing to ours, there'll be a floating charge on all the Nile Authority assets, and of course the usual negative pledge clause provisions. What it ultimately rests on, as we all realise, is "full faith and credit". But we know that Cairo really wants this one, *and much more*: that's the ultimate sanction.'

There was a pause. Someone fumbled a pipe alight.

'What happens if there's another war?'

'That's the Egyptians' problem,' said Condon. 'Obviously any investor knows that risk when he buys the bonds.' He was beginning to crouch low across the table, which meant he was getting interested. 'Personally, I doubt whether the Israelis would knock out something as big as this. No matter what noises they make, they care too much for world opinion. And if I remember my military days'—he glanced at Lord Magnus, who had a chestful of medals from the War—'they're in a position of military superiority.'

'It's quite a gamble.'

'For Christ's sake!' I exclaimed, and saw several eyebrows go up. 'Of course it is! What did we expect? Most of the big investment projects have been precisely that. A gamble! We could keep going, if we had to, on the standard Scandinavian issue, but those aren't as interesting as they used to be, as we all know.'

'If we don't do it, someone else might try,' said one of the younger directors, a take-over type we'd recruited recently from journalism. 'Griegson's would love to show us their paces.'

Lord Magnus intervened with the tact of Solomon. 'I don't see any reason not to let Thomas carry on for a few weeks and see what the result of further soundings may be. If he can't make headway, that's that. If he can—and he'll look in some unusual places, I hope—then damn me, we've got a coup on our hands. He may as well be in Cairo as kicking his heels in my office—he's no use to any of the rest of you.'

He ho-ho'd jovially to show he was joking. It was a little close to the knuckle for my taste.

KK stirred himself at the bottom of the table and said, 'What do you mean by "unusual" sources? Nothing disreputable, I trust.' Lord Magnus gestured at me. I said, 'Condon's the expert.' Guy grinned, as though he enjoyed the thought of funds being thought disreputable.

'First of all there's the Arabs' own cash,' he said. 'And we know what that means. In the present atmosphere it ought to be easy to persuade them to put up a good bagful. They're deeply involved in Eurobonds already, and down in the Gulf they'll jump at any way of keeping Cairo Radio under control.' He paused. 'Then I thought Thomas or I might take a look at some of the funds from the under-developed world which have been flowing so merrily back into the developed world—the Chinese merchants, for instance, who buy US company overseas bonds rather than put their cash into a situation nearer home where the political prospects are not so good. I've been in Bangkok recently and it's obvious that millions have been flowing out of Thailand and Vietnam by the back-door as fast as the Americans have poured them in at the front. Apart from that, you can add the usual sources—Latin America and so on.'

Lord Magnus said, 'Guy, you don't give enough attention to Kuwait. I'd like to see Thomas in Kuwait the next trip.'

Condon nodded. 'He can do it after Beirut. Though the Lebanon is still worth a couple of days: the information is as good as ever even if a lot of the Gulf funds seem to have been withdrawn after that last bout of guerrilla fighting.'

Suddenly there was silence. We began to look at our watches. There was nothing else to be said. It was the moment Magnus had been waiting for.

'So you go!' announced our Chairman, as though there had been a unanimous vote. 'Watch your step, Thomas! Lots of interests involved. They'll all be trying to have you on.'

Sir Felix smiled amiably at nothing in particular; Magnus was chortling; KK was already beating a retreat through the door; I was grinning, too, God knows why; only Condon was looking sour.

'Cheer up,' said the ex-journalist. 'You convinced us, didn't you?'

Guy shook his head. 'We're making it sound too easy,' he said. 'We'll deserve the Order of the Nile if we get within a mile of it.'

FOURTEEN

Zürich was a steady slog, if brief. I checked in at the
Dolder, looking enviously at the cars going up to the
Wellenbad as my taxi slid down Waldhaus-Strasse and
into town. The city was hot, the heavy moist *Föhn* blow-
ing in from the lake, and the bankers at first were snappish
and sceptical. I worked my way methodically down the
Bahnhofstrasse, calling on the big boys first, then on to the
smaller private banks. Not for the first time, I discovered
that Zürich had heard about my business before I arrived.
I fielded questions on the project, the possible size of an
issue, how it could be done, who might be in, what guarantees were on or not. Even those banks which I guessed
to be sitting on Gulf sheikhs' accounts were polite but
distant; Eurodollar issue pipeline clogged perhaps, or the
war, or just the *Föhn*. Yet through all the needling and
the cool ironies I detected at the end a faint whiff of
interest. Yes, a good solid coupon at a hefty discount. Fat
yield and the World Bank were in too; perhaps the sort of
paper for high-yield portfolios. All the banks had plenty
of those.

I was sweating by mid-afternoon, and dropped in at
Sprüngli for an *Eiskaffee* and a chance to use the loo.
Sprüngli never changes: brown wood panelling and ladies
in toques eating heavy cream-cakes. I picked up a *Tribune
de Genève*, read of a brokerage firm which was rumoured
to be in *'difficultés plus ou moins graves, à la suite de la
baisse générale de la bourse de New-York'*. Which of the
banks in Geneva I wondered had already been contacted
by the informants in Zürich about TR's latest caper.
Enough of them, I'd bet; they'd be expecting me. I paid

the bill and went back to my rounds. There was a wild geometric tie in the window of Cravates Nelly in Bärengasse, but I resisted the temptation.

I resisted the usual dinner invitations, too, and was back at the Dolder at 6.30, breathing in the smell of the pine trees as I kicked off my banker's greys to put on a thin shirt and slacks for the walk to the Wellenbad. There were still plenty of people around, staring at each other's well-oiled bodies in a discreet Swiss way, but I headed straight for the water and plunged in. Nothing changed. Life was cool order. The mini-tidal wave still came rolling down the pool each half-hour with Swiss precision, preceded by a warning bell.

Geneva.

Amsterdam.

Brussels.

Paris.

Frankfurt.

More of the same, without the Wellenbad. Interviews, explanations, queries, endless telephoning, elaborate lunches with Herr Generaldirektor or M. le Directeur-Adjoint. It was getting easier, though, the word was getting around, and somehow the whole notion of the Nile issue didn't seem so far-fetched any more. At least, that's what I reported to Lord Magnus by telephone before boarding the Lufthansa flight to Cairo. 'The ball,' declared Magnus across the wire, 'is in the Egyptians' court!'

'Let's hope they know what to do with it,' I said.

And it was only there, in the Boeing, with the Greek islands turquoise far below, that the pressure began to catch up with me and I noticed the nerves began to twitch. So I had another drink. It didn't help, or didn't have time to work, because Cairo was below us.

There was no joy in it this time. I found trouble at Immigration. Toby Underhill didn't meet me. The taxi was as slow as a camel and nearly as dangerous. There was a dust storm over the city and the air was dry and soiled. A dwarf sat on the pavement, roaring with rage or laughter, I couldn't tell. I felt like a spent gigolo.

FIFTEEN

The Egyptian economist said, 'You see, there are the figures,' and pushed the pile of papers across the desk so I could check he hadn't added them up wrong.

'But that's impossible!' I exclaimed. 'Quite impossible! You're showing a deficit of a couple of million.'

He smiled faintly, like the commander of a garrison who hears the bugles of the relief force when half his men are dead.

'Precisely,' he said. 'And I have included the maximum potential of the Nile Cascade. We get a thirty per cent boost to irrigation acreage—if we are lucky—and the gain will be wiped out in four years. As you say, sir, it is impossible. An impossible situation.'

'What then?'

He looked at me, indulgence touched with exasperation. '"Then?" Why, "then" a lot of people will die. No—I mean they will not live. Will not survive. Their expectation of life will not improve, if you prefer.' He didn't bother to inject a Westerner's tincture of grief into his voice.

'You're telling me I ought to be getting you twice the money at half the interest rate?'

'I'm telling you simply that we *need* this project, by whatever criteria you examine it. And we'll meet your terms, whatever they may be, and pay up on the nail, as the expression goes, because we have one score more projects still to come and every one is as important as this and probably bigger.'

I said, 'OK. Get back to the ancillary engineering item.' I still didn't see how it came to $25m. He'd taken me through the maps a dozen times but I was short on the basic engineering training and it was hard work for me, this computing of cubic metres and water velocity, evaporation percentage and seepage loss.

We were working in his flat, out in the relative greenery and quiet of Maadi. The furniture was jammed into three rooms, a reminder that this was another affluent bourgeois family expropriated by the Revolution yet working for it and even honoured by it. There were books spreading across every wall and photographs of London School of Economics post-graduates in the bathroom, and every hour he broke off from cramming me with obscure facts and figures to call for tea from his spinster sister and tell me lurid tales of the intrigues in the Department which perpetually threatened him with loss of his post. One of the Somerville girls had said she would call in, but there was no sign of her.

I said wearily, 'Let's get back to the schedule. If you can vet the draft of the Offering Circular, when can you tell me who would come over to New York to sign the Purchasing Agreement and the Fiscal Agency Agreement?' And SEC Form 18, I remembered. If we ever got that far . . .

We worked on into the evening cool.

SIXTEEN

The Ambassador summoned me to tea, so I had my Hong Kong suit pressed and went off on foot into the afternoon heat, out on to the Corniche and up the road towards the Nile Hotel. Cairo is surprisingly convenient for a big city. The main hotels, the Nile Hilton, the Nile, the Semiramis and Shepheards, are grouped together overlooking the river and many of the embassies are within a mile or so across on the top of Gezira.

The British Embassy is embarrassingly vast, laid out with lawns and pilasters over a whole block; it can be compared in the empire of the Min. of Works only with the Consulate-General in Istanbul, and is about as unnecessary. It's well known to the mob, so the police are usually much in evidence at the gates. I avoided the British Council Library and aimed for the Residency.

Sir Wilfred looked younger than his years and smaller than his photograph and bounced up and down like an urchin. He was waiting for me in the enormous, high-ceilinged, cave-cool study, ruffling the tissue pages of the airmail *Times*. He sat cross-legged in his socks on a sagging sofa. It was proof that he had once been one of HM's Political Agents in a sheikhdom of the Persian Gulf, an experience which is guaranteed to turn a smooth diplomat into a romantic Arabophile for life.

'You know how anxious we are...' he began. I was getting tired of this line. I said, 'Yes, of course, the Secretary of State...' and tailed off as though to suggest that the Foreign Secretary and I had an understanding that could only be hinted at even in the presence of one of Her Majesty's Ambassadors Plenipotentiary.

The Sudanese servants (or were they Nubians?) brought in tea. We chatted, delicately, of London and the weather until they had left.

'How is it going?' said Sir Wilfred. 'If I may ask ...' His socks were very clean and I couldn't see where he had left his shoes. I wondered if he entertained Egyptians in bare feet.

I told him, then said, 'You see, so much depends on whether the prospective underwriters can be persuaded that the guarantees mean anything, and of course primarily on what the Egyptians are really thinking. That's where I need your advice.'

HE munched his rock cake furiously and washed it down with a swig of lemon tea.

He said, 'I had rather a curious encounter with my Soviet colleague yesterday. It was done very discreetly of course ——' I made what I hoped were suitable diplomatic noises '——but the upshot was that he wanted to know if we were serious about the Nile project.'

I said, 'He knew?'

'My dear fellow, of course he knew. There is no such thing as a secret in Cairo. They get hopelessly mixed up with the gossip so you never know which secrets are the *real* secrets.'

'Did he take the idea seriously?' Very few other people seemed to.

'Most definitely,' said the Ambassador, and began to wave his hands at me. 'He'd be very foolish not to. The Soviets would undoubtedly be most embarrassed if we took over where the High Dam ended. I'd be the most popular man in Cairo. Which would be a pleasant change.'

'How's that?'

'It's very simple. The Russians have been calling the tune here since the Six-Day War. They've paid the piper well, I admit, but they're getting a bit of a bore—for the Egyptians I mean. It's not their fault, they've behaved very well, but inevitably they have been forced to appear the masters and that's always difficult, as we know so very well.' He paused, sighed, sipped again. 'And these Soviet Air Force officers on the missile sites...' His voice tailed away. He paused while the Nubians came in and poured out more tea, then carried on. 'It's true, you know. The West—despite everything—is astonishingly well thought of out here—quietly, of course, behind the façade of invective.'

Ambassadors often fall into these delusions, I thought. It's splendid if you can persuade yourself you are loved deeply whatever insults the mob may shout at your wife. But in this case, I wondered whether he might not be right. I said, 'At least we allow them to feel they can make a choice.'

He said, 'Precisely! We're a credible alternative.'

'And you believe we're credible?'

'My dear fellow, you know it already,' said Sir Wilfred. 'The Cabinet here have talked about nothing else for the the last two weeks. If they're not showing you their enthusiasm it's because they don't trust capitalist bankers— at least, until they see the colour of their money. They probably think the harder they make you sweat the better the terms they'll get.'

'It's not like that at all,' I said gloomily, and tried to explain about floating an international issue, where the likely sources of funds were, how timing and first-class sponsorship and careful soundings in advance were all-important.

Sir Wilfred looked appropriately intelligent as he listened, then rose to shake me warmly by the shoulder. 'I wanted to cheer you up,' he said. 'If the Russians have their wind up you must be getting somewhere. It looks as though you're over the first fence.'

The first fence was always the lowest, I remembered. There was probably something in the Koran which put it even better. As old Füssli at the Swiss Bank Corp. had once breathed at me: *'Aller Anfang ist schwer,* my dear young colleague.'

I ran into Toby Underhill and his Jag outside the Chancery, where he was gossiping with the security officer. He gave me a lift back to Shepheards; he didn't seem surprised to see me back.

'HE still the determined optimist? he inquired.

I grunted. Casual as a QC about to spring I said, 'How long have you known that Tal girl?'

'Not very long. Nice, isn't she?'

'Very nice,' I said. 'How long?'

'Couple of weeks. Seen a lot of her recently.'

'What's her first name again?'

'Mara.' He spelled it.

'Is she in town?'

'Afraid not. She's just popped over to Rome for a few days.' I was absurdly angry.

'Congratulations, anyhow,' I said.

He smiled, and looked quite handsome for a moment, in that English sort of way.

I said, 'I'm leaving the day after tomorrow.'

'I'll take you to the airport.'

 SEVENTEEN

I went East.

The form was the same everywhere. Heat shimmering

67

off the airport buildings. Bored or sullen or obstructive officials, armed guards, taxis shuddering through dusty streets, cold air pushed through anonymous luxury hotels by grinding wall fans. Telephoning and more taxis, charging their kamikaze way down crowded narrow streets.

The banks marble-cool, and curious looks from the outer office babus crouched over their tiny desks. Smiles, invitations to sit on low sofas, sticky coffees, protestations of eternal friendship. On my part, explanations in that *haute banque* manner which conveyed what a privilege it would be for the Banque Anonyme to associate itself with us on this deal, a privilege with 'a not uninteresting yield'. They liked that, the bankers, I could see the nerve pulsing in the flesh of their necks at the very sound of the phrase. And for us, TR, of course what a great pleasure to be working again with our good friends of Banque Anonyme.

After three days, I could have given the spiel in my sleep. By the fifth day I had begun to dislike the sound of my own voice. The trip lasted twelve days.

But the issue was on.

EIGHTEEN

Pimlico was blooming bravely in the morning sunshine when I got back to London, but the nannies in Kensington Gardens were doubtless right, it was too bright too early, the damp began to rise from the Thames, the cumulus was scudding overhead and I decided to give the House a miss for one day. I rang the Foreign Office and said to Sue, 'You're back then,' and she said, 'What d'you mean?' and I said, 'Lunch at The Garden? With the admen and the lawyers?'

'And the journalists. And that hideous carpet.' I took it she agreed.

I walked all the way to Henrietta Street, head down and hands in pockets, along the Embankment. The police were keeping a careful eye on the traffic at Westminster which meant there was an all-night session in the Commons and they never knew when an MP in pyjamas would be making a dash for the division lobby. The tourists outnumbered the natives and Whitehall was a stage-set for a long-running farce. The Life Guards looked as miserable as their horses, enduring the flashbulbs. London was like an old vaudeville hoofer, I decided, going through her paces one last time for the benefit of *Time* magazine. The strain of swinging, however briefly, had begun to tell and the tourists were already tired of Portobello Market and the King's Road. They would soon stream away to Copenhagen or Sofia, and London would be as passé as Paris. I looked forward to the day.

Sue was tired and shabby too, wearing a linen suit whose cut was inferior to the material. So I hugged her in front of the waiters and tried to say all the right things.

We sat down and she looked downright pretty and confessed she loved her Minister of State with a sad and unrequited passion. I did my melancholy Slav bit, pressing my head against the wall until the customers looked at us and groaning with the pangs of jealousy. She said, 'He's so *sweet*. So gentle and aristocratic, and so shy with all the official visitors. He has a terrible time at home—he's a widower and he told me he has to cope with two teen-age daughters. But then the car calls for him to take him away from it all. He enjoys that part of it enormously, going down the Hill with the policemen saluting, so he never gets through his papers completely. Then we're all waiting for him, all nice and smart and respectful, to take him upstairs.'

I said, 'You've got him under control, then?'

'At first he was scared stiff of us, but now he wallows in it. You should see him, he's six inches taller by the time he reaches his room.'

'And then there's Palmerston on the wall and Miss Carew hovering over him all morning with a bit of shoulder showing and a healthy dash of lavender water.'

'Don't be rude. He told me I was as good as a daughter to him.'

'Wait till he asks you to be a mother to his daughters.'

'You're just jealous.'

'I have a right to be. There's only one woman in my life.'

'Don't tell lies.'

'My word is my bond. My floating-rate convertible bond of course. It's not for want of trying.'

Sue opened her menu and began to study it as though she was looking for spelling mistakes.

She ate the avocado without the shellfish, a double lamb cutlet and green salad, and irrigated the mixture with the house claret and black coffee and brandy. I accompanied her. She said she was slimming and I told her she must be joking.

Out again into Covent Garden and the smell of fresh air and tomatoes, Woodbine cigarettes and onions.

She said, 'Lend me fifty p. for a taxi.'

'I'll drop you,' I replied, cutting down towards the Strand. I had to go up West.

The commercial section of the Egyptian Embassy is in South Street, hard by the shadow of the Dorchester, and manages somehow to summarise in a quarter of an acre the atmosphere of the country it represents. Go through those doors and from the point of view of the Metropolitan Police you are on Egyptian territory. They are more right than they know. It looks, feels, effectively is, Cairo.

The carpets are threadbare and wheeze dust. The corridors are long and gloomy like a hotel without guests. The paintwork is chipped and stained, the late President looks out gloomily in granite from the entrance and the welcome is as warm and vague as an absent-minded great-aunt. I'd lost count of how often they had broken off diplomatic relations; but I couldn't manage to get angry with people who hadn't realised for years that they had a Tiepolo on their ceiling.

The Ambassador and the Commercial Counsellor were delighted. They had convinced themselves that all was over bar the signing. There would be HE's photograph in the papers and then the inauguration. The Counsellor said, shyly, 'Perhaps the Prime Minister will want to come out and push the button.'

'We'll ask the White House as well,' said the Ambassador, a saturnine gentleman heavy with Clark Gable charm. The chickens were having their grandchildren counted while the eggs were still cold as Tutankhamen's tomb. I said, 'There are still a heap of details to be sorted out. We shall need your help.'

I explained patiently about the international bond market, the institutional investors and others, how an underwriting syndicate is formed, the selling group, where the bonds might be listed, and why it was important to have a good after-market. They listened carefully, asked the right questions, looked impressed at the end. We worked happily for an hour, then they let me out past the lone policeman back into London. There was sand in my hair and I would have had an arak if it weren't for the British licensing laws.

Back in the House they were all fussing over a new computer, a piece of hardware which was to connect all our European associates instantaneously and process and control Eurosecurity transactions. KK kept talking about the software problem. He was grinning like a kid with a new electric train-set. Monica told me Mr Condon was in Paris. I called on Mr Bullen, our accountant, to ask for more travellers' cheques, and he complained that I hadn't yet submitted an account for my Peruvian advance.

'I warn you, Mr Kane,' he said wearily, 'I don't want it back in a bundle of escudos like last time.'

'There's nothing coming back,' I said, and he looked at me as if I had revoked. He said, 'I look forward to receiving the statement,' as though I had run amok at the casino. He was one of KK's men.

Miss Spielter said that Lord Magnus was at the Bank of England. He would be arguing the toss about ending the float. There was a scrawl of green ink on my desk. 'None of my business—but why not marry Susannah? Just been lunching with the Minister of State.'

I crumpled it and threw it at the wastepaper basket and missed. What girl needed enemies with friends like that?

Six days later I left for New York. Sue came to the airport. 'I still haven't seen your New York flat,' she said. 'Apartment,' I said. The duty-free shop had run out of quarts of Chivas. Again.

It was the best time to leave London. I was going to escape the English weekend. I kissed Sue in front of the Special Branch desk and let myself be carried away on the conveyor belt of international travel. A package for the New World once more, I climbed into the nose of the 747.

'Welcome aboard, darling,' said the Chief Steward, and gave his greying curls a last pat in the mirror.

NINETEEN

New York was in aid of two big pieces in the jigsaw: a possible registration of the issue with the SEC, and co-ordinating the whole deal with the World Bank. The SEC are niggling and difficult, everyone knew that, and American lawyers compulsive comma-hunters whose services come very high, but registering securities with the SEC appeals to Continental investors, and the information required in the prospectus would be valuable in helping to re-establish Egyptian credit.

So Condon and I went through the exercise, endless sessions with the lawyers and the Transworld statistical boffins on the whole Egyptian economy, the debt situation, Government revenues and expenditures, the lot. Hours of drafting and re-drafting, till I couldn't tell the public health bilharzia statistics from the country's IMF gold tranche. We worked New York lawyers' hours, till eleven or even later most evenings, with dinners sent in from Eberlin's or an hour's break at Oscar's where the bond traders propped each other up along the bar missing successive trains to Great Neck, and the food in the dark-purple dining room was vaguely Italian, overpriced, and definitely inferior to the martinis.

We would emerge into the street to the dividend of a cool breeze off the Battery: a hint of clean ocean salt after the day's exhaust fumes. Streets nearly empty now, the battalions of Polish and Ukrainian office cleaners mopping their way down miles of marble floor, bank windows lit up where the night computer teams and cheque sorters were reducing the mountain of the day's paper. Unlike the City of London, Wall Street never entirely closes down.

Some nights I'd be too tired to go back to 81st and would drop in on Rosa. She is intense and small and fiercely committed to causes, from California grape pickers to the rehabilitation of junkies. 'R. Vitale' it says on her mail-box in the front hall of the three-storey house in St Luke's Place, because if you put 'Miss' on the mail-box that would be an invitation to obscene letters, threats, perhaps worse. Rosa accepts that about New York, as she accepts the astronomical rent she pays for her single large room overlooking a soot-blackened garden, the noise from the endless police and fire sirens, the dirt and danger everywhere. But St Luke's Place is pretty special, a little enclave amid all the Village squalor: a row of old gingko trees, the 1840s houses with front steps and neat white-framed windows, and the view of a little park where the old Italian men play *bocce* every evening and the neighbourhood kids splash in a swimming pool dark-green with chlorine.

Rosa accepts other things, too, and has few illusions about who I am or where we two may be going. She manages to live in the present, reminding me that her people tilled a vineyard on the slopes of Vesuvius before coming to New York. How she reconciles our relationship with her membership in the local Women's Lib seminar I don't know, and I don't ask.

We would look up at the garlanded plaster ceiling of her room, watching the mobile catch puffs of air from the ancient air-conditioner, sometimes listening to music, occasionally talking. She never asked me about my work or my absences or my London life; we lay together on the slopes of the New York volcano, taking and giving without explanation and without looking beyond each night.

By the beginning of the second week there was enough of a skeleton prospectus to warrant a trip to the World Bank, so Condon and I caught the shuttle and headed once again for the shrine at 1818 H. The news was good. The Bank, said Larochelle, would be prepared to make a loan of $30m simultaneously with our issue of $50m, as we had asked. As for the shortfall of $45m to cover total first-stage project costs, the Bank would enter into a standby commitment to ante up the remainder when as and if all went according to plan. The commitment would be for half the usual charge: everyone, manifestly, was bending over backward to get this one launched.

Condon left at once for London and from then on he was sending me daily telexes while I battled it out in Wall Street. By the end of the second week we had a pretty good idea of what the preliminary interest in the issue might be. The Swiss were in for very sizeable amounts, and so were the American institutions, hungry as ever for a good yield and no Interest Equalisation Tax to pay. Even the Scandinavians were biting. Barring a blow-up in the political situation, we might just have a success on our hands.

The only disappointment was from the Middle East itself. A lot of that money, of course, was in Switzerland already but the Beirut banks hadn't been over-enthusiastic. Condon's telex read SUGGEST PROCEED DIRECT BEIRUT PROUPGINGER BANKS. There was no need to use cablese in a telex, but Guy enjoyed that sort of thing. Joe Larochelle was flying out there anyway, so we co-ordinated moves and I took the Saturday Pan Am Jumbo all the way through to Beirut.

TWENTY

The orange juice they serve at breakfast-time in the Beirut St Georges isn't Israeli but I'm sure they'd produce the Jaffas if you insisted. It is a great hotel. I sat on my balcony the next morning for an hour and more, brushing up my tan and reading the local press. The Church and the Club were across the way, the Club barred and shuttered against the next riot. The port was beyond the church tower; someone had put up a new restaurant near the sea, or perhaps it was just a fresh coat of vermilion paint that disturbed the familiar landscape.

To maximise the satisfaction of the guests the management had allowed the swimming club to take the area three storeys below my bare feet, though the only swimming was being done by a potbellied American tourist who had strayed across the road from the Phoenicia. The Lebanese ladies lay in formal rectangles across the terraces, their towels, umbrellas, mattresses and skins gaudy as a child's paint-box. They gossiped, schemed, yawned and lusted after the trim, brown-tanned Beirut playboys who paid their calls like fashionable physicians, bowing, inclining and snapping thumbs at the waiters.

The lay-out of the St Georges is old-fashioned in thick carpets, the lift comes complete with a boy to save you the effort of leaning on a button, and there is a teasing choice between the red-leather bar where the Lebanese politicians do their work or the terrace and the sun and no one to see you drop the pistachio shells on the floor.

I asked at the desk for Joe Larochelle and because the name was French the hall porter switched into French,

76

then snapped a query across the room in Arabic, and told me in English that Monsieur had checked in in the middle of the night. I let Joe sleep: lying in all morning must be a luxury for a man with five children and a boss called McNamara.

Time hung heavy, and I helped the feeling along with a short walk to the terrace and a slug of Pernod; since Beirut is still a French city, it seemed appropriate. In a minute I would send a postcard to Camden Passage. I let it wait.

A voice from across towards the bar said, 'Remember me?' and I knew I had been expecting her. Sometime, some place.

She came across the terrace and her eyes were touched with kohl, very lightly, and she looked lost and found at the same time so that she needed holding very tight.

I didn't. I said clearly, 'Just a minute,' and pretended confusion.

'Wasn't it in Lahore, the time the General got drunk? No? Give me a clue!'

She said, 'I'll have a grenadine please,' and sat down, not opposite but next to me, and propped her legs on the next chair. She had a high instep, no stockings, a tiny heart-shaped birthmark just below the sandal strap.

Then she swung round anxiously and said, 'Do you mind? Perhaps you're busy? What are you doing here?'

'Questions again,' I said, so that she crossed her hands in contrition over her heart, like a ballerina dancing Giselle.

I relented. 'I'm looking for Baedekers.'

'Baedekers?'

'Yes. I collect them. Old editions.'

'Are they valuable?'

'Not particularly, except for a few rare ones. There's

77

the 1914 *Konstantinopel und Kleinasien*, for example. If you ever see that on a bookstand, don't leave it behind. Or the *Russia* 1912 which is still the best guide to Russia and includes a side-trip to Port Arthur and Peking. The very early ones are also good. Not because they're so rare —they aren't—but because they're so funny. "Don't drink the Paris water", "Steer clear of the Neapolitans", and that sort of thing.'

'Tell me more about the Russians.'

'I've got the *Russia* 1912,' I said. 'Splendid stuff on Leningrad. St Petersburg I mean.'

'My parents came from there. How wonderful.'

'D'you realise that's the first thing you've ever told me about yourself?'

She shrugged and frowned fractionally as she stirred the ice in her drink with a straw. The waiter refilled the plate of nuts.

'There's nothing much to tell. White Russians; I've lived all over Europe. Do you smoke?' She produced a packet of Gitanes. 'Anyhow, you know what I'm doing down here.'

'It wasn't you who told me that. It was the belted Earl with that sex symbol of a car.'

'Oh, Toby,' she said, so that the subject was opened and closed like the lid of a tea-caddy.

'Have you just come in from Cairo?'

'No, I went back to Rome to deliver some Coptic embroidery and my dealer gave me a lead in Beirut and said to see what was going on here.'

'There's nothing going on,' I said. Too soon.

'Yes there is,' said a third voice. 'Reconstruction and Development has hit town. It still hurts.'

Joe Larochelle eased himself into a chair then struggled to his feet and waited to be introduced. He kissed her hand and I wished I'd thought of that first.

'Lovely morning,' he declared, and signalled the waiter.

'Don't play the Canadian clown,' I said. 'There are enough of them about.'

'Not in this town,' said Mara and smiled at him as though she had decided to like him. I noticed Joe's ear flapping as he tried to pin down her accent. He was a better man than I if he could trace it within a thousand miles of Paris.

'I'll start with breakfast and catch you up later,' said Joe as the waiter hove across the horizon. 'Thomas, you seen that guy who hangs out in Starco yet?'

'Waiting for you,' I said. 'Wasn't that what we agreed?'

Mara gulped her drink and made a face as the glass tipped up and a bit of ice splashed out on to her bare shoulders. 'I'll go,' she said, and got up as though she meant it. 'You two have things to talk about. I'm—how d'you say?—I'm a gooseberry.'

We both made violent protests. Joe put his arms round her shoulders and pretended to force her down into the chair. She gave in with all the reluctance of Nureyev for another curtain call.

The waiter came again. Joe forgot about breakfast and she said, 'Well, now I'm here I can't pretend not to listen to you, only I won't understand a word you say. You're obviously working together on some scheme and I guess it's the Nile barrage loan or whatever you call it.'

I said, slightly too fast for it to be casual, 'Who told you that?'

She said, 'Toby of course. He said everyone knew except me. But please, I'll change the subject if this is all top-secret.' There was a touch of pique in her voice. Her body seemed tense, more aggrieved than her words.

'It depends on what Thomas has been doing,' said Joe, without seeming to notice. 'That's why we arranged to meet here. He probably told you he's just been pretty well round the world. You can put two and two together and presume he's been trying to slot together this bond issue.'

I said warily, 'There's really no reason for the cloak and dagger. It's just that I don't want the Egyptians to hear garbled details on the grapevine before I can tie it all up and tell them myself.'

Joe said, 'You mean you've had good news?' and sounded surprised and pleased at the same time.

'Let's say I'm beginning to hope we can pull it off. I talked with London again last night. We need some more European calls and a long talk with Condon who's been up in Scandinavia. Then we need some careful investigation into the treaty undertakings. There's a lot that could still go wrong, but the odds are shortening, and we're up with the deadline which I was given by Cairo, you remember.'

'He's still hedging,' said Joe to Mara, as though he'd decided to relax. 'So be a good girl and keep this to yourself. But as you say, everyone in Cairo has been talking their heads off about it. I'm surprised it isn't all over the papers.'

'There *was* a piece in *Al Ahram* two days ago,' said Mara. 'It said the Soviet Ambassador had called on the President and they discussed the possibility of "major amendments" to the High Dam extension programme. That was all.'

'You see *Al Ahram* in Rome?' I asked.

'No, there was an old copy on the plane yesterday.'

'So you read Arabic?' asked Joe, sounding mildly scandalised. Perhaps he was just careful.

Of course,' she said. 'A little. I need it for my job. Don't you?' and smiled at him mischievously.

'You win,' he said, and gave her a hard look. 'I was about to say that it looks as if Thomas Kane Esquire has pulled off the only miracle in this part of the world for the last two thousand years. He'll tell you all about it if you ask him nicely.'

'Start at the beginning,' she said. 'And keep it simple.'

'There's no need for a long lecture,' I began, and watched her as she smiled privately at my expense, but not privately enough.

'The Egyptians need to go ahead with the extension to Aswan. It's usually called the Nile barrage scheme or the Nile Cascade. They'd prefer to hang on to what's left of their non-alignment status and not rely on the Russians for this one too.' Every time I explained it I sounded simpler and less plausible. 'So they looked to the West for help and have given all sorts of promises of good behaviour. I've been trying to raise the money from the private side and Joe here is from the World Bank and has been trying to make my money more respectable.'

'How much is it?'

'$125 million for the first stage.' She didn't look as surprised—or as impressed—as I had expected. I went on: 'We're raising it in what we call Eurobonds—an international issue in Eurodollars. They're a non-money —they're dollars floating round outside America which bankers are now using to finance all sorts of projects. It's less theatrical than it sounds.'

'These bonds will be what we call bearer bonds,' Joe added, to illustrate the explanation. 'Anything from $25,000 upwards and the actual bit of paper is worth that amount of money, at the year of redemption, to whoever is holding it. Tom's job is to put together an underwriting group of banks which take the risk by buying the issue and then selling bonds through a selling group to other banks, insurance companies and so on all over the world.'

She was very alive and excited, out there in the sun. I looked at her again. Most women would have been giving us the dazed expression after the first two sentences. But she was taking it all in without fuss. No furrowed brow. For Christ's sake, she was *listening*!

'What's the interest rate going to be?' she asked next. 'Do you know yet?'

Joe said, 'That's enough, if you please. This is getting too technical.' There was a touch of irritation in his voice. He made a fuss about getting the waiter back, trying to demonstrate that he had lost interest in the conversation. 'Tell me about your little flat in Paris. Best of all, give me your address—and your phone number.'

'Yes, go on,' I said. 'He's got three daughters and an Eskimo au pair girl back home in Quebec. They keep him busy.'

'No man is a hero to his au pair girl,' said Joe, and looked round for applause. Mara was looking faintly bewildered. 'It's all this rubbing noses,' I said. 'It gets him down.'

'Tom didn't even mention that I can use the Bank flat in Paris,' said Joe. 'So you needn't worry, I promise never to ask you to put me up.'

'You've got it wrong,' she said and laughed in his face so I felt jealous of his age for the first and only time. 'Mine's in Rome.'

'Ah! That's different.'

'And I'm hardly ever there.'

'Better still.'

'Join the queue,' she said, still smiling. 'There are fourteen on the waiting list.'

'Including the famous Toby?' I asked

'Don't be nasty,' she said, and called a halt. 'Someone told me you're British yourself but I can't believe it. You're always so hostile to other Englishmen—people like Toby.'

'Come and see for yourself. I'll show you my club and my old school tie.'

'Funny you should say that,' she said. 'I may be in London at the beginning of next week. Shall I call on you?'

I liked the way she could switch from laughter to sobriety in the space of a sentence.

I gave her my card and added my Pimlico phone number. Joe played the Trappist and I mentally thanked him for it.

After she had left—because this time she insisted we had private business to discuss over lunch—he said, 'Who *is* that girl?'

'She's a dealer in Islamic art, whatever that means. Decorative, isn't she?'

'*Jolly* decorative,' said Joe, in his county voice, and pushed me in the ribs as we went in to lunch. We had both drunk too much, out there in the sun.

TWENTY-ONE

When Miss Spielter showed me into the Parlour, which was the name Lord Magnus had given to his office, the Chairman of Thorne Reinhard was in the far corner of the room, bending over the furniture and rubbing away with what looked like an oily rag. He strengthened with a gasp, pink and white with the exertion, and waved the rag in my direction.

'Ah!' he said, which is a City greeting.

I replied, 'Good afternoon, Sir', which is the way they do it in Wall Street. 'I've just come in from Kuwait,' I started, but was brushed aside.

'What d'you think of it?' he demanded and gestured vaguely but forcibly towards the corner.

'Think of what?'

'There. The chair.'

'It looks like a chair to me.'

'Then look again! Closer! No, come over here.'

I said, 'It still looks like a chair.'

'Yes, yes,' said Lord Magnus, who was beginning to get exasperated. 'How d'you like it. It's mine!'

Obviously it was his.

I said, 'I'm sorry, I've been on a plane ...' then I got the point. 'You mean, you did that? You *made* it? Sir?' Lord Magnus trumpeted triumphantly, his irritation forgotten.

'Right at last, m'boy. It's my new hobby. Carpentry! The Chancellor told me about it—nothing like working with wood to relax the busy mind in the evening. You should try it yourself.'

'It looks,' I ventured, 'rather Chippendalish'. A charitable view was evidently required. The object had four legs even if the whole thing seemed to tilt sidewards. Perhaps there was a loose floorboard.

'Are you an idiot, Thomas?' Lord Magnus shouted. 'It's supposed to be. It's a copy of a chair you can see in the V and A.'

I wasn't in a mood for Lord Magnus as Renaissance man. 'What's the point of making a copy of something?'

I asked him. 'You could go to Aram and get some up-to-date ideas.'

Lord Magnus snorted like a thoroughbred hunter. 'I am not a complete fuddy-duddy,' he declared, and threw the rag to join the linseed oil on the window sill. 'I do my modest best to keep up with modern living or whatever they call it. I happen to prefer what I see in the V and A. What's the use of all that chrome and plastic to me?'

I said, 'Quite. You'd blunt your chisels.'

We got down to business—I with a summary of the state of play in New York, Washington and Beirut, Magnus with some brisk questions on attitudes, amounts, even technical drafting points. I had to hand it to him: he hadn't missed a trick in all those telexes and memos. He was right on top of the situation.

The deal was coming to the boil. Even KK greeted me benevolently. We were on the 'phone most of that afternoon to Zürich and Geneva. I wanted to go up to Stockholm but Lord Magnus overruled me. 'Ring them,' he said, 'Or send someone else.' He was right. Condon or I had to be available to go out to Cairo at short notice. Monica stayed behind late, with her usual sullenness, and we worked into the evening until the City was deserted as a football ground in mid-week, the sun had gone down over Westminster and the sky over St Paul's was a Union Jack in flames. When even the Swiss bankers had gone home to their chalets we started on the transatlantic line. Lord Magnus came back to the House in tails and a breastful of decorations to talk to New York for half an hour. KK hovered in his office, too, doing a quick switch deal in forward dollars.

In the end I gave up and let myself out into the crumpled London evening. I started to walk to clear my head, up through the asphalt jungle of Barbican, dodging the City Corporation's watercart, on through the back-streets of Finsbury, tattered as Baltic bonds, and up into the drab bright lights of the Angel. The cut-price electricity shops still out-numbered the antique dealers, but only just, and the accents in Sainsbury's and the Council chiropodist were getting smoother week by week. It was getting to be one of those areas where if you ran out of cigarettes you called a mini-cab to go and get you more. I wandered around for half an hour, past the bakery and the building that says 'By Appointment to HM Queen Mary Organ Blower' and the VD posters near the bus queues. Then the bingo crowd was let out and I escaped into Sue's.

She said, 'Oh, it's you,' as though I'd just come back from Reading. 'I thought you came back tomorrow.'

The danger flags were flying. She was wearing one of Biba's mistakes; it was the sort of evening she read *Nova* and wrote to her mother. There would be undies drying over the bath and period pain-killers on the mantelpiece. If it was breakfast time she would be crunching her toast in bed like a parrot eating caraway seeds. The thought of breakfast decided me. I gave her a perfunctory kiss. She didn't respond. I knew what was coming. But my heart wasn't in it, we'd been through it all so often before: my lack of involvement, my withdrawal, my refusal to feel committed. Her bloody tiresomeness, I thought, staring at her. I kissed her again. She turned her back on me.

'Oh, Thomas, don't you see it's no good,' she was of course saying. I knew that the scenario called for tears before long, and I wasn't about to have any, not tonight, not from her, thank you very much.

'I'm rather tired,' I said. 'Mind if I desert you? I need to do some work in Pimlico.'

'You can go where you like,' she said. 'You're your own master. And you're not much bloody help, come to think of it, are you?'

So I took a cab back across the city, through the cinema crowds. A winter of discontent was looming ahead. Maybe I was just tired.

My flat was clean and cold as an operating theatre. The antiseptic order soothed me. I turned on the Sony, drank whisky and milk and woke an hour later in the armchair to catch 'Late Night Line-up' still droning on. Then I went to bed and slept heavily, dreaming of Lord Magnus chasing Mara round the Pyramids.

TWENTY-TWO

I was woken by the telephone and Mara's voice. The morning was trying to creep around the heavy curtains. The accent sounded heavier and I still couldn't place it. She said, 'I've just got in! I'm in a 'phone booth at Heathrow and the queue is full of Pakistanis. I think I'll turn round and go back.'

I said, 'Are you colour prejudiced or something?' and she shouted 'No!' very loud. 'But I'll never get through Customs, they're searching everyone's toilet bag.'

That would teach her to fly cut-price by Syrian Arab Airlines.

'I can't collect you, I don't run a car,' I said.

She laughed. 'I suppose I'll manage. But it's *awful*, it's as bad as Jeddah in the Haj.' It was the sort of remark I sometimes tried to carry off, and usually dropped with a dull thud.

'Come and have lunch,' I told her. 'See you at my

office. Oneish. The grey marble with roses in the window, not far from the Bank.'

'I know it,' she replied. I wondered how.

The morning looked up and cheered. It was the day for Annie the Char so I threw the bedclothes on the floor and took a shower without closing the curtains. Then I waded out of the bathroom, put the Jolly coffee pot on the cooker and poured myself a pint of orange juice from the fridge. I added a Vitamin C tablet, just to be sure—we're all hypochondriacs after our fashion. It was a breakfast calculated to make a man look forward to his expense account lunch, and today I looked forward to that with an appetite that had nothing to do with the *Good Food Guide.*

The *FT, Express, Times, Listener,* and *Spectator* were waiting on the mat. Chase Manhattan informed me that they were opening a branch in Brno and invited me to the ceremony, no expenses paid. The coffee was good and the saccharin didn't taste as bad as usual. The flat was blessedly quiet. I was supremely alone so I rang Sue, feeling benevolent. There was no answer, which made me feel virtuous too, and readier than ever for my lunch.

I beat Monica to the post and stole the stamps off the letter from Angola. She took a memo to Mr Bullen attaching Sols 2.75 as the rebate due on the Peruvian expenses and requesting the renewal of my air credit card. Lord Magnus sent me a note querying the repute of a bank in South Dakota I had never heard of—he assumed that I was an expert on all things west of Shannon. Condon had vanished for the day to Geneva. KK was reported to have broken his toe in his bath.

Mara was early. She came through the door leaving Monica glaring in her wake; she was carrying a small parcel and a Leica M-3 with what looked at a distance like the 120mm Elmar lens.

'How very nice,' I said, rising from my desk with what I hoped was a banker's decorum. I remembered too late that I might have kissed her hand. She was wearing something pale and mauve, silk and simple, which looked as if it came from India. Silk, superb silk. The Malabar in the Taj, Bombay, I guessed. And another Hermes scarf. The door closed.

'You look ridiculous behind those papers,' she said, and to my utter astonishment reached up and kissed me on the cheek. It was like the shock of a cold shower on a hot day. She smelled of sun and warmth and there was a touch of some herbal scent.

She said, 'Hullo,' and I, stupid as a schoolboy, goggled back. The kohl had gone but the eyes were deeper, darker than ever.

'I've brought you a present,' she announced.

It was the Baedeker *Egypt and the Sudan* for 1914 and she untied it herself, triumphant, and opened a page already marked.

' "Intercourse with Orientals," ' I read aloud: ' "The average Oriental regards the European traveller as a Croesus, therefore as fair game, and feels justified in pressing upon him with a perpetual demand for *bakshish*. Travellers are often tempted to give for the sake of affording temporary pleasure at a trifling cost, forgetting that the seeds of insatiable cupidity are thereby sown, to the infinite annoyance of their successors and the demoralisation of the recipients themselves. The traveller should bear in mind that many of the natives with whom he comes in contact are mere children, whose demands should excite amusement rather than anger, and who often display a touching simplicity and kindliness of disposition." '

'Come here and let me thank you properly,' I said and advanced round the desk. She retreated, not too fast, and that was the moment Lord Magnus chose to march into the room.

'Ah!' he said and I replied, 'Good morning, Sir.' It was our usual morning exchange.

'Visitor, I see,' he declared, not a jot put out. He was introduced and they charmed each other busily for a space of some minutes. 'How is what's-his-name in Shiraz, the Governor-fellow I met when I was there?' and 'You must come and give me some advice on my own Persian pieces. Mainly ceramics you know,' and 'That would be very interesting, Lord Magnus, but I don't claim to know much about ceramics,' and 'Of course, you're here for the sale.'

She said, 'What sale?' and Lord Magnus said 'Sotheby's. Tomorrow. Oriental miniatures. The rest of the Bardekian collection.' She murmured 'How very stupid of me, I hadn't realised it was tomorrow.'

Miss Spielter rescued her and carried him away to return the Chancellor's call. 'Bring her along tomorrow morning, Thomas,' he said.

'That's an order, Sir?'

'That's an order. Sotheby's at ten-thirty. I'll probably look in myself.'

'No comment,' I said when the door had closed. 'Now you know it all.' She was inspecting the small Gris behind the filing cabinet.

'Why are you here,' she asked suddenly. 'Because of him?'

'I suppose so.'

'And the job interests you?'

I began to hesitate. 'It fascinates me and gives me the life I enjoy. I wouldn't say it interests me.'

'You don't get excited about this—the extraordinary *importance* of all this? The power? The mischief? The way you really can command governments?'

'Sometimes. Not really. Less and less.'

'If I were you,' she said, and paused, looking out of the window across at Price, Waterhouse, 'If I were you, I'd *adore* it.'

'You'd better ask Lord Magnus for a job.'

'He's nice but not that nice.' She swung around and said, 'You're giving me lunch?'

'If you're free.'

'Where? At your club?'

I laughed. 'If I belonged to a club—which I don't— they wouldn't let you past the front door.'

'Why not?'

'Because you're a woman. Very obviously so.'

I wondered how liberated. There was a pause.

'I'll take you to Sweetings,' I invited, 'so long as you eat fish and don't drink coffee.'

TWENTY-THREE

Sweetings is where the City man goes for lunch when he's nostalgic for his schooldays, so it's usually pretty crowded. Public school of course—the rest of us don't need these artificial aids. For us, Sweetings means superb fish, not instant nostalgia—oysters in season, lobster if you like it, enormous grilled sole, haddock and halibut and herrings, salmon smoked, steamed, stewed, hot or cold, sweet or sour, fish pie, fish curry, fish kedgeree; everything but fish fingers. Bread and butter, brown and thin and damp, a memory of cricket on the lawn before

91

Evensong. Ginger beer and lemonade. Sherbet. Rice pudding, apple pie, jam roly-poly and treacle tart. You don't see many women eating there which I suppose isn't surprising; they haven't the tribal memories to nourish.

Mara surveyed the décor and said, 'Good,' looked at the menu and said 'Good' again. She was squeezed next to a notorious property developer, wide as the Green Belt, who was spooning sago pudding into his face, well down into a bottle of champagne. He paid her not the slightest attention.

'Bit like an Israeli kibbutz,' I said. 'One of the less spartan ones where they allow you to wash your hands before meals.'

'Promise me the food is better,' she said, as though she knew them too well.

'How's Toby?'

'Shut up. You've got it wrong.'

I said, 'Poor Toby.'

'He's rather sweet,' she said, 'but really, he's just a bit limited, our Toby.'

'You mean he thinks the Hermitage is a restaurant in Chelsea?'

'Not precisely ...'

'Ah, you mean he's the English playboy? The great unsexed?'

'A tiny bit too virginal,' she murmured and kept her eyes modestly lowered. She squirted half a lemon on to her potted shrimps. 'Am I supposed to eat the yellow part? No, I like these Englishmen, you don't. That's the difference between us.'

'We're going to be incompatible,' I said gloomily and the property developer came up from the pudding and gave me a startled glare. It was time to move him on.

I said, 'Are you *sure* it's safe for the weekend? Perhaps you ought to lay off it for another week or so. It's only a few days ...' She took the cue at once. 'But of course, darling,' she said, raising her voice slightly. 'Did I tell you about the doctor who fixed me up? He was very sweet but then he had the impertinence to ask me if I'd go out with him.'

The property man swallowed his glass in one gulp and left abruptly.

'Sorry about that,' I said. She grinned. I decided I liked her.

Someone behind me was saying, 'Did you say you were going back into Gilts?' in the elaborately casual tone of voice in which one would ask about the weather, and an answer, nasal and fluting as an oboe: 'I'm stuck with those bloody Australians and oils are looking poorly.' The waiter said, 'Just one moment, sir,' and nearly tipped the tartare sauce down Mara's neck. A voice came lofting over, 'But dammit man, I said *one* grilled and *one* poached. And spinach with the poached.'

The most remarkable thing about the top-drawer City-type is his voice. They all have it at the House—they aren't hearties up this end of the City, only their first cousins; the voices are loud, of course, but it's the pitch, rather than the volume, which cuts through a crowded room like a chain-saw across a valley.

'Tell me about your Russian ancestors,' I said. 'And Rome and your wretched childhood and how you ever managed to learn Arabic.'

She spat bone elegantly and waited for me to pour the Chablis, the icy water trickling down my hand and under my shirt-cuff.

'Later,' she said. 'There's plenty of time. Tell me about the City.'

'There are thirty-one livery guilds,' I began, 'and two Sheriffs, a Lord Mayor and the Common Council ...'

'No,' she said. 'I've read the Baedeker too. I mean the real facts. For instance, how much money do you make—not for yourself, don't look so shocked, I mean your bank—out of a project like the Egyptian issue?'

'We usually don't boast about it,' I said. 'But assume 2½ per cent spread. The managers—that's us—take ½ per cent, the underwriters ½ per cent between them, then there's another 1½ per cent split up between all of us as selling group commission. You see, the real money is made in the distribution, not just in shouldering the underwriting risk.'

She said, '2½ per cent of what?'

'Of the issue's face value.'

'$125 million?'

'That's right.'

'That makes—let me see, 2½ per cent of $125 million, about $3 million. Why! that's *fantastic!*'

I said, 'Let's say Thorne Reinhard will take a minimum of half a million dollars. If we pull it off.'

She seemed as impressed as an Australian in the Ginza. 'So that's why you live it up.'

'Nonsense. I'm not the one with an XK-150.'

'With first-class travel every week and a Patek Philippe chronometer you don't need it,' she retorted.

I said, 'Don't give me the nouveau riche stuff. I'd have been a serf on your summer estate back in the good old days.'

'America? The land of opportunity?'

'Perhaps. Look at these idiots all around us. Why d'you think I'm sitting in the middle of them, with the most desirable woman in London?' She looked down, for the form.

'I'm not one of the dividends of the capitalist system,' she said curtly.

'But you aren't exactly in rags right now, are you? You can't hide the shoes and the handbag, those are the sort of things that give a woman away—whatever the slip of Indian silk she's wearing.'

'I buy my make-up at Woolworths,' she said. 'It's one of the reasons I come to London.'

'And the lipstick? That's not from Oxford Street.'

'Well all right. But I travel tourist class on the planes ...'

'And buy your underclothes in Marks and Spencers?'

'Of course,' she smiled quickly. 'But that's a point to you. It's a very snob thing on the Continent.'

'Better take off the St Michael label ,before you go back to Cairo.'

We went in search of coffee and were going out into the street when a heavy man squatting by himself on a stool at the counter called out to me. He was grey-haired, shrewd-looking, a bit crumpled in his dark City suit. He said: 'Is it true, this rumour you people are going ahead with the Nile issue?' I said, 'Of course. How much do you want to come in for?' and he laughed and said, 'Are you maybe joking?'

'Who's that?' asked Mara, when we had found coffee as black as the Poulbot can do it, which is the darkest you can get in London.

'One of the Moscow Narodny directors.'

'What are they?'

'It's the Russians' foreign trade bank. They've been in London since the Revolution and have a branch in Beirut as well. In Paris it's not the Narodny but something called the Banque Commerciale pour l'Europe du Nord. They operate on strict capitalist principles and make a packet for their shareholders, a clutch of Soviet foreign-trade organisations.'

'I suppose they have to be here because of all the trade that goes through London.'

'Not exactly,' I said. 'They claim to specialise in East-West trade, it's true. But they also play the banking game as if they were any other bank. They're as enthusiastic as anyone and in on every new development. They appeared as underwriters, for example, in one of the new floating-rate issues.'

'They've got some pretty good textbooks on the capitalist system, of course.'

'And they've been checking it out for fifty years.'

'Perhaps they're going to turn out better capitalists than any of you,' she said. She seemed to find that funny. She was smiling to herself.

'Dinner tonight,' I said, trying to make it a statement, not a plea.

She wrinkled her nose over the cup and said, 'Sorry, I've got to see someone. To do with work.' I was far too disappointed, and at the same time angry with myself for being so.

'Don't be in too much of a hurry,' she said gently, suddenly looking full at me. 'There's plenty of time. I'll see you tomorrow morning and then we'll be seeing each other back in Cairo.'

'Tomorrow at Sotheby's, then,' I said. 'Ten-thirty.'

'That's right. Though I'm not sure it's going to be my sort of thing.'

TWENTY-FOUR

The Bardekian sale was being held in Sotheby's Book
Sale room, and I climbed the Bond Street stairs and
pushed my way there past two other sales in progress
and an exhibition of old violins being pawed over by sad-
eyed baggy musical types. I arrived at ten-fifteen, and
immediately spotted Lord Magnus, seated near the
dealers' green-covered horseshoe table wearing his 'what
I want I get' look. The room was already crowded, and
I was just able to commandeer two chairs near the back
wall whose dusty lower shelves were already full of cases,
umbrellas and other clutter. The mutton-chop whiskered
auctioneer, looking like some Victorian headmaster about
to rebuke the school, was in his pulpit appraising the
house, flanked by the usual trio of smooth blond Sotheby's
acolytes; the dealers were exchanging the wary greetings
of wrestlers about to spring at each other. Just after ten-
thirty Mara appeared at the double glass door, causing a
flurry in the back rows but no reaction among the dealers,
intent on bidding for the first lots of Persian calligraphy.

I mouthed a silent greeting, motioned Mara to the seat
I'd saved, squeezed her hand. She leaned towards me and
I smelled herbal scent again. I looked and thought I
detected a pallor under her tan, a certain tenseness in
the way she was sitting. She was wearing a simple terra
cotta linen suit, all business. But she had no catalogue,
and bent like a novice over mine, beginning with the
green cover which proclaimed 'Highly Important
Oriental Manuscripts and Miniatures'. Lord Magnus had
noticed Mara now, and gave her a courtly seated half-
bow, which she received with a vague smile.

The bidding was brisk, latecomers standing at the side walls, a few determined private collectors giving the dealers quite a run for their money. Kraus bought a leaf from a fourteenth-century Mamluk manuscript for £3,800 and were battling with Maggs over a Persian miniature, a Tabriz portrait attributed to Bihzād.

'Who the hell was Bihzād?' I whispered at Mara. She appeared not to hear me. I tried again, pointing at the catalogue. 'Bihzād. Who was he? When did he live?' Mara jabbed at the catalogue, pointed silently to the reference to A. Sakisian, *La miniature persane*, Paris, 1929. She certainly wasn't casting her pearls of expertise before this particular swine. Maggs bought the lot for £1,400.

Later on, Magnus, outwardly imperturbable, bought himself three Persian miniatures in rapid succession, including one from Isfahan described as 'A Youth Faints During a Drinking Party in the Country'. I noticed the minute signs of his excitement: a tapping of his pencil on the catalogue like the tail-switching of a stalking cat. Magnus looked full at me, savouring his triumph, then stared briefly at Mara. I followed his gaze. She was twisting her watch, looking at the door.

'I *am* sorry, Thomas,' she whispered, 'but I really must run. I'd have loved to stay for the Indian miniatures, but I have an engagement with a dealer ...' Her voice trailed off, she was tensing herself to rise. Something didn't tally; for the first time since we'd met she seemed ill at ease.

'We meet when?' I ventured, trying to catch a smile. But she wasn't playing. 'I'll ring you, Thomas. Soon.' She was gone.

The morning session was over a half hour later, and Lord Magnus gave me a lift to the City, bouncing in the deep leather back seat over another last-minute coup, a sixteenth-century Persian lion composed of gold script on a deep blue ground. I vaguely heard him expounding the difference between *naskhi* and *nasta'liq* script, but my mind was on Mara. The girl worried me and I couldn't even say why.

We worked late again the next evening. The American lawyers had a query about the negative pledge clause and kept us on the line for an hour or more until I couldn't tell the big bad wolf from the SEC and Monica was on the verge of hysterics. At long last the lights were turned down and the cabinets locked and I was casting around for cigarettes in the sudden calm of the empty office when the phone rang again. I let it ring for ten seconds, hating the lawyers for their stupidity and their caution, then relented and went over and answered.

It was Mara. She sounded tense, almost breathless. 'I wanted to find you,' she said. 'I have to get back to Rome at once. A client is there and wants to see me.' I said, 'Hell,' and meant it. She said, 'I'm sorry. I'd planned to stay until the weekend.' I was as irritated as a schoolboy stood up by his new girl-friend, though with even less justification. 'When are you leaving?'

'At once. There's an Alitalia flight at midnight.'

'I'll take you to the airport.'

'That would be nice. But you haven't got a car.' I said, 'I'll collect you at the hotel in three-quarters of an hour.'

It was Sue's night for Indian music but I rang her on the off-chance and she answered at once. 'No evening Raga tonight?' I asked.

'The tabla has got flu so it's postponed.' She sounded relaxed and sleepy; I could hear a TV set in the background.

'I need to go to the airport,' I said, the cool con-man.

'One of the New York people is flying through in transit. Can I have the car?'

She said, 'Of course. Why don't I drive you out?'

I said in my firmest bank-manager voice: 'It's not worth it. I'll only be a few minutes. And it's raining again. You stay inside and find me something to eat when I get back.'

The Mini-Cooper had lost half a silencer back around the time the speedometer hit zero and I drove through Regent's Park with the din knocking the stucco off the terraces. Mara was waiting in the foyer, wearing a scarlet travel-cloak and carrying a single leather case. Your complete accomplished lady globetrotter. The flunkeys were so impressed they put down the Cooper to eccentricity.

We didn't talk much, out on the dual carriageway where the sky still held a shadow of the summer dusk over beyond Wales.

'You're cross with me?' she asked. The eyebrows were high, now arched in query; the eyes were pools of dark distress. I said, 'Despite my better judgment—yes.' I added, trying to be honest, 'I suppose *I'm* usually the one who flies off too soon into the night.'

'We'll meet in Cairo, then, shall we?' she said. Her voice was a promise, but not enough to soothe me, it was too controlled for my liking. I felt out of my depth.

Terminal 2 was heavy with shadows where porters skulked, smoking rebelliously. The ground hostesses were blotched and weary, indifferent as if some party had just ended. The taxis were beginning to give up and go home and the police had long since stopped taking the numbers of cars parked in the entry lanes.

When her bag had been taken away she said, 'Don't come any further,' and led me back to the car. The fender was buckled and rusted. 'Thank you for taking me,' she said, polite as a god-child. I muttered something about disappointment, bleakly. 'Oh Thomas!' she said. 'Don't you understand at all? I'm feeling so happy— quietly happy. I'm so glad I came. And I want to see you in Cairo, I do.'

She was fingering the button on my jacket, looking up into my face, trying to force me to look at her. I resisted her. 'That's why I wanted you to stay longer,' I said. 'Just a few days longer.' She was smiling into my eyes, knowing how much she was wanted. I blundered on, despite her recognition. 'I'd have shown you round. Taken you out of London for a few days ...'

'Thomas——' she said, and the beginnings of a laugh were in her throat. 'Thomas, you silly man. It will be all right, I promise you. But let's walk before we run', and abruptly she was in my arms. She kissed me with gentleness, skill and control, for twenty-five seconds timed by the ticking of her watch behind my ear, her body moving softly against me.

At last she broke away and repeated, lightly, 'Walk before we run.' Then she ran into the shadows of the building and I drove home to Camden Passage.

TWENTY-FIVE

I was back in Cairo within the week and the man at Shepheards rolled his eyes in welcome and said, 'Your usual room, sir.' Even the chambermaids were smiling, shy as novices, in the corridors.

Shepheards isn't the same as it used to be, of course, back in the carefree days of the War, with the Duff

Coopers, the pashas, that chap Rommel out there in the desert, picnics at Sakkara and the boy Farouk. Nor is Cairo the same. Don't let them fool you. It's become a sober, serious capital city after one Revolution and three lost wars. There are fewer touts, for one thing, fewer child prostitutes, less hypocrisy, more self-respect. The road to the Pyramids still has the *boîtes* which infected the whole Eighth Army but the Egyptian belly dancers haven't been allowed to expose their breasts since the Revolution so they bring in girls from Lancashire to demonstrate the real thing to the few tourists who are left.

Shepheards went with so much else, burned down in 1952 by the mob. It has been rebuilt without flair, without passion, a strangely bleak and cavernous building where servants move rapidly about your business: the polish on the wood fittings gleams as brilliant as the smile of the dead President, the rooms are frozen by American air-conditioning to the temperature of Forest Lawn, and the shops in the arcade are always closed.

Toby turned up while I was still in my room. Because the day was hot and we didn't particularly trust each other we went across the street to the steam massage parlour and watched each other's faces turning red and our skins running with sweat. His body was lean and bony and more muscular than I'd guessed, and I was jealous of him for Mara until I remembered what she'd said.

Afterwards we sat in the bar and put the liquid back into our pores with arak and lemonade. It's a foolish mixture and he ought to have warned me. He said, 'HE wants to see you again. We think the central bank are at last prepared to be cooperative.'

'The attitude of the Bank of Egypt is very important

—from the point of view of our friends in Zürich especially,' I warned him.

'There's apparently no longer a problem there. Full availability of foreign exchange, principal and interest, right down the line.'

'Can we start to draft that part of the prospectus then?'

He grinned. For the first time I realised that this deal could be a feather in his cap at a time when the post-Duncan Foreign Service officer had to be able to demonstrate he was something more than a dab hand at the *placement*. So the Nile issue was going to help to give Toby an embassy of his own, one day twenty years ahead. There is no justice in this world, I thought; Toby had done nothing but chauffeur me and take me to Son et Lumière at the Pyramids. On the other hand, Condon and I earned a hell of a sight more money than he did, or his Ambassador for that matter. And there was Mara, too.

I said, 'Seen that girl—the antique dealer—lately?' and tried to make it as casual as a remark about the weather. He said, non-committal, 'She was here a few days ago. Then went off to Teheran, I think.' He relented. After all, he was drinking on my account. 'She's probably coming back tomorrow morning, arriving quite early.'

I thought, walk before you run, you fool, you're meant to be at the High Dam Authority at nine and the Finance Ministry an hour later.

To hell with it.

'Meeting her?'

He replied, 'Thought I might.'

'Let's go together,' I suggested. 'Give her a surprise.'

Toby gave me a brief blank diplomatic stare, then began to talk about the latest UN peace moves. Cool customer, when he tried.

She came in from Beirut on the daily UAA flight that keeps Egypt's national airline solvent and allows it to squander the takings on a prestige service, empty, to Moscow. I liked the way she came down the steps of the Electra, slim and quick and self-assured. There was an assurance of sensuality about her that had no need of jewellery. You could see that she was aware of her body, she held it erect and ready. You knew that she would never wish to deny it.

She pecked Toby on the cheek and made faces of surprise at me over his shoulder. We shook hands. Her wrists were strong and tough. She smiled, gravely. Her eyes were now her defence—severe, almost stark. Her lips were painted very pale against the tan.

She said, 'How's the famous loan? Is it going to be a great success?'

I let her play it as she chose. Toby clearly didn't know that we'd met in London or Beirut. I heard them chatter together and dreamed of how Mara would console him and how I would apologise punctiliously and encourage him to curse me and how Mara and I would tactfully offer to help him find a new girl.

She was booked into the Semiramis, which is right next door to Shepheards and a damp-shirt's distance from the Embassy.

'Dinner,' he said to her, and I marked him two out of ten; there was no authority in it.

'Toby darling,' said Mara and sounded little-girl contrite, 'I'm awfully sorry but I'm booked.' She didn't offer to explain and sped away from us in the lift. Toby gazed at the counter which sold Real Kohl and seemed to be about to say something bitter to me about the nature of woman. But the training held firm, the upper lip stiffened in time, and we both went away.

I was in my room ten minutes later when the phone
rang. 'It's me,' said Mara. 'I hope I wasn't too cruel.'

I said, 'Never try that sort of trick with me,' and knew
my voice lacked confidence.

'Take me out to dinner,' she asked.

'But I thought you said you were booked?'

'Yes. I am. I'm having dinner with you ...'

We met on the Semiramis roof restaurant because she suggested it. I said, 'Is this discreet enough? We don't want
Toby to find us,' and she laughed and said, 'Not just yet.'

'Seriously,' I countered, 'why don't we go somewhere
quieter?'

'I know Toby's type,' said Mara. 'He won't come here
because it's too pricey for a lonely bachelor dinner on a
diplomat's salary.'

'He might turn up with someone else?'

'There isn't anyone else.'

At this rate I'd soon be feeling sorry for the man.
Mara was wearing white, cut high to the neck, with a
silver medallion on a chain and the same heavy clasp
in her hair; I decided it must be Yemeni but I wasn't
going to risk mentioning it in case it turned out to come
from somewhere like Finland.

'And I checked with the head waiter,' she was saying.
'There aren't any official dinner parties up here this evening so he won't be squiring the Ambassador's wife.'

It was certainly quiet, if you managed to ignore the
loudest pop-group between Tripoli and Tokyo. It was a
warm night softened by a faint breeze drifting down
from the Citadel. In a moment of silence the hooting
of the traffic came up to us from far below, muted and
unreal. The candlelight was soft yet true also and I could
see she wasn't all that young, and I welcomed the discovery. But there was something else.

She fiddled with the silver, snapped the grissini into stubs, swirled the wine in her glass, looked round the room past me. I said, 'Relax, Toby's not coming—I believe you.' She flicked me a smile of thanks which was curt and very tense and said, 'I know. It's not that, it's just— oh damn! I think I ought to tell you something ...'

It's a nasty line from a woman at the start of an intimate evening and I listened to the alarm bell jangle somewhere in my skull, anticipated husbands, lovers, criminal past, debts, took a swallow of wine, forced myself to savour it, paused till my pulse was normal and said, forced-casual again, 'You'd better get it over then.'

She gave me a startled glare, then put her head back and laughed out loud so that the waiters and the Secret Police man in the corner turned and stared at us. 'My dear, I'm sorry,' she said. 'It's nothing like that. No confessions, I promise. It's something else.'

She paused, grinned again very briefly at the thought, and asked, 'Just how important is this loan?'

I must have reacted without intending to because she said at once, 'No, I don't want to pry, please let me explain. But you'll have to help.' She was leaning forward, ignoring the food, her arms set square on the table.

'It's very big. Very important to the Egyptians. A major part of their development plan.' I didn't know what she wanted me to say. 'It will make big headlines. Certain people—certain governments—will be angry. Others will be happy.' My Chairman thinks it will give him his place in history, I thought, he's been looking for it for forty years. 'It will make the firm a fat amount of money and at the same time the Egyptians ought to be very grateful to us. Is that what you mean?'

'Is it all fixed and settled? Is it definite?'

'No. Not by a long chalk. But we know now the funds

could be available if terms are attractive enough. The Egyptians have to guarantee foreign exchange availability to service the loan.'

'Which they will?'

'Almost certainly.'

'So nothing can go wrong?'

'A hundred things can go wrong. The President can be shot. The Nile can dry up. The Israelis can bomb Cairo. The Swiss can have second thoughts.' I could also fall under a camel, I reflected, but I was remembering my kerb drill and it could soon be over bar the signing.

She listened, intent and worried. I didn't know why she should be worried. I said, 'Look, you seem to think something's wrong. Why don't you tell me what it is?' We should have been whispering but I discovered my voice was forced high and loud by the din from the band. 'Can't we change this bloody table or something so we can hear ourselves think? Oh Christ! here's the belly dancer.'

We waited like a married couple exhausted by a family row. The belly dancer came swooping and sweating past our table, her flesh fat and glistening, leaving us with a painted grimace and a whiff of flesh and cheap scent.

Mara said, 'Perhaps I'm silly but it's this. I was in the lounge here on my last trip—after London, before you got here—and I got into conversation with a man.' I tried to interrupt and she brushed me aside. 'Just a man. I suppose he wanted to pick me up, but he was more tactful about it than most of them and after a bit he gave up and we started talking. He'd been drinking, I think, which helped ...'

'What sort of man?'

She shrugged. 'As I said—just a man. Middle-aged. German, though we were talking French. He said he was a businessman, an exporter from Munich. I didn't know what he was selling. At least, I didn't bother to ask him and then he started boasting. You know how they do—they want to impress me so that I'll go to bed with them.'

'Are they as stupid as that?'

'Most of you usually are. Never mind. As I was saying, he was talking too freely. He might have been annoyed that I hadn't asked him about his business because he said to me all of a sudden, "I've got what the Egyptians want, you know, and they want it badly"—something like that. And I asked, "What do you mean?" and he said, "Why do you think they are so cheerful these days? Simple—because they've got some money in the post and they know what they are going to do with it." I said, "What are you talking about?" You see, I was half in a mood to leave him to his drinking. Then he said, "The Government of course. They've got a packet of money on the way. They've fooled the smartest bank in London and they're going to get millions and millions." '

'What nonsense,' I interrupted, very firmly. 'He was a drunk, talking drunk. You shouldn't have stayed.' I hoped it sounded more convincing to her than it did to me. The pulse under my watch strap had begun to throb and I was afraid she would see the sweat beginning to seep into my shirt front.

She went on in the same worried voice, 'You're probably right. But I didn't see why he should invent this for the benefit of a strange girl late at night. So I asked him something about how he knew all this and he laughed, in a *German* way if you see what I mean, and said, "Because, my lovely lady, they're going to give those fat millions to me." And he lifted his glass and said, *"Salut aux banquiers du City"*, only he pronounced "City" properly.'

'You'd better go on and tell me the rest,' I said, and Mara looked at me and put her hand across the table and traced the faintest pattern on my wrist with her nail.

'I still thought he was drunk and I went on, "Why give millions to you?" He said, "Because I've got what they want," and I asked, "What's that?" And he replied, "What do you think they want more than anything else in the world?" and suddenly, at that moment, I understood what he meant—it just came to me—and I asked, "Weapons?" and he raised his hands in the air, like this, and I said, "The Bomb, perhaps?" and he clapped his hands together but shook his head and said, 'Not exactly, my little girl, but you've got the right idea," and lots of other things so I had to leave him. But he was quite cheerful when I saw him in the lobby the next morning and he didn't pretend he didn't know me. He's staying here in this hotel.'

She paused, then said, 'Give me some wine. I've been talking too much,' and pushed her glass forward.

I poured it to the brim so it spilled on to the cloth. I sat there silent, worried as hell. She murmured, 'It was all nonsense, of course, but I thought I ought to tell you.'

The belly dancer was still on the stage, driving herself towards her tatty climax. She might have been swimming naked in the Nile for all the attention anyone paid her. The band was a continent away, a dim memory of the Jazz Age. I had started to think very hard. Mara sat silent and her eyes never once left my face. Her hand was still tracing a mechanical pattern on mine.

At last I asked, 'Did he mention a figure?'

'No. Just "millions and millions". But surely, Thomas, all this money in your project is tied? It's all allocated?'

I said, 'How can we tie it? Refuse to close the deal till we see the dams in existence? After a certain point it's impossible.' One item was hammering away in my brain, denting the consciousness, demanding acknowledgment. I didn't believe it. I refused to be taken in by saloon-bar gossip. Yet the thought was there and wouldn't go away. The issue was tied, fixed, undivertable. But what had Sir Felix said at lunch all those weeks ago? His query about the 'Ancillary Engineering' item of $25 million in the overall project memorandum?'

I asked, 'Do you want to dance?' and she shook her head.

At that moment desire was driven out. I had not believed it possible. I recognised that the evening was over. I wanted Mara to go away and leave me alone, to think.

Instead, she said, 'Listen,' so I listened and she started again, very slowly, picking every word.

'I was right to tell you? Yes?'

I nodded.

She said, 'We both think it's nonsense. It doesn't make sense. I didn't believe him then and I don't now. But admit it, you're worried—and darling, for some reason so am I. I'm scared for you and I don't know why.' She was holding my hand, suddenly intimate, and the waiter probably thought I had wooed her and won her. 'You aren't going to relax again until you've got to the bottom of this and nor can I because I'm the one who told you. So there's only one thing to do. I shall have to talk to him again.'

I had thought of it five minutes before but I could never have asked her to do it for me. I said, too quickly, 'Yes, I agree. And I have to hear him.'

She frowned and said, 'You could join us for a drink, I suppose, casually, and I'd introduce you. But he probably wouldn't say anything to anyone else.'

It had become a minor diversion. I was ridiculously

confident of what I needed to do. 'That's easy,' I said and believed it, briefly, that evening. 'We'll fix up a tape recorder. You'll have to make him talk.' I didn't doubt her willingness. I didn't doubt her sympathy. I assumed she would do it for me.

She looked steadily at me, then said, 'If you can fix it, then I'll be nice to him. I'll need a few hours. Better get him to take me to dinner. What about up here—if you can square the head waiter?'

You can square any waiter in Cairo and the Semiramis roof restaurant is no exception. I almost relaxed. 'We can invite Toby to listen to the tape,' I suggested. 'He'll like that.'

'As a consolation,' she said. She didn't smile. She was still holding my hand.

TWENTY-SIX

STRICTLY CONFIDENTIAL

To: Chairman, with copy to G. Condon
From: T. Kane
Re: Nile Issue

There follows: transcript of a conversation, recorded on the night of August 7 in the Semiramis Roof Restaurant, Cairo, between Miss Mara Tal (see file; acting on my behalf) and Dr Karl Dietrich (West German passport No. HA267567) described as 'Businessman'. Transcribed from the French. Recording supervised by self and parties kept under personal surveillance. Charge: Eg£150 to head waiter for arrangements. Restaurant bill charged by Dietrich to his room account. Tape begins...

MT: '——so I said why shouldn't I if I want to? Thank
you. Yes. Of course I'll have a drink. (Laughter.)
I warn you, I'm thirsty tonight after the trouble
I've had with a real villain, a dealer in old brass, up
on the souk.'

KD: (indecipherable)

MT: 'Well, let's start with one bottle, anyway. Oh, all
right...'

KD: (to waiter)

MT: 'That's good then. But I'm sorry I was so late. You
must have been sitting downstairs for an hour.'

KD: 'It was no ordeal, Mademoiselle...'

MT: 'You mean?'

KD: 'The barman knows me by now. I don't even have
to raise my finger. That's why I like this hotel. They
can see when a man's glass is empty.'

MT: 'Better than Kuwait?'

KD: 'Kuwait is no problem if you know your way
around. They can't turn a place dry if it's desert,
whatever the Prophet said. And they know it themselves. I know them. They all drink like—like
Bavarians!'

MT: 'You're Bavarian?'

KD: 'No, I am a Rhinelander. A very long way back.
(Pause.) You care to dance, Mademoiselle?'

MT: 'Only if you will call me Mara.'

KD: 'So we dance, then—Mara!'

Interval.

KD: 'You permit me to say these things?'

MT: 'Of course. Why do you ask?'

(Pause.)

MT: 'It was so nice to see you when I came downstairs
this morning. But I was quite shy. You might have
forgotten me...'

KD: 'Mademoiselle—I'm sorry, Mara...' (There follow personal remarks deleted from record as irrelevant.)

KD: 'You wish to dance again?'

MT: 'Not quite yet. Let's stay here and try the second bottle...'

KD: (to waiter, in English)

MT: (to waiter, in Arabic. Laughter.)

KD: 'You must know the Near East well if you speak the language.'

MT: 'Not so well as you do, I'm sure. Do you spend much time in Cairo?'

KD: 'More and more. Damascus is crazy. Baghdad is vicious. Amman has been destroyed. Cairo is getting better. More sane. More clever.'

MT: 'How do you mean?'

KD: 'They understand business better than they used to. They are more—more realistic.'

MT: 'Perhaps they have been told to be by the Russians?'

KD: 'Nonsense. The Russians are barbarians. They are the new pashas. Or they would like to be.'

MT: 'And the Egyptians know this?'

KD: 'That goes without saying. They will soon be hating the Russians.'

MT: 'But how does this make them more—more realistic, you said?'

KD: 'They are more polite to people like me. (Laughter.) No. I am serious. There is a perfect example here this week, though it is not yet public, you understand...'

MT: 'Yes? Some financial transaction?'

KD: 'You know it? Those English bankers? Ah yes, forgive me. We have discussed this before.'

MT: 'I was at a diplomatic cocktail party last night and people were talking about it quite openly. The Nile barrages, they said it was. It's an enormous amount of money.'

KD: '$125 million just for the first stage. Yes, it is a lot of money. You have to be very realistic—you understand?—to persuade the City of London—or even my own Frankfurt—to lend you so much money.'

MT: 'No! No more wine for me. You carry on, though. I shall be drunk and we don't want me to be indiscreet...'

KD: (Further personal remarks. Deleted.)

MT: 'Now you're being ridiculous. But go on, tell me, how do you know all about these banking negotiations? Are you a banker too?'

KD: 'No! Bankers are parasites or fools, usually fools. Which is fortunate for men like me...'

MT: 'Are the Egyptians being more realistic with you, then?'

KD: (Inaudible.) 'My dear, it is so comic, so amusing, that I think I shall tell you. Though you must promise me first that you will forget it at once. I tell you because it is a joke. We shall laugh together, and then forget it, no?'

MT: 'Oh yes, of course, a joke.'

KD: 'But how do we know no one's listening to us? This restaurant is probably bugged. What I am telling you is not for everyone to hear...'

MT: 'Nonsense. There's too much noise and we're in the open air. Go on—we'll talk very quietly.'

KD: 'Very well. What was I saying? Ah yes. I was saying I am not a banker. I am a salesman. I sell things the Egyptians and others want very much. The bankers are providing the Egyptians with a lot of money. The Egyptians say they want the money to build dams and irrigation canals. Very well. But

how can the bankers be so certain that the Egyptians will spend their money the way they say? If
you give a child ten piastres and say "Buy a kite",
how can you be sure that when he goes to the
bazaar for his kite he will not change his mind and
take sweets instead? If you are angry or surprised
when he comes home with sweets, then you are a
fool. Or a banker!'

MT: 'But these are surely not children or fools involved
in the Nile barrages affair.'

KD: 'Not at all. You don't believe me? Then why am I
in Cairo tonight? I do not sell kites, nor sweets
either. Nor do I sell machine tools from the Ruhr,
nor tea biscuits from London, nor perfumes
from Paris. My dear, I sell the things they want
most.'

(Pause.)

MT: 'That's obvious: weapons. (Pause.) No, don't look
surprised, you mentioned arms when I saw you
that night in the lounge.'

KD: 'That is true. Perhaps I said too much then. You
seem to have that effect.'

MT: 'But I thought the Russians gave them all the
weapons they could use or need, in fact more than
they know how to use, from what people have been
telling me.'

KD: 'My dear, "weapons" can mean all sorts of things.
Certainly the Russians have been giving them
MiGs and tanks, Sam 2s and 3s and Soviet soldiers
too to make sure they use them properly and don't
get beaten again. I am not that sort of crude butcher
who sells guns and knives. I am *au fond* a scientist,
I even have a doctorate, you know. But not in pure
science. Also a very long time ago.'

MT : 'You said you had what they wanted more than anything.'
KD : 'Precisely.'
MT : 'Which is some sort of process? Some device? Some very advanced bit of technology?'
KD : 'You are very quick. I do not carry these things in my pocket of course. But there are things they need—sophisticated technologies, advanced skills, certain computer programmes—which they are willing to pay for handsomely. But please, you must not ask me more. We are here to enjoy ourselves. More wine?'
MT : 'A little. No, you finish it. Tell me one thing more and then I'll want to dance again. These bankers may be stupid but they're not going to give the Egyptians $75 millions—is that what you said—?'
KD : '$125 million.'
MT : 'Yes, $125 million without having some sort of control over where it goes.'
KD : 'I am not interested in the $125 million. The Egyptians can spend most of it on their precious irrigation. They are welcome to it. I only ask them for a small part of it—a part that they can divert without the bankers realising until it is too late and I am back in my villa in the Algarve.'
MT : 'How big is that part?'
KD : 'Let us say, well under one-third. Less than one-quarter perhaps. Now who is going to begrudge an honest German businessman $25 million? Now we dance please or I shall wish I had not said all this ...'
MT : 'Yes, let's do that. How fascinating all this is. My job seems terribly dull in comparison with what you've been saying ... Dance now? Yes, of course. Careful! Can you manage? Oh, fine. (Laughter ...)'

(The rest of the tape is either disjointed or irrelevant.)
Ends.

TWENTY-SEVEN

Mara sat in my room the next morning making grim-
aces of embarrassment as she listened to the tape recorder.
'It seems even worse than it was,' she said. 'I sound like a
chorus girl in search of a good meal.'

'You seemed to make the most of it,' I said, jaundiced
as an overworked confessor. I had been watching them
all evening. 'Did you have to dance with him quite like
that?'

'I was doing it for you,' she said. 'And you know it. So
don't get jealous.'

She had been wearing a shimmering cool green evening
dress cut high at the neck and straight to the ground. But
when she turned, her back was bared to the waist, and I
had sat at the other end of the terrace all evening looking
across at the muscles rippling beneath the brown skin as
she played with him and led him on. I had not dared look
at her face nor at the stocky, fleshy man who sat opposite
her, facing my corner, so I had tried to remain incon-
spicuous, ignore those shoulders and the long-fingered
hands resting around his neck, ignore the palpitations of
the head waiter and get the whole thing over.

We listened to it again, then again. I got more and more
depressed. She said, hesitantly, 'He'd been drinking again.
But it doesn't sound quite like the last time. He's still
boasting, but it sounds more convincing here...' She
looked at me, then asked: 'It's the $25 million figure that
worries you?'

117

'Yes. It's exactly the figure we were worried about in London and New York. These big projects are always broken down into stages and sectors, and there's always a lot of guesswork.'

'So this breakdown of the financing must be fairly vague?'

'Very vague. In this case there was the figure of $25 million for what is described as "ancillary engineering work". One of the things I've been doing here is trying to find out what that means.'

'The Egyptians told you?'

'Yes, but I'm not an engineer. The Ministry of Finance talked about bridges and pumps and road installations and showed me a map. It's all in the project plan. But we were worried about the figure being so high.'

'That is the $25 million the Egyptians are talking about? The cream off the milk?'

'*They* are not talking about it,' I said. 'One drunken pot-bellied Bavarian is talking about it.'

'Rhinelander. And he hasn't got a pot-belly.'

'Kraut,' I compromised, suddenly unreasonably angry. 'And you ought damned well to know.'

I needed advice from London badly and I didn't want to admit it. I jumped up and began to pace the room, from bed to window and back. After a few minutes, I said, 'Look, Mara! I can't go back to London and produce the tape and tell them the deal is off. It's just one man talking to a girl he wants to make, late one night in a Cairo hotel. So what?'

'Can't you check again the $25 million with the Egyptian planners?'

'It's too risky unless I'm sure something is wrong. The deal is poised, now, at this moment. The prospective underwriters will smell something rotten if we hesitate. This is why we have tried to move so fast. We'll start losing what we call my "indications of preliminary interest" if we're not careful, and once the big institutions start to fade away it'll be like trying to shore up a sand-dune.'

She said, 'Do you *believe* him? Is he trying to sell something to the Egyptians?' It was the question that mattered.

I paused. I said, 'Yes, I do. On balance."

She asked, 'Do you believe the Egyptians are negotiating to buy—whatever it is—from him?'

Quite simply, I didn't know. I couldn't risk a guess at that one. It was too important. 'I'd have to have more evidence. That's the $25 million question: are the Egyptians going to throw his ball back?'

The chambermaid knocked and I sent her away. There was a woman in my room but the atmosphere was as chaste as a board meeting. Mara shivered as the air-conditioning blasted away and got up to open the balcony door. The hot Cairo air seeped around us like smoke. With it came the nerve-shattering din from the streets below, intrusive and harsh. I felt my head begin to pound.

She was saying, 'He's bound to have some sort of evidence of a deal. Documents. Plans. Letters.'

'Something from the Egyptians,' I muttered. 'That's what we need.' The 'we' came naturally; neither of us noticed it at the time. I was sitting on a sling-back chair looking out on to the Nile and watching the Hilton felucca go drifting past with a party of camera-carrying middle-aged American tourists, as grotesque in their parrot-coloured shirts as a Yankee at the court of the Pharaohs. My head felt worse. Mara came and stood behind me and then I felt her hands begin to massage my neck, digging deep and hard into the muscles of the shoulder. Her fingers were strong, supple, and I felt myself drift under their rhythm. She stood close to me and supported the weight of my back against her thighs so I could feel her warmth move through me, through the thin skirt and the cotton of my shirt. Her hands kept kneading slowly and steadily.

I heard her say in a low voice, 'Do you really need those documents? If they exist?'

'God, yes! I'd give my right arm for them. A year of my life. A lot of money. I'm scuppered without them. And I have to have them fast.'

What I really wanted was to know that they did not exist. But we are all today so prepared for the worst, so hardened against disaster, that I already assumed that they did.

She said, 'Then I shall try to get them for you?' Simple. Just like that.

The fingers drove down the length of the shoulder and back again to the spine, smoothly, firmly. 'There must be something in his room to prove it one way or other.'

'And how will we get into his room? Climb up the drainpipe?'

She said, 'How do you imagine a girl like me gets into a man's bedroom?'

I must have tensed, almost shuddered. 'Don't do that when I'm massaging you,' she snapped, and there was harsh anger in her voice.

I turned away from her body and got up abruptly. 'It's absolutely ridiculous,' I said. 'I wouldn't dream of it. It's— it's just ridiculous!'

She laughed at me, except that there was no humour in her voice. Her eyes were now very dark. 'Why is it so ridiculous?' she asked in a tight voice I'd never heard before. 'Isn't it the best way? The traditional way? Why the English gentleman all of a sudden?'

I said, 'I'm not a prude, and I know you're not a child,

but it's—it's out of the question.' She laughed unpleasantly again and the thought flashed through my mind that perhaps the idea excited her. They're all whores at heart and men have always known it and never trusted them, said a small voice inside me before I could silence it.

She came round and faced me. She was wearing a silk sheath in grey and blue, crisp, sensible. I realised she was damned angry. 'You can't do it yourself, if that's what you're thinking. *Ce n'est pas ton type!* And I don't suppose he'd much go for you either.'

She wasn't being flippant. I could see why she was irritated. I said, 'I'm not a pimp and wasn't exactly born yesterday. I can't kid myself that you're under any obligation to do this.'

'All right, then,' she said, and the eyes were still hard though the mouth was smiling. 'Let's say I'm doing it for you. Don't you see? You need help. I want to help you. That's all. No more than that.'

I had a sudden fantasy of myself explaining to the directors over lunch in Fredericks Place how I had got hold of the vital document, and KK's expression. Perhaps that was what decided me.

'You won't push yourself at him unless you have to, I suppose?' I said tentatively. She looked at me, still angry but with a mixture of condescension and the other thing, the exciting hint of her perhaps caring.

'I'm not a professional,' she said, too coolly, 'and he's not precisely my type either, you know. A bit on the mature side, if you know what I mean.' She moved towards the door, paused with her hand on the knob and added, 'No need for you to worry, my dear.'

A warning light lit up somewhere in the back of my mind. That Distant-Early-Warning radar console, the one that always reflected people's motives. What was her interest? Why the hell did she suddenly care so much? Or, as they like to say in Wall Street: 'What makes her so goddamned hungry for the deal?' I didn't know the answers, and I didn't like it, any of it. But I couldn't figure out any better way to get the evidence I needed. And what the hell, she volunteered, didn't she? It was her idea in the first place. Which left me in the clear. As usual.

When she left I kissed her on the mouth. It was as perfunctory as the salutation of Mediterranean cousins at a railway station. Yet I felt closer to her than before. She had now become my accomplice, and accomplices, like trapeze artists, must commit themselves to each other wholly lest they fall.

TWENTY-EIGHT

Mara came across the road into Shepheards at eleven the next morning. She found me first go at the bar and slipped on to the stool next to mine. 'Good morning,' she said, matter of fact as Monica and one hell of a lot more desirable. I said, 'Hullo,' and held on to her, hard, when she reached over and squeezed my hand.

'Sleep well?' she asked coolly.

'Yes I did. I've got a hangover like a hurricane to explain why.'

'Try a Fernet Branca.'

'They don't have any. They never have any.'

She was fresh and gleaming, her hair still damp from the shower and her embroidered blouse a crisp triumph of laundering. I saw her breasts rise and fall, strain and relent, under the thin linen, and my body tightened.

I said, 'This isn't the place to say it. But I want you to

know that I won't forget last night. I want to take you away from here and make it up to you somehow.' Her eyes were wide as windows, clear, smiling now. She said, 'That was what I was thinking. All the time...'

The barman listened scrupulously from his corner and polished a glass to keep his hands from my throat. An American sat at the other end of the counter and gazed greedily at Mara. She must have felt his eyes on her, she looked around and froze him arrogantly into a humiliated departure.

'I was with Toby,' I said. 'We sat here till eleven. He was drinking like a fool. Then he insisted on driving me to one of those places near the Pyramids. It's a wonder he didn't hit a camel on the road. We got back at two, then he wanted to talk about you.'

'What did you say?'

'I was past caring.'

'Don't you want to know what happened? To me I mean?'

'No.'

'Whether I discovered anything?'

'Yes.'

'Then listen—and carefully.' Her voice was tight, cold again, all business.

'Go on.'

'There weren't many papers there. He must have an office somewhere, or hide them, and I didn't like to risk searching the place. He's a light sleeper.' I tried desperately to look matter-of-fact.

'So it was a waste of—effort?'

'Wait a moment. I said there *were* some papers there, a batch of letters in his briefcase. I wondered whether to bring them...'

'God no!'

'Exactly! So I took them into the bathroom to read.' I was thinking to myself that she was an adult woman, she must have known what would have happened—to both of us—if he'd discovered what she was doing.

'That was risky. He might have woken.'

'I could have distracted him.'

'Of course.'

'I had to be very, very quick. You didn't think I could memorise them, I hope.'

I said, 'No, never mind that. What's the gist of it? Are we right?' Again the 'we' and it wasn't the royal plural.

She nodded firmly as though at an auction.

'Yes,' she said. 'We're right.'

The air whistled as the tension went out of me. I suppose I was relieved. Mainly for her. Then for myself. And for Lord Magnus and the House and all my banker colleagues and the Western capitalist system which had nearly laid an egg. For the history books that wouldn't mention the Nile issue. For the shadow of Anthony Eden, unreprieved. For the future of Anglo-Egyptian relations. For the President who would not be inviting the Prime Minister to the inauguration. For the *fellahin* who would breed and hunger in peace. For the Israelis who, perhaps, would not be attacked.

She was saying, 'At least, I *think* we're right. But I don't really understand these things.'

'You mean it's not clear—absolutely clear?' I struggled to regain perspective. Life is never so simple, I reminded myself.

'Read this,' she commanded, and put a small envelope into my hand. 'I thought I could take one risk. There were a couple of carbon copies of the same document—it's a sort of sales letter. I decided he wouldn't notice if one were missing.'

'You're crazy,' I said, but it was too late to complain, the deed was done, and I tore open the envelope, unfolded the single sheet of coarse yellow copying paper. No letterhead, of course; one sheet only, the later sheets missing.

Memorandum to: Chief of Weapons Procurement
It is commonplace that complex equipments used for crucial tasks must be adequately reliable. Unfortunately reliability is not a disposable design parameter. As long as human beings have access to the equipment it is wasteful to attempt to provide more than a certain level of reliability. The purpose of the surveillance radar, therefore, is to give in conjunction with a SAGW system the earliest practicable warning of the existence of a target and the least amount of information necessary to put on the tracking element. The ambit and accuracy of the associated data will determine the performance characteristics of the radar system.

The best missiles in the world are no good if a target cannot be found and localised. Vietnam has demonstrated to the Americans at last the importance of good target designation and acquisition aids. A greater ground-to-air delivery accuracy for point targets has been one of the principal achievements of our company's recent development activity. Increases in lethality of various warhead types give us another factor that can be played off against accuracy, size and cost. Very significant strides have been made in the past two decades in the lethality of conventional and nuclear warheads, particularly against soft targets. But there is much yet to be accomplished in the selection and design of warheads for various classes of targets.

If therefore the following proposal development can survive the concept formulation, DCP and contract definition processes, the chances are excellent that it is feasible and ready to be put into hardware form as a significant additional component in any fully-fledged weapons system. The missile complex already emplaced at the Canal

I read it three times, cranking my brain like a rusty tractor. She was so quiet I might have been alone there at the bar.

'I still don't know what it adds up to,' I said.

'How?'

'I don't know what he's *selling*, for God's sake.'

She looked worried. 'Surely, some sort of missile system. Yes, there you are—"ground-to-air——"'

'Not for twenty-five million,' I said. 'Anyhow, they've got plenty already, from the Russians.' I needed Condon. This was all Dutch to me but Guy was supposed to have known about these things in the days when he was something mysterious in BAOR. I said petulantly, 'I wish it wasn't so typically long-winded. It's just a German sales puff.'

'I'm sorry,' said Mara, almost sullen for the moment.

I reached across and touched her hand, apologising. 'It's not your fault. Look, I'm pretty sure he's talking about some sort of surveillance radar system. Where he talks of an "additional component to existing systems" he must be offering the Egyptians a sort of gadget—on the side, a private-enterprise extra—which they think will help them make their Soviet system more effective. Probably some way of overcoming the inefficiency of their troops.'

'That's what he means in the first paragraph?'

'Yes, and the Egyptians would jump at it if it makes

them less dependent on the Russian technicians who operate most of this hardware they've got lined up along the Canal.' I paused. 'But hell, I still don't *know* that Dietrich has *sold* his gadgets.'

Mara looked around cautiously. The barman had vanished. We were quite alone.

'There were the other papers ... I only had time to glance at them.'

'Can you remember anything?'

She frowned, scowled at the polished wood opposite. 'Something about illuminators, an optional infra-red homing system. And a "horizon-searching CW acquisition radar"—at least, I think that's what it said...'

'Go on.'

'There was a letter from the Defence Ministry, signed by an Under-Secretary. Confirming the conclusion of the fourth meeting, trusting that at the fifth meeting it would be possible to finalise contracts or something like that. And —yes, a reference to "financial clauses": some phrase about "pending conclusion of third party negotiations".'

'Any figures?'

'Only one I can remember. Just a minute—I think it was $2.7m. for some element in something else called a volume-coverage pulse system. Oh yes, and a couple of letters pinned together from a bank in Zürich, very technical, about the arrangements for handling "sums of the scale you refer to".'

'That's better,' I said. It was much, much better. The more I thought about it the better I felt. Though Heaven alone knows why I should feel so good about a disaster.

She turned and looked at me, directly.

'Is it enough?'

'Enough for me,' I said.

'Enough for your people?'

127

'That's my next problem.'

I knew already that it wasn't categorical. I still had no primary document. No confession from the Egyptians. But it was the best I could do. It was enough for me.

Repeat. It was enough for me.

'Relax,' I said. 'It's over. I want to give you a present— yes, Lord Magnus wants to give you a present, a very extravagant one. What would you like?'

She leaned over, almost toppling on the long legs of the stool, burrowed her head into the crook of my shoulder and murmured in my ear so I felt her breath moist on my temple and my senses struggled, drowning in her warmth and her perfume. 'Don't give me a present,' she said. 'Just take me away from here. Not now but later—as soon as possible—when the whole thing is over. When we can relax and be together.'

I groped my way back to land. 'I'll take you,' I said. 'Whenever you say, wherever you like. But you realise I shall have to go away at once, back to London? For a few days——'

She nodded. 'You can't cable?'

'No. I've got to go and explain to the Chairman. It's going to be difficult.' I didn't know which way we would have to play it. Too many elements were involved for me to risk unilateral action.

'Then you'd better go at once,' she said, and I could see her relax suddenly as though something had been seen through, completed. 'We must ask Toby to take you to the airport.'

The BEA Trident came down over London at midnight. We broke through cloud, the night sky vanished into the English mists and the engines started to turn themselves on and off in noisy spasms. It meant that the Captain had switched over to the automatic landing system, ignoring our unanimous hope that he might do it himself. The reservoir and the lights of the BOAC workshop slid under our wing, the stewardess sprinted for her seat, the engines gave a final despairing roar and we bounced, once, twice and a third time, gently. Then there was the scream of reverse thrust and a racing turn on to the first runway, our tyres stamping black smears on to the wet tarmac, and we rolled, bumping, heaving, to the Arrivals ramp.

Fifteen minutes later I was through Customs. I aimed for the Hertz desk then changed my mind, bought a paperback for the sake of the change and went to ring Condon. He told me Magnus had just left on holiday for Sardinia. I 'phoned the Spielter for the address. It meant waking her up, but she was very kind.

So I turned round. Just time to get the night flight, Economy Class only, to Rome. An argument with the Alitalia desk. Alghero or Olbia? We agreed on Olbia. They said Alisarda would take me from Rome in the morning. Who the hell was Alisarda? 'You can spend the rest of the night at the airport,' she said, 'if you're in a hurry.'

'Not on your life,' I told them. 'I'll stay at the Hassler.'

I did, too.

татататататата TWENTY-NINE татататататата

'Bit overdressed, aren't you?' said Lord Magnus, who definitely wasn't. His pot was hanging obscenely over the lip of a pair of scarlet bathing trunks, the kind which must have been the rage of Deauville back in the days when the Duke of Windsor was living it up. I took off my tie, my jacket, my shoes and my socks, opened my shirt to the navel and sat down next to him under the awning. I'd have carried on with the strip-tease if he insisted but the Aga Khan wouldn't like it. 'Nice tan you have,' said Lord Magnus. 'Do they have a sundeck at the Ministry of Finance these days?' I ignored him. He was smeared with a grease that smelled like the entrance to a tannery. 'All this travel to the tropics, eh? Where the sun never sets? The rest of us have to pay through the nose for it.'

I had tracked him down at last after reaching the pepper-pot villas and silver beaches of the Costa Smeralda. It took me an hour in the taxi I'd picked up at Olbia airport. He was sitting under a bamboo awning in the piazza in the middle of Porto Cervo half-naked and alone, engrossed in the front page of the *Nuova Sardegna* where the latest bandit folk-hero told all, complete with photographs of his manacled stance in the courtroom. A mint copy of the *Neue Zürcher Zeitung* lay unopened on the table next to a glass of amber liquid. It didn't look like Malvern Water.

'Vernaccia,' said Lord Magnus indulgently. 'The local hooch. They call it wine but it kicks like a horse.' He was riding it without visible difficulty.

Smeralda is one of the places the rich go to these days to get away from it all. But not each other. They get away from campers, trippers, tourists and work, but stay in touch with running water, elegant villas, nightclubs, Bain de Soleil on every counter and boutiques selling Pucci dresses—gaudy Florentine pageantry for the long cool evenings. They put up with second-rate dance bands, exorbitant prices, the rudest service south of Clermont Ferrand, and the sullen age-old stupidity of the Sardinians. The villages are artful in faded apricot and peach, the villas are white and orange-roofed, the mountains dramatic with tumbled masses of rock and the whole ensemble is undeniably, remarkably, frustratingly beautiful, more beautiful even than the Swiss printers can manage in the publicity brochures. It has the authentic smell that seems to emanate from the ground in only the most exclusive resorts— sweet and salt at the same time, as though a beautiful woman has just passed by and they're making crêpes suzettes in the restaurant next door and the sun has been shining for a thousand years.

Lord Magnus was relaxed all right, which didn't mean he wasn't bored. He seemed to be glad to see me. 'My wife's gone up to Maddalena today in the Kedgworths' boat,' he said, as though assuming I knew the Kedgworths intimately. 'Can't stand this sailing lark. Thought I'd catch up on the papers.'

We were directly above the port and the sea was as emerald as the Aga Khan had promised. It looked less polluted than any sea I'd seen for years. We sat on basket chairs and squinted out over the incredibly blue-green water. The Yachting Club was carefully battered and patched so it looked mediaeval, and lying at anchor were two enormous white yachts, a three-master flying the German flag, and a long white motor vessel with the American ensign. The mountains behind us shimmered in the heat; the haze had fogged the dark horizon but the islands just off shore shone pink and startlingly clear in the transparent water. The architects were a collective genius; they had taken every risk on offer and yet the result wasn't phoney. I began to think there was some point in having money.

We drank more vernaccia, which tasted warm and oily and tightened the gut so I felt I was ready to slay dragons again. Cairo receded over the horizon like love and hope and childhood and I was tempted to let it go and take my shirt off. The waitress was beautiful, not just pretty, her face the oval of Sardinia, her eyes spume-white against her tan. She refused to smile. Perhaps she also had the stunted teeth of the islanders. I saw Lord Magnus observing me indulgently and said nonchalantly, 'I wonder how long before she'll have the local moustache...'

'You've got your working suit on,' said Lord Magnus, when his curiosity finally got the better of him. 'You haven't come for a holiday, I presume.' I said, 'I had hoped to report to you in London. Condon told me you were here.' I tried to give it an edge suggesting, 'I was surprised you could come away at a time when the Nile issue was coming to a head.'

'Everything is under control,' he said. 'Isn't it?', suddenly harsh.

'I suppose so.'

'Then why are you running round as thought you want me to change your nappy?' His voice was unmistakably curt. I must have given it too much edge—he had decided I was criticising him for sitting in the sun in scarlet swimming trunks.

'I need advice. I need your authority.'

'To carry on?'

'To call it off.'

There was silence.

'May I ask precisely why?' He turned and looked straight at me. I didn't know where to begin.

He added, 'You and Condon told me it seems to be in order. Trouble with the guarantee clause?'

'No.'

'Then what in the name of hell are you moaning about?'

'There's something wrong.'

'Yes,' he said, with heavy irony, waiting.

'With the whole deal. We've been conned.'

'Rubbish.'

'Yes we are, I know it.'

'How?'

I said, 'It's hard for me to expect you to believe this.'

'It is indeed. But do proceed, if you will.' It was his bloody Westminster manner, and I didn't like it at all.

'You know the $25 million ancillary engineering clause?'

'Yes. You checked it. So did the World Bank fellow.'

'I know. But it's phoney.'

'How d'you know?'

'Because I know of a man—a German—who's got a $25 million arms deal coming through and the Egyptians have told him they'll be getting the money through a London bank.' It sounded as frail as Thor Heyerdahl's reed boat.

Lord Magnus said, 'Ah!' and his tone changed. I couldn't tell in what direction. He peered at me again.

'How do we know about all this? What evidence? Through whom?'

I said, 'You remember that girl in London? The girl who came to Sotheby's?'

Lord Magnus said, 'Ah!' again, which is an enigmatic sound at the best of times, and I told him the whole story. It got us through another couple of glasses, and the sun started to melt the paving stones and kindle the hair on my chest. The man at the next table was peeling for the second time. The other tables were now full. I could smell Fabergé Brut from several of the men. A yacht glided alongside the quay and discharged a cargo of women with long peroxide hair.

Lord Magnus said, 'Have you checked up on him? Dietrich? And what of the girl?'

'Not yet.' I hesitated and went on. 'He looked real to me and we've got those figures, which are enough to make me feel pretty sick.'

'She isn't just a whore, I presume?' asked Lord Magnus, which was an old-fashioned way of putting it. I said, 'No,' very firmly. He inspected me with faint distaste.

'May I ask why she did this for you? Another of your conquests Thomas?' There was no praise in it. He was not amused and not convinced, and far from pleased. I shook my head.

Lord Magnus made a grimace. 'And who the hell *is* she?'

'She's an art-dealer. Lives in Rome. She stumbled on something. She's trying to help.' I wondered whether to suggest she might not refuse some compensation if we offered it, but decided the moment was inopportune.

He said, 'We must check on her I suppose,' and then seemed to put the idea out of his head. 'And the arms stuff? What about that?' His tone was edged again.

'That all makes sense, especially now that it's so clear that the Israelis are producing plutonium at Dimona, down in the Negev.'

'$25 million too low?'

'For the development of an armoury, yes,' I said. 'But it's enough to produce something very crude and perfectly effective for blackmail purposes.'

Lord Magnus scratched the grey hairs on his chest and pondered. It's a strange business, banking, and I knew enough about it to know that he wasn't using his intelligence in the sense that an American strategist would understand. He was a banker, so he was waiting for a hunch just like a Quaker waiting to be moved. We sat there and I allowed him to justify his extra £30,000 a year. I was off the hook. I had come to the Chairman and he would tell me what to do. For the moment, I was utterly, blissfully, at ease in the sun, content to sit there watching the sails on the horizon. We stayed like that, silently, together, for a long ten minutes.

Lord Magnus stretched himself, pushed back his chair, delved into his trunks, discovered a couple of notes, pinned them under the vernaccia bottle and strode wide-legged towards the car park. I trotted beside him, clutching my clothes, and said, 'What now?'

'Go and have a swim,' ordered Lord Magnus. 'I'm going to sleep on it.'

He vanished into a large Mercedes, then reappeared. 'Dinner this evening,' he commanded. 'At the Romazzino. You can wear your suit!'

I went back to the basket chair and the wide-eyed waitress. Most of the population were sleeping; the rest were eating before sleeping. I ate a pizza and guessed it came from a packet. The waitress didn't perjure herself by denying it.

The charm went away with the coffee cup and the bar was suddenly crowded with pink-skinned visitors. The men were plump, in shorts, drinking beer, and the women were either very fat or very thin with painted hair and heavy jewels. They had loud voices and their vulgarity was unmistakably Belgian. 'Tu sais, tu bouffes toujours trop, Maurice!' one of the hard blondes was saying to a man with a face like Paul-Henri Spaak in middle-age. Maurice ignored her.

So Smeralda, too, was other people. I felt tight and damned tired, too. Then I remembered I had left a taxi clocking up the lire behind the post office.

We dined badly but in style up at the white cliff of the Romazzino and Lady Magnus told me all about the Kedgworths' yacht and Garibaldi's tomb on Caprera. Her husband was sceptical of Garibaldi and hostile to yachts, but from the glint in her ladyship's manicured eye I guessed that they'd be packing the Kwells by next year. She went away to play bridge and we went out to the terrace and lay on wicker chairs, our feet stretched before us on stools like first-class passengers on those pre-war Cunard crossings, and looked down on the sea and the long lawns and the

135

glow of the fire from the barbecue on the beach. The Mediterranean was the colour of polished pewter; a yacht sailed slowly past, trailing a phosphorescent wake across the smooth surface. Around us were the sandy hills of the bay; the mountains behind, silhouetted sharper than any shadow-play; the smell of pine, strong Italian coffee, perfume and a memory of suntan oil. There was inoffensive music, vaguely nineteen-thirtyish, in the distance, and a hum of conversation; the sea and the cicadas beyond.

'Nice place this,' said Lord Magnus and his arm took in the entire coast of north-east Sardinia. 'Pity the people are so rough.'

The guest at the feast does not comment so I stayed silent.

'How long are you staying?' asked Lord Magnus, as though I were paying a social call. I began to feel I wasn't being taken seriously.

'I suppose I go tomorrow. But it rather depends on you.'

'Take a few days if you like,' said Lord Magnus, as though it was a gift in his granting, which I suppose it was. 'Do you the power of good.'

I said, 'Look, Sir, I've rushed out here to bother you because I thought it important. What am I supposed to do? Do I go back to Cairo and call the whole deal off?'

'Dear boy? Of course not!' cried Lord Magnus with the greatest energy he had shown since his butterfly stroke before breakfast. 'We mustn't be rash, not at this late stage. Don't let a little thing like this panic you into precipitate action.'

I felt a tang of bitterness in my mouth. 'You're saying this is all a cock-and-bull story?' I had the hopeless feeling in my stomach that warns me when I've lost.

'No, no, *no*,' said Lord Magnus, so reassuring and solid that he nearly soothed me again. 'I merely said we mustn't do anything *rash*. We shall have to look into the whole story.'

'But we haven't got the time. I'm already up against our deadline. We have to finalise the documents. I've already sent out drafts of the agreements and prospectus. We have a timetable too as you know.'

'Never mind, just do as I say. You must play for time— just for a little longer.'

It was easy to say it in Sardinia but I could see ahead of me an interminable round of not-so-casual meetings with puzzled and suspicious underwriters whose bewilderment would turn to scorn—for myself, for the House—when the truth came out. The first cables of query would be on my desk in a few days now. And I thought—very briefly before I pushed it away from me—of what I should say to Mara.

I said, abject now, 'Please, Sir, be frank with me. You think I'm wrong.'

'No,' he said. 'Not at all wrong. Not *wrong*...'

I knew what he meant. Two bankers have to have the same hunch. His hunch went the other way from mine.

He said, 'You, Thomas—you obviously think this deal has gone rotten.'

'Yes, I do.'

'I don't,' and didn't bother to explain. 'Now you'd better save Sardinia for another occasion. Go back to Cairo to-morrow if you can, while we're doing a check from London. Don't let anyone think we've got cold feet. Just stall them a little while longer. Do you understand?'

I said, 'Yes,' but hardly meant it.

At midnight I was alone in a bar down in the port. The shelves were crowded like the walls of a museum: Anisette and Aerol and Amaro Cora and Arquebusa. Cinzano, Martini and Ramazotta in threes and fours. Campari Cordial, Coca Buton and cognac in seven varieties. Sambuca Negra, Marie Brizard and Scotch. Fernet Branca,

Punt e Mes, and Diesil Tonic. Grappa in ten separate bottles and Beefeater gin. The vernaccia was too humble so it was hidden out of sight. A symphony of alcohol. God, I was tired.

THIRTY

Back through Rome, where Leonardo da Vinci was like Coney Island on Labor Day, in time to pick up a seat on the East African Airways flight down to Cairo. I sent Sue a postcard of a Sardinian peasant sitting outside a *nuraghe*. I felt grubby and my head ached. The glamour of my life was wearing thin, I reckoned; I was ready to quit, to go firewatching in the Rockies.

Yes, for that instant, as the pilot took us low over the ochre-green of the Delta, the cosmopolitan romance was ended. Never mind the mysteries of the Orient, the majesty of the Pharaohs: it was all a fraud and I was arriving over yet another city like the others—the same wretched roofs, the same blocks of grey and hideous apartments, the same shanties on the outskirts, the same dinky traffic, the same poverty, the same misery, the same stink. There would be the usual defences against all this. The same luxury hotels; the same servants; the same expensive food; the same alcohol; the same taxis; the same touts; the same drab offices; the same financiers; the same officials; the same fat Minister. Then another plane out again, another airport, the same relief of escape—until the next time.

Shepheards was full of tourists chattering about Abu Simbel in three European languages. The receptionist gave me a harassed nod so I left my bag and went across the road to the Semiramis to look for Mara.

I found her faster than I intended. She was sitting in the lounge talking to the German, Dietrich.

He saw me first, gave no sign of recognition and went on talking. I stood by the door, hesitating. After a moment she looked around and gave an ambiguous little wave. She made to turn around in her chair as though to dismiss me, then turned back to me and waved me across to their table. It was done casually, cleverly, and I understood she had kept her head.

'Why, it's Mr—I'm sorry,' she said coolly and looked me straight in the eye. 'I'm afraid I've forgotten your name.'

'Kane,' I said and reached for the accent. 'Thomas Kane, Ma'am. We met at the French Embassy, you remember? You were with that nice English diplomat.'

'Of course!' she said, and almost overdid the grace and favour. 'Forgive me. I'm being rude. You should meet Mr Dietrich, he's staying here in the Semiramis.'

Dietrich rose with dangerous agility for so heavy a man and clicked heels and bowed. Mara sat back in the chair, her bare arms splayed, and twisted back to look up at us. 'You're both here on business,' she said. 'Mr Kane does something to do with banking. He's an American.'

'Not quite,' I demurred. Dietrich tuned up his small talk.

'I hope your business is going well,' he said. We were talking English, presumably for my American benefit. I bet you do, you bastard, I said to myself and smiled modestly.

'And you,' I asked. He waved his hands as if to dismiss such matters, gave a *malesh* shrug, and said, 'Well enough.' Mara shuffled about in her handbag, head down. 'The atmosphere here has greatly improved,' said Dietrich, whose voice sounded deeper away from the tape recorder. We agreed that there was room for further improvement.

139

We gossiped a bit, warily. I didn't like him at all, I decided. As soon as I decently could, I left on a mission in search of the *International Herald Tribune*.

I found it and sat down in the foyer the way they do in spy films, watching over the masthead and wondering whether I ought to cut a hole in the middle of the page and peer through that. Dietrich left soon afterwards. They shook hands; she seemed to have some trouble extracting her hand from his. He came straight past me without noticing and out into the street and I saw him jump into a taxi and disappear. He was wearing a crumpled linen suit the colour of a faded Afrika Korps uniform.

Mara came towards me a few minutes later and leaned over my chair so I could remember her perfume.

'Oh damn!' she said, 'Oh darling, damn!' The accent was an entrancement but I sometimes thought she had the vocabulary of an astronaut.

I asked, 'What are you so upset about?'

'It's obvious. He's seen us,' she said with her voice for high tragedy. 'He might guess why I was so interested in his work.'

'You were clever enough,' I reassured her. 'You treated me like the man who takes the dog for a walk.'

She said, doubtfully, 'I suppose there's no reason why I shouldn't have met you briefly?'

'None at all.'

'But it's terribly risky. If he sees us together again he's bound to get suspicious.' She touched me, tentatively, her fingers scudding across my wrist, asking to be grasped in mine.

'Oh hell,' I said. 'That's the last bloody straw. You mean you're not going to help me forget all this?' We had retreated into the shadows and stood side by side like strangers in a bus queue, gazing at the counter selling artificial kohl in four colours and watching the hotel entrance.

'My dear,' she said. 'I'd love to, but it's too risky just now.'

'I suppose you're right,' I mumbled and I guess I meant it. This affair was getting off the ground as slowly as an Irish engagement.

'How long will you be?' she asked. 'How long have you got? I shall have to go back to Teheran eventually, but I can take my time for the next week or two.'

'I don't know. It could still drag on...' I hesitated to tell her. I don't know why.

She understood. 'You mean they don't believe you in London?' She sounded incredulous.

'It's not as simple as that. They want to think about it.'

'Think about what?'

'About the meaning of the jigsaw.'

'They can't be expecting us to find *more* evidence...' Her voice sounded angry as well as bewildered.

I said helplessly, 'The Chairman was on holiday when I found him. He has to get in touch with the other directors.'

She scowled, like a child denied a present, and said, 'Dietrich was bubbling over with glee today. He wouldn't tell me why. He kept laughing to himself. I think he's probably made his deal.'

I said loudly, so the girl behind the counter looked across at us, 'Jesus, I can't help it! I can't *do* anything. I just work for them. I do what they tell me.'

It was useless to try to explain that I had gone to Lord Magnus for advice. He had given it and it was wrong. It was his responsibility. Let him be wrong. Let me be in the clear. I just knew that he was wrong.

She looked up at me and said, 'Why?' very softly. I looked at her.

She repeated it.
'Why not? Why can't you do anything?'
I didn't know why not.
I began to think about it. Then, as she looked up at me,
I began to draft a cable.

CONDON 39DRAYTON GARDENS LONDONSW10
UNABLE REACH YOU TELEPHONE MUST REPORT HAVE DIS-
COVERED FACTOR MAKING DEAL IMPOSSIBLE STOP NONO
TIME CONVINCE MAGNUS WHO IMMOVABLE NILEWISE ALSO
SKY HERE AZUREST BUT ESSENTIAL YOU INFORM LEAD
UNDERWRITERS SOONEST POSSIBLE BLOWUP SPHINX STOP
PLEASE RELY MY INSTINCTS AND ACT SPEEDILIEST REPEAT
SPEEDILIEST EXPLANATION FOLLOWS THOMAS

THIRTY-ONE

Joe Larochelle arrived in town three days later and must
have made for the hotel with an escort of outriders. He
was waiting for me in the foyer when I got back. He looked
harassed and tired and hot, like the man who runs up and
down the Pyramids for the benefit of the tourists. His suitcase was still parked by the desk.

'Boy, the wires are humming,' he said. 'I don't know
what you said to your boss, but if you have a spare half-
hour I can tell you what mine said to me, and he wasn't
reminiscing about his days in the Pentagon. Where've
you been, anyway?'

'Listening to the British Ambassador wag his chin,' I
said. 'He wanted to know whether he could go ahead and
take soundings with Number 10. For the inauguration.'

Joe fired me a doubtful glance, all business and all suspicion.

'What did you say?' he asked.

'That our lawyers were having trouble over the drafting of the guarantee clause.'

'Did he swallow it?'

'Of course.' I never know whether to believe a British diplomat, they are too well schooled in mendacity.

'What's the gospel he's getting from the Egyptians?'

'He says they're pressuring him to know why we haven't produced a final date for the delivery of their loot.'

'That tallies.'

'Yes. In any two directions.'

'You'd better fill me in.'

'How much do you know?' I needed to know whether Joe's arrival was Condon's doing or Magnus having second thoughts. But it couldn't be Guy, he would be killing the issue from the underwriters' end.

'Look, fellow,' said Joe, wearily patient. 'I was minding my own business in Paris, planning to take a little vacation back home, when the 'phones started to ring and here I am. That's what I know.'

'So Lord Magnus didn't waste any time?'

'Cable and Wireless have covered their dividend. Let's put it like that.'

'Have you heard from Guy Condon in all this?'

'Not a word. As far as we're concerned, it's His Lordship in person.'

'Why come out here then?'

'To watch over the interests of the Bank. What else? Don't forget the World Bank has a holy reputation to look after. We'd be as embarrassed as a bishop in a brothel if we found ourselves guaranteeing an arms deal.'

I said, 'Joe, do you believe me?'

He shrugged. 'Would you, in my position?' he asked. It wasn't an answer. 'Tell me all,' he said, 'and don't leave out the sexy antique dealer.' We sat down, in a quiet corner, and I began.

Half an hour later he announced, 'Time for a drink,' and whistled at the waiter. Two of them raced towards him as though it were the Farouk Gold Plate.

'The trouble is, I don't know what I'm supposed to do next,' I confessed.

Joe grinned and scraped a hand through his thin blonde hair. 'Nor do I,' he said. 'Your guess is as good as mine. Let's start by having dinner with that girl of yours.'

'No good. She and I can't risk being seen together.'

'Then I'll take her out without you.'

I said, 'Don't be crazy, Joe. If Dietrich sees her with anyone else who looks like a banker he'll begin to put two and two together.'

'But I don't look like a banker.'

'Yes you do, you've got 1818 H Street written all over your worried face.'

'Why is the woman still hanging around? She's not still having it off with Dietrich, is she, and coming to tell you all about it?'

'Be careful, Joe,' I said. 'I wouldn't like to throw you in the Nile.' I must have looked as though I meant it because he shrugged and said 'Sure, sorry, you must have had a bellyful of this town.'

I said, 'I still want to know what I ought to *do*. Do I sit here waiting for Moses to come out of the bulrushes? I can't stall for ever while Lord Magnus gets on with his hols.'

'We do as we're told, Tom,' said the Canadian. 'We'll

swim the Canal, you and I, and ask for asylum if our masters tell us to. They sent me here to hold your hand; they sent you back to keep the Egyptians happy. That's the way it is.'

'So we have to twiddle our thumbs while the Egyptians put together the biggest double-cross since the Japs bombed Pearl Harbor. You know that, Joe, the House will never live it down. Lord Magnus will get his place in the history books OK, he'll be another Ivar Krueger, our banking colleagues will decide we're dangerous cretins—yes, you and I—we're both in this—and certain governments will be so livid they could be tempted to back all manner of idiocy in the Middle East. The Russians will be laughing fit to burst.'

Joe squeezed the lemon so the juice hit him in the eye. He crossed and uncrossed his legs, began to struggle with the low cushion, then changed his mind and subsided with a groan.

'I don't give a brass monkey for your precious Thorne Reinhard,' he said. 'Sir Felix is one of the old-style City relics and Lord Magnus deserves another bloody nose if he thinks he's going to pull off a coup here in Cairo to avenge his bruises for what he went along with in 1956.'

He paused, as though wondering whether to say it or not. 'But OK, I admit it, Tom, I'm scared—shit-scared. I was having nightmares on the plane. I told you before: the joy of this issue is that it reverses this wretched business where less developed countries borrow wildly expensive money to finance prestige they don't really need. All right, it's oil sheikhs and Latin American generals and Lebanese rentiers who are going to buy your bonds in Switzerland and London, but that doesn't alter the fact that the proceeds are going to the have-nots who are ploughing them into a project that may feed a few million people. I don't know why I'm giving you my Rotary lunch lecture, you know it as well as I do. Only it's on my mind more often than yours because I'm a do-gooder development banker. So that's what I'm thinking. If the deal *is* rigged, then all development financing will get more difficult than ever. Everywhere. None of the big boys that you and that Condon guy have persuaded to trust the Egyptians are going to forget the lesson—the example will be catching.'

'Very eloquent,' I said. 'So are you with me or against me?'

Joe stopped. 'I don't get you,' he said. 'How d'you mean, am I with you or against you?'

'You believe I'm right? About Dietrich?'

Joe said, 'I don't think the issue can go ahead until the Bank is entirely satisfied.'

'So what do we do, for Christ's sake? Ask the President? We can't risk alarming them. They'd fly off the handle if the wind changed.'

'Why is this girl still hanging around?' Joe asked abruptly. 'If she can't look forward to your romantic attentions ...'

'She's just completed some deal. We planned to go off somewhere.'

Joe said nothing but raised one eyebrow. I said hastily, before he could put it down again, 'We've been waiting for this to be cleared up.'

'Why wait?' said Joe. 'It could be a long business. Won't do to keep the lady waiting. I could look after this end for a few days—I'll go and see the Ministry and so on.'

'But I've been sent back here ...'

'You've been sent back to stall them as long as possible. They had this out on the 'phone before I left. I said to London, wouldn't it be less suspicious if you kept out

146

of the way—easier for you to keep them waiting peace-
fully if you're not in town. They said they supposed so,
whatever that means.'

'Joe,' I said, 'you tempt me.'

'Then go ahead. There's nothing I can't do in your
place. Except what the lady's waiting for, if you see what
I'm getting at.'

'You can't?' I said innocently, and he grinned and
said, 'My Eskimo wife wouldn't like it.

'I thought it was an Eskimo au pair girl.'

'What's the difference? It's rubbing noses, that's all.'

'Okay,' I said. 'Stop the slapstick. We've got to decide
what to do.'

'Tom, what do you *want* to do?' He said it as if it was
the one question that mattered.

I paused, then I pronounced, slowly and carefully,
because now I understood it at last.

'I want to stall the issue. Stall it *safely*, you understand.
No risk of the thing slipping through our hands. If our
masters are being stupid—blinded by their political
regrets—then we've got to use our own initiative.'

'Don't include me in this,' he put in. 'You work for
a cosy little bank. I work for an institution. And I have
a family to support.'

'Then play safe if you have to,' I snapped, 'but let me
risk my own neck if I want to. I won't drag you down
with me, I promise.'

'OK! OK!' said Joe. 'Take it easy—you were saying?'

'It's got to be stopped at the underwriters' end as well,'
I said. 'All those banks have come in because we sold
them the idea. They can't be left up in the air like this
while London scratches itself and looks for Dietrich in
the Frankfurt 'phonebook.'

'Never mind the sob stuff,' said Joe. 'These boys in

Geneva and Zürich can keep their hair out of the mangle without your help.'

'It's more than that. That's where the timing is tightest. You know it as well as I do, Joe. They can't sit on their funds for ever waiting for the sponsors to condescend to float the issue.'

'You're going to bust it up if you're not careful. Then look a fool when Dietrich turns out to be a nut case.'

'That's my headache,' I said, 'not yours.'

'You're going to make the underwriters bite their nails?'

'I've put my own head on the chopper. It's a fair exchange.'

'You're gambling on the arms deal becoming a fact. You realise that's the only way you'll be proved right?'

'And if Dietrich gives up and goes off with his tail between his legs, no one will ever know what nearly happened.'

'Or why the Nile barrages were built by the Russians after all.'

I said, 'Then we can always put the deal together again.'

'Tom,' said the World Bank man. 'Have you actually *done* anything about this? Something rash? Something I ought to know about?'

I hesitated, but only for a moment. The cable had gone. I had made my play. It was up to Condon now. This was no time to spread the risk.

'Don't worry,' I lied. 'I'll give you plenty of warning. And who knows? I'll probably live with it in the end.'

Joe said, 'I don't know what you're doing. I've never seen you. I never want to see you again.' He rolled his eyes and said 'Help!' very quietly.

'You agree with me Joe? In your own fat gut?'

'Perhaps I do,' said Joe, but he evaded my stare. 'Perhaps I do.'

Do-gooders had always been yellow.
So I was on my own.

I stood under the shower for five minutes the next morning until my chest hairs stood up and my belly tightened and went numb and I could kid myself it was a wet February in London. A triumph of mind over matter. The thudding on the door could have been the water pipes and I ignored it. There was a telegram on the mat when I groped my way back to dry land. It came from Sue and I did a double-take straight out of the Hollywood 1920's. We sent postcards, and never, but never, letters—it was our agreement—and here she was sending a cable as though she were pregnant and my intentions weren't honourable. It said: COLLEAGUES ADVISE ME CANCEL PURCHASE AGREEMENT SINCE ISLAMIC ART BEAR MARKET LONDON CAUTIOUS REGARDS CAREW

I went back under the shower to work it out. She was trying to tell me something and it wasn't a reminder to change my socks. A warning? A bear market? What agreement? What was she talking about? Or was it simple jealousy? No, Sue wasn't a fool. She knew the Cairo police read every cable. She was telling me something important.

I thought about it all the way to the airport and on to the Cyprus Airways morning Viscount to Nicosia. Then I eased it out of my mind like last year's Annual Report. I was sitting next to a familiar perfume. 'Good heavens, it's you!' I said with a tolerable effort at surprise. 'What a coincidence! Are you going to Cyprus as well?' Mara

149

took off her dark glasses and said, 'Please! Can we stop this charade? You're behaving like a married man with a conscience.' She smiled to make up for it and I kissed her hand and helped her fasten her seat-belt—she didn't say whether or not she'd flown before so I thought it best to show her the ropes.

She was reading Heikal's weekly article in *Al Ahram*. 'Where are you supposed to be?' I asked. 'If anyone looks for you ...'

'Cairo thinks I'm in Rome. Rome thinks I'm in Beirut. Beirut thinks I'm in Teheran. Teheran thinks I'm in—I forget where. Does that satisfy you?'

'Then we forget it. Forget everything. If we can ...'

'Of course we can,' she said. 'That's my part of the bargain.'

Cyprus is quiet and small. It's a Mediterranean island, which just about sums it up, a distant province slumbering in the sun. The Greeks have long since scrubbed out the blood on Murder Mile, bottled up the Turks in a handful of enclaves and turned the UN troops into a big foreign exchange earner. The place bristles with soldiers, and it doesn't matter. The locals have more guns than are good for them, and so what. It's a great place to get bored, and that applies whether you are a Turk, a Greek, a Finn in a blue beret, a Tommy guarding Britain's A-bombs down at the sovereign bases, or a tourist in search of night life and suntan lotion. Everyone speaks a civilised language, the food is execrable, the wine slightly better, the beer very good and even the Scandinavians now take a nap in the afternoon.

Three superannuated EOKA terrorists were gunning their taxis when we went out of the shiny new terminal. I chose a driver I knew and said to Mara, 'Where now?' That was as far as my plans had stretched. She said, 'You mean I have a choice?' and laughed so that I guessed she was happy. I said, 'Mountains or sea?' and she laughed again and said, 'Sea. Please.'

'Where?'

She shrugged, free of care, and our gunman sighed heavily, loud enough to be sure we heard. 'You know the place better than I do,' she said, which was strange because we went into Nicosia to make inquiries and when we reached the Ledra Palace the porter nodded at me vaguely, as though he'd seen my face before and couldn't remember whether I tipped well, but snapped into life when he saw Mara and said, 'Welcome back, Miss Tal' and 'How long are you staying?' and the manager came out of his room to join the festivities. Bloody strange, I thought.

'We're not staying,' Mara announced to all and sundry, as though it had all been fixed by Horizon six months before. 'It's too hot up here—we're going down to Kyrenia. Is the flat above the harbour free? You know, the one you used to keep the keys for.' Ah well, I said to myself, I hadn't expected that I would be the first, nor the last either, I must remember to carve my initials on the table. I'm not possessive. A pleasant thought.

We sat in the bar and watched the journalists getting drunk on pink gin while the porter made 'phone calls and swapped the taxi for a self-drive Morris. It had a tricky insurance cover in case we got shot up by the UN or someone else, and a gearbox that jammed like a Bofors gun. Then everyone swore eternal gratitude, I got my chance to remind them that I am a good tipper, and we ambled off past the roadblock into the Turkish enclave and north to the sea.

It was the noisiest part of the afternoon, when the cicadas try to deafen the sound of the UN convoy coming up the hill from the coast. The Turkish Army in St Hilarion were doubling as guides for the tourists and the black-suited policemen sweated like London bobbies in a heat wave but looked twice as relaxed. The pottery was still making souvenirs for the UN men, the shepherds did what shepherds have always done, and thirteen English tourists visited Bellapais Abbey, sat under the Tree of Idleness and asked the waiter if he remembered Durrell.

The Morris was better downhill than up, as we all are, and freewheeled down the mountain past the Maple Leaf camp and the favourite ambush corner so Mara's hair was streaming like bunting on a flagship by the time we regained Greek territory. No one paid us any attention. Kyrenia is a port with a fine sturdy fort above the harbour where the fishermen are being pushed out by the international yacht set. Kyrenia will soon be spoiled, but it hadn't happened by that afternoon. The siesta went on for a damned long time, even for the mad dogs, and it took us an hour to find our two rooms and a shower above a café looking out towards Antalya. It wasn't the finding that took the time, Mara hadn't forgotten, it was waking the rentier-Greek who owned it and persuading him to take his arms from around Mara's neck long enough to part with the key.

She threw her bag on the bed, which looked serviceable, and said, 'Come and swim.'

I said, 'It's not wise to swim when the stomach is full.'

'You haven't eaten properly since breakfast.'

'Why don't we wait until the wind drops?'

It was true, the wind that greeted us on the hillside had been coming from Crete, even in the harbour it was butting the dark-green water into wavelets big enough to make the yachtsmen keep a tight hold on the main-brace. Outside the harbour wall, beneath a vicious looking gunboat, the sea was beginning to pound against the stone like an angry tenant on the wall.

She said, 'Swim!' in her Catherine the Great voice, and led me down the stairs on to the quay. By the time we had refused to drink with the proprietor and to buy fish from the newest arrival it was early evening. 'It's getting late,' I said. 'I'm tired, let's wait till tomorrow.

'I want to show you my own beach,' she said.

'That's pretty good for a girl who doesn't know Cyprus.'

'I never said that.'

Four miles west of Kyrenia, on the road to Paphos beyond the vineyards and the tomatoes, there's a lane that will admit a mule ridden sideways and that's the lot. We pushed the Morris through the rushes and then suddenly came out on a silver beach. The sand was coarse, fragments of rock and shell which need another million years before they will go through a sieve, and the sea was very green and very loud and near. The air was salt and full of the smell of the Mediterranean, rosemary and myrtle and wild lavender and mint and asphodel. There were wild irises growing white and frail on the bank where we left our clothes, bamboos surrounding us in a screen and a freshwater stream flowing softly past our feet into the sea.

She was running, barely glimpsed, into the spray. It was cold, but if you're naked on a strange beach you don't dawdle on the edge and we were both in the waves, struggling to reach beyond their crest where we could ride them out. I reached her, spitting salt, and grasped at her but she was ready for me, my hands slipped on her body and she was away, under the wave, and beating through the current in a fast classy crawl. The next wave was the one in seven, it tossed her back to me and this time she let me hold her, laughing, then dragged me down through the pale and clear water so my lungs pumped and I kicked her away and escaped, almost frightened by her strength and skill.

The sun toppled behind the hill with a last flare of jagged rays through the pine trees and the water began to punish us, tirelessly. Dusk was moving in and the bamboos turned dark and menacing round the cove. We gave up and let the sea carry us in and smash us sprawling on to the sand. I had forgotten we were naked. We were both staggering like cross-channel swimmers when we climbed up the beach, our arms around each other, our flesh cold and slippery. We shivered even as we pressed our bodies against each other. There were goose pimples on her shoulders. Her breasts were larger than I had expected, and her nipples had turned the colour of a long Campari. We lay on the beach, embracing statues strewn with sand, and for the second time since Groppi we were unready for each other.

'Walk before we run?' I asked, and she said, 'Let's go back to the flat,' and pushed me away.

Back in the room the shutters were open and her skin was strangely pale, milk-white in the evening air. The sea sounded like an express train with a million coaches beyond the breakwater. Her skin was salt on my mouth. And her body was ready now, eager, and the breeze blew straight in through the open window, cool-laden with perfume and with salt.

Afterwards our stomachs were protesting hunger, growling like jealous dogs and she threw a kaftan of towelling around herself and we went down on to the quay to eat fish and drink retsina and local brandy, to feel the alcohol in our veins and gaze at each other with the surprise and delight of new lovers who have waited a long time.

She forced me out, those next days, on to the beaches,

154

into the hills. We made friends with a Canadian major, with a Greek lieutenant homesick for Salonika, and with a black donkey tethered near our own bay. We drove into the mountains and climbed with the goats up the crags and balanced and looked down on to the rich broad valleys of Cyprus, brown in the summer heat. We ate cheese and fruit and stopped drinking spirits, and in the evening there was fish or lamb and rough dry bread, and wine to make us gently drunk in each other's arms. Once, one evening, we were miles away beyond Lefka when it began to rain, very softly almost like a fine English rain. It pitted the sand with tiny craters like a small-scale moon landscape, and the grains felt soft and cool under our feet. The sea was warm and gentle, almost oily, and we swam slowly together into the eye of the setting sun as it tipped towards the horizon at the level of our eyes, the orange streaking deep across the swell.

She laughed a lot but even when the mouth curved in a smile the eyes were calm, silent, eternally clear. When I looked at those eyes, under the high-arched brows, I was afraid. I didn't know why. I was afraid of inadequacy; afraid that she was still beyond my grasp; afraid to tell her of my fears.

We talked for hour upon hour. About being brought up in Paris. About Rome and New York. About how we'd met. About men she'd known and women I had known. About the Arabs and learning Arabic. She spoke Russian, of course, and talked about Moscow and Leningrad, which she knew, and Berlin and Africa and Peru which I knew better. We scarcely spoke at all about our work. It had been left behind as if by a pact and for these days I tried to put it out of my mind. We didn't talk about Sue and I didn't mention the cable, folded and damp in my hip pocket.

Then one day we went out into the hills above the sea and made love on a bed of pine needles and woke to see a herd of goats being driven past us oblivious as *sadhus*. We stopped at a café with a view and it was there that the doubts, the fears, the instinct, caught up with me at last, and when she said, 'You won't know Shahsavar. It's a small village on the Caspian ...' I knew what I was going to do.

I studied the line of her jaw and the soft twist of the neck under the collar and talked—charming as a Borgia at the feast—and made up nonsense and lies about Qazwin and Sarvestan, the Shah and the court artists of the Indian Moghuls, and wanted so much for her to laugh me to scorn.

But she let it all go. Then I knew the bitch had framed me, and hated myself for my stupidity. I think I forgave her without realising it. And if she was a fraud, I could not begin to understand what it meant, except that I was betrayed and lost.

We were very quiet that evening and she wondered why I was so tense. In the morning I told her I had had a cable calling me back to London at top priority. She didn't bother to ask how they had known where I was. Perhaps she hadn't thought of it.

THIRTY-THREE

I had an errand in Zürich and sat glowering and depressed in the Athens transit lounge utterly oblivious for once of the tommy guns the Colonels' police were waving around.

The new terminal building is small and squat with

padded shoulders, like most Greeks. I drank coffee, spat the grounds out of my teeth and tried to get a grip on myself. Tranquillise the jerky nerves. I tried to remember Pericles' dates, and the name of the man who stole the Elgin Marbles. Augustine had found God by digging in the sand. The Grande Bretagne is always booked up. Where the hell was Condon? The Peruvians had been nice though debauched. Merida was the main town of Yucatan. Good bankers when they die go to ... where?

Sue had said LONDON CAUTIOUS. Perhaps I'd imagined it, out of guilt or something stupid. Perhaps this was the week that Kane shot his bolt. No obituary in *The Banker*, by request. Where was Mara, what sort of idiot did she think I was? Would she wash away my memory in her shower and pick up a tall, blond Finn to make sure? Or go back to Toby and shrug me away? All right, so she didn't know about the Indian Moghul princes and the Qazwin school of Persian art. Perhaps she was being kind, letting me talk nonsense rather than correct me and humiliate me. Or perhaps she just hadn't heard me properly. A banker who loses his hunch is like a one-armed violinist. I was in this bloody airport because the hairs had flapped on my neck, I'd listened to another hunch and now I couldn't make out the words. So what if she were a cheap fraud, a silly girl, a whore out of *Vogue*? What if she had been playing at Freya Stark in a mini skirt? Who the hell *was* she anyway, at long last? So what, I said to myself, and I knew the answer to that one. A fraud is a fraud is a fraud.

But I couldn't get it out of my mind, I'll never get it out of my mind, her lying there, lying across me, and the way she said 'It's never been like this before', her voice so still, so soft, and I believed her, sweet Jesus, I believed her.

157

My bloody heart was still overdoing it. I said to myself, cretin, dupe, slow down. Take time to think. Think of a Latin tag and multiply it by Makarios. Where shall I build my next home?

Then I did think calmly for a moment, went to the Olympic desk and said, 'Drop me off in Rome,' so the girl scowled and began to remake the ticket, doubtless wondering if I was one of the Palestinian guerrillas. I was almost brown enough. The sunburn prickled across my shoulders and I almost forgot where the sun had been, when.

On board the Boeing I read the London papers carefully, and discovered the Middle East had nowhere made the front-page. I slept a bit after lunch, unwisely, collected a headache and toppled into Fiumicino in the heat-smog of the Roman summer.

Rome was empty if you don't count the tourists, which was getting hard even for me. The all-American boys were sprawled down the Spanish Steps, scratching or cruising or sleeping and every single one of them was turned on. Some of them were trying to look the girls up and down and then up again, the way Italian males do, but they didn't have the trick, there was no admiration in their stare and the girls knew it and hated them. And others looked inexpertly at the Italian boys. The ladies in Babingtons tut-tutted like their sisters in Cheltenham and the *carabinieri* leaned on their swords and posed for the tourists and dreamed of the happy days of Mussolini.

Up in the Piazza del Popolo the Italians were shrugging through the traffic, handing off the Fiats like Welsh rugby three-quarters and making for Rosati, where a poet's daughter had turned up wearing a topless dress. Rome's a village, word travels fast, and everyone crowded the pavement tables waiting for her to re-emerge. There was another government crisis and the beautiful people were talking about the chances of a military coup. These days the Romans are always talking of a military coup.

Nothing happens in the summer. The Pope makes the same speech in three or four languages in Castelgandolfo. The *pépées* have their month of power: the wives are away at the villas or on the beaches and the husbands shack up with the girlfriend and the wives pretend not to know, putting down their husband's exhaustion at the weekend to the effects of the heat and the city and the travelling.

I checked three times. First, in Via del Barbuino, in the shop with the shutters near Knoll International, where a middle-aged princess sells everything from Kyoto tea-cups to Patagonian shawls and had never heard of anyone like Mara. Second, in the Via Giulia in a first-floor office where the Arabists argue about *mihrabs* and their host deals discreetly in ceramics and hash. Third, in a street behind the Station where the buildings are as dreary as the Civil Code and an old man who used to run the Italian Liceo in Alexandria is coughing himself to death and wondering whether to embrace the Prophet before it's too late. None of them had heard of her. The princess said, 'She could work in Paris? The prices are better.'

It was no good. I knew Mara had always said Rome. I asked, 'Do I need to go to Milan?' and she smiled, a weary principessa smile, and said, 'If she looks the way you describe her, I'd know her even if she dealt from Milano.'

It was getting to be sordid and I flew away from Rome. The heat haze over the sea beyond the airport was as heavy as woodsmoke and the beaches below the vineyards were black with bodies roasting in the bonfire of the sand. I still had that other errand in Zürich.

Which was clean and cool so I felt better when I saw

the sturdy Swiss queueing at the pedestrian crossings. The bankers were virtuously with their wives in the mountains, and the Dolder Grand was still the place to stay in summer, cool and high up, rich and remote in its pine woods. I stayed there that evening, very quiet, and drank Vichy water, went to bed early and sent a cable to Sue: THANKS LOVE. It was less than the minimum wordage and the Swiss clerk told me I was wasting money, so I made it THANKS STOP LOVE which seemed to say it all and still cost me wasted money.

Breakfast in bed. The waitress was blonde and smelt of honey. Her waist was very slim as she reached out to clasp the shutters open. Bright sunshine. Bread and cherry jam, cheese and bitter coffee with creamy hot milk.

I showered, dressed, took the long taxi ride into town down the steep cobbled hillside. Japanese tourists, businessmen, the lake lively with little sailing boats, a few milk-chocolate-ad. clouds in the blue sky. Chimes from the church near Stadthausquai.

The man I wanted to see didn't waste money on premises near the Bahnofstrasse, but every senior bank manager knew him all the same. He was formerly a German Jew and had his office in his apartment in one of the modest buildings in Waffenplatzstrasse. Old Friedrich Bauer ran a finding service, a very special one, had done since the war. Miss Spielter had put us on to him years ago, before he'd become well-known, and he'd served us well, giving us helpful information on the pasts of some of our more amnesic German banking friends. And not just the Germans. Bauer's superbly catalogued files were very far-ranging, and kept up to date with all the skill of an expert on medieval manuscripts, which the Spielter once told me he had been, before the Nazis.

After the usual brisk preliminaries we began the search.

We found her on the fourth try. The photographs flicked before my eyes like a Feuillade experiment and—suddenly —there she was. A little severe. Rather young. Very white, mouth prim, eyes secret.

The card was very brief.

MIRIAM ABRAMOVNA TALOV (or MARA TAL)
Born Moscow 1941 Parents dead.
Kiev University and Moscow Institute for Economic Analysis.
1965-1966 Gosbank.
1966 Moscow, editorial staff of *Voprosy Ekonomiki*.
1966-1967 Paris, Banque Commerciale de l'Europe du Nord.
1967-69 Beirut, Moscow Narodny Bank.
1970– Unknown. Observed Cairo.

That was the only moment I panicked. I think that's true. Just one brief moment. He had to ask me twice whether I wanted his fee billed the usual way and still could get no sense out of me.

Outside in the street it was all right again. I watched a kid on a tricycle, saw shoppers emerging laden from the corner Migros, and felt better. I let myself think about it for a little while, probing my brain to assess the new discovery with the delicacy and curiosity with which the tongue explores the empty socket after a tooth has been pulled, and with something of the same sense of relief. Bruised, dazed, happy!

The buffet at Klothen Airport was half-empty, and the waitress stood there smiling at me nervously until I realised I was grinning like a fool.

THIRTY-FOUR

BEA gave their usual demonstration of how to make a £100 flight at 30,000 feet as unpleasant as a 3p. ride in the No. 11 bus down the Strand in a winter rush hour. London was wet and grey, the rain was a fine mesh of water, dripping from every lamp post, rushing down the gutters. Everything was dirty, stained, crowded. Monica was reading *Angélique* in English. 'Goodness! You're brown,' she said, which was intimacy coming from her. I said, 'Yes, brown all over,' and she went pink for some reason, then angry: another arrow for St Sebastian.

Miss Spielter was lecturing a temp with a plunging neckline and shaky shorthand about the traditions of the House. I jerked my thumb at the Parlour door. 'He's not coming in,' she said. 'My, what a lovely tan you have!'

'For Christ's sake,' I said. 'Is he still in Sardinia?'

Miss Spielter peered at me briefly. 'No, he's driving up from the country and said he'd be stopping at the Victoria and Albert for a lecture. Is it urgent?'

'Very.'

'Then you could try to catch him there.'

I said, 'Thanks. Sorry to be so rushed,' and turned on the Connecticut grin and she smiled and said, 'How nice to see you back.'

So I was still the blue-eyed boy as far as Miss Spielter was concerned. I wondered whether she would still be smiling next time she saw me. When the shambles would be common gossip and I was being posted to Helsinki.

The City was empty for the summer. The men from the Bank of England extension were crowding their wine

162

bar as though sterling could be left to itself. Austin Reed had a sale. Farther along Cheapside there was a choice of gas, oil or electric central heating at special prices. Wallace Heaton were trying to sell Japanese darkroom equipment cut-price. They even had time to be civil over the silver hairbrushes in Mappin and Webb. It wouldn't last. The girls were hideous, thick-thighed yet under-nourished. Malcolm Muggeridge was preaching a sermon at Bow Bells.

Plastic macs and German tourists in Fleet Street. The cab driver thought it quicker to try the Embankment. He was wrong. Green Park was at its greenest, the deck-chairs drooping in the rain. Some diplomat type alighted from a car in the middle of Belgrave Square and kissed the hand of a lady walking a dog. The French First Secretary and the Spanish Ambassador's wife? I wondered as we rattled through Beauchamp Place, more chi chi than ever, and with less reason. Oh God, oh Kensington!

The V and A was defended by a trio of West African attendants but I broke through their protests and sneaked up into the back of the lecture theatre where the lecturer had already started. She was a formidable Frenchwoman who kept darting furious looks at the projectionist. Lord Magnus sat happily in the middle of a scrum of dis-tinguished looking ladies, a few frayed old academic gentlemen, a group of slightly baffled Dutch tourists who had gone in through the wrong door, and a miscellaneous bag of scruffy unisex students.

'The Bamyan carpets are finer,' the Frenchwoman was saying, 'and usually made of yak's wool. Late eighteenth century drifting over into the nineteenth. What I call the Regency yaks.' She tapped on the floor and the lights went off. A pattern of rectangles and crimson triangles blurred, then focused on the double screen. Lord Magnus sat high on his wooden bench, lapping it up with the relish of a New York slum kid in Macy's. I let him be. Once, he took a silver pencil from his pocket and made a note on the back of an envelope. 'The yaks died out in the 1850s,' said the Frenchwoman, and we all suffered for them. The lights went on. No applause, like in church.

Lord Magnus growled, 'You're making a habit of this,' and gripped my arm, in greeting or admonition it was hard to tell. I said, 'Habit of what?'

'Habit of tracking me down off duty.'

I nearly said how nice it must be to be able to take in a few museums after a weekend inspecting the estate, but thought better of it. His eyes took in my tan, appraised my grey-dot tie, flickered to my shoes, then back to my face.

'Trouble?' asked Lord Magnus in his Headmaster tone. I nodded.

'As bad as that?'

'Worse.'

Lord Magnus tore a giant hand down through his jowls in the visual equivalent of a sigh. We went out to the Armstrong Siddeley with the chauffeur, Dobson, watchful at the wheel. The car was long, with those unmistakable, war-influenced slit-like windows, sleek in gunmetal, grey and black, the sexless sphinx-like creature crouching at the tip of the bonnet. That car said a lot for Magnus. And it made sense—he didn't have to search through the herd of Rollses and Daimlers when he came out of some Establishment function.

I pushed the glass panel shut and leaned back in the cushions, trying to frame my opening sentence.

'Well you'd better get it over hadn't you?' said Lord Magnus, now a brisk surgeon about to operate. He stared ahead, then briefly at me, his eyebrows raised.

I chose that moment to remember his war record. A

dashing brigadier—Crete, Sicily, the lot; the worst his enemies could say was that he wouldn't have minded losing more men in one day than Auchinleck in the whole campaign, although of course he hadn't. I could feel the sweat start at the small of my back, and my stomach muscles tighten as I sat straighter against the fawn leather upholstery.

'Well, come on,' said Lord Magnus, and actually took out his spectacles and his wallet and started to read a dog-eared letter handwritten in black ink with the House of Commons crest on the top. 'Out with it, Thomas.'

I said bleakly, 'The Nile issue is off.'

I left it at that.

There was a long pause as we slid past Harrods and caught up with the traffic jam at Knightsbridge.

Lord Magnus said, 'Explain yourself,' very quietly, without looking up.

'It's bust. We've been had. I've made a balls-up.'

Lord Magnus was still reading his letter. He said, without looking up, 'Thomas, you are being remarkably incoherent, and totally uninformative. Have you done something foolish?'

I said, 'I suppose so. Yes, in fact I have.'

'Then we shall both need a drink,' said Magnus dryly and knocked on the glass and told Dobson to stop at Brooks's. I looked at him and decided he was enjoying himself, that's for sure, furling his upper lip like the seadog Englishman. He'd have his game of bowls, but I'd be the one to steer the fireship.

'Useful, these V and A lectures,' said Lord Magnus evenly. 'The place is much livelier than the BM. Ever tried looking for those carpets when you're over in that part of the world?'

I said, 'I've rather gone off Islamic art.'

165

'Ah!' said Lord Magnus. 'So that's what it is.'

We went in behind the great picture window of Brooks's and he took a moment to glance at the ticker-tape. When we were in the library and the waiter had brought the bottle and syphon for me and a pale India tea for Lord Magnus, I said, 'It's not as simple as that.'

'I gather it's the girl. Beautiful, I'll say that for you.'

'She's a fraud,' I said. 'A great gaping beartrap. I fell in.'

Silence. No hint of disapproval yet, nor rage.

'She's working for the Russians. She's with the Moscow Narodny. She's played me for a sucker.'

It wasn't the place for a big scene. No breast-beating in an Englishman's club. The traditions of pukkahdom have their uses. I said—in the same mutter that we were both using, because there was a quick-tempered Tory MP writing a letter, probably to *The Times*, at the corner desk —'I'll resign of course. I've been the biggest idiot ...'

Lord Magnus ignored me.

I began again, more feebly, 'I'm most awfully sorry ...' and the stupid English cliché was the truest thing I'd said since Kyrenia.

'Ah well,' said Lord Magnus, still ignoring me like a general his bootblack, 'I had my doubts about the lady all the time. How did you spot her?'

'Her cover story got to look pretty thin. So I checked her out in Rome, then with Bauer in Zürich. Cost us a fat fee but it's her all right ...'

'Money well spent,' said Lord Magnus, who hadn't touched his tea. I realised dimly he still hadn't reproached me.

I said miserably, 'I should have seen through her at once. I'd do anything to put it right.'

'Then you'd better not waste too much time in London,' said Lord Magnus. 'When are you flying back?'

'Flying where?'

'Cairo of course.'

I shook my head like a meths drinker. 'You mean you want me to go back?'

'Well of course you must. No point in having you moping about in Fredericks Place.'

'What do I do in Cairo?'

'You carry on with the job.'

'But the deal's been bust. By her. By Moscow.'

Lord Magnus said, 'Why?'

I said, 'I beg your pardon ...'

Lord Magnus said, 'Why should you think the deal is over?'

I said, 'The Russians ran rings round us. Round me. It's all over.'

He waited. I risked a glance at his face and the old, cold, grey eyes were gazing down on me, unsatisfied, impassive, waiting.

I stumbled on. 'So you see, Sir—we've been operating under a misapprehension ...' For Christ's sake why didn't he make it easier for me? I said, 'All the stuff I told you about—the tape recording, the German salesman called Dietrich—it's—it's unreliable ...'

Lord Magnus said, rather gently, 'You were vexed with me in Sardinia, Thomas, because I didn't want to cancel the project.'

I grabbed at the straw. 'You admit, Sir, it was clever. They must have planned the whole thing. To keep the West out of Egypt they had to discredit the deal. The Moscow Narodny must have loved it—a chance to beat us at our own game.'

I was talking too much. I could hear myself. I knew why. I was putting it off. It. Off.

'So I told you to procrastinate,' said Lord Magnus, and

actually smiled at me. 'That has always been my policy in a sticky situation. *Play for time*, I always used to tell the Cabinet, and I still say it today.'

Oh Christ, I thought. How do I get out of this one. I hadn't even got to the confession yet.

How could I tell him about the cable from Cairo to Condon? How confess that I had taken the bit between my teeth, rushed back in a pique from Sardinia, and buggered up his precious issue without even a carbon to Fredericks Place.

I opened my mouth.

I lost my nerve.

I drew a long breath.

Lord Magnus spoke first. 'Just as well you found out,' he said briskly. 'Now you'd better hurry back.'

I said, 'Where? What for?'

'Thomas, the girl must have made you stupid. You go back and pretend nothing has happened.'

'That's ridiculous.'

'Why?'

'Because the deal is off.'

'Why is it off, pray?' His voice took on an impatient edge.

I began to flounder. 'Because the Russians have been writing the script,' I said, since I couldn't bring myself to tell him the real reason it was off, and it was so tentative that I thought I noticed a glimmer of hope.

'So now you know it. Go and let them think you're as ignorant as before.'

'With Mara too?'

'Naturally.'

'The underwriters ...' I began. 'The cable I sent ...' But I said it to myself, the words never became flesh. I had my chance again and fluffed it. I swore never to set foot on Smeralda again, never to drink, never to assert myself, never to sleep with non-WASP women, never to think that I knew best, never to look down on KK, never to pretend to know my trade.

And I never told Lord Magnus.

'Do what I tell you,' he was saying. 'Go back and play for time. Do nothing. Wait. Do you understand me? This time?'

I said, 'Yes', helplessly. Then I added, 'I still think it's hopeless. The whole thing stinks and I can't see how we get it off the ground in the end.'

'Look, boy,' said Lord Magnus sharply and grabbed a handful of my terylene and worsted like a New York cop making an arrest, 'I *want* this one. I want it very badly. I mean to get it too. You know what I've said to myself, every day since I took over from Felix? I've said that I don't believe that banking is about money. It's more than that. Even now. It's the stuff of power. The warp of history. Why did I leave Westminster to come down to TR? And was *happy*, mind you! Happy to have given up government. I came back to the City because I knew that was where I had my real job to do.

'I had an honest dream. A patriot's dream, though that's an old-fashioned, unfashionable word. You know how, in the nineteenth century, it was the British merchant banks that developed the world. Railways, ranches, factories, ships—it was all done by the City, by men like us. From London. All of it risky; some very high risk stuff. A few of us lost out. Even Barings went to the edge. But it was England that did it, and then England went tired and twisted, God knows how, and turned her back on the world. Not just on the Continentals, but on the whole damned lot. The Empire hung on, all right, but the imagination had gone.'

169

I stared at Magnus. I'd never heard him speak like this. He was standing on the carpet in front of the great marble fireplace, a big fleshy man, wrapped in double-breasted navy.

'That's what I wanted to do,' he said. 'Take England back across the seas. *That's* why I wanted this deal. And if you sit there snivelling, Thomas, and tell me that the House is scuppered because a clever girl gave you the glad eye, then you can go back to Boston tomorrow. Either that or the plane to Cairo. Tomorrow!'

I said, 'I'll take Cairo,' and when he snapped, 'What's that?' I said 'Cairo!' too loudly. And I said to myself, please God don't leave me in the dark too long. Because now I was well and truly in the labyrinth.

There was only one thing to do.

I went to find Condon and told him everything.

THIRTY-FIVE

Sue said, 'I've been to the dry-cleaner three times and they swear they've never seen a light blue featherweight suit with a Hong Kong label and a hole in the left-hand pocket.'

'Oh shit,' I said and kicked my suitcase where it stood in the corridor in Camden Passage. 'The one I've brought back with me is filthy. I should have washed it in the bath like they said in the shop.'

'He's got three and a half hours before his plane,' said Condon. 'I vote he gives it up. He'll have to wear his tweed.'

'In Cairo? In August? You must be joking: I'll buy another.'

'Try and charge it on expenses,' said Sue who was in a domestic mood and sometimes worried about our extravagance.

'Mr Bullen will never stand for it.'

Condon said, 'You can always describe it as "Bribery of Cairo Officials". Not even Bullen will expect a receipt for that.' Sue and I had always assumed that Condon had none of these sordid problems.

It was the evening of my day. Sue and Condon were like brother and sister and I tried to remember to be nice to Sue. It wasn't much to ask of a twelve-hour stopover. And after all she'd sent me the cable when the bells began to jangle in the Office, which must have broken seventeen sections of the Official Secrets Act; but I was feeling so ragged I couldn't be bothered to ask why.

'Let's eat,' I said and added, 'Carriers?' hopefully.

'Nonsense,' said Sue firmly. 'Much too expensive.'

Condon shrugged like a man who's never heard of surtax and said, 'You choose. I'm paying.'

'I would if I could,' I said, 'but I've only got piastres.' Sue snorted and grabbed us both by the arm, propelling us out past the clobber into the street.

Islington was dazed by the August heat. She threw Condon the keys of the Mini—for some stupid reason she always said he was a better driver than I—and we sidled through Clerkenwell past the Wells and down to Holborn.

'Oh my God,' I said. 'She'll want to go to one of those pizzerias near the British Museum. I can see it coming.'

'Wrong again,' said Sue. 'We'll go to the place next to Charlotte Street!'

Condon raised an eyebrow in a hammy attempt to be supercilious as we went into the thumping heat and the babble of au pair chatter. Sue stuck her elbow into his ribs, hard. 'Don't be outrageous,' she said. 'You're not at work now. You can drop the poise.' The trouble was we were both wearing suits, which was enough to mark us off as outsiders. The waitresses were all Italian women, though only just, and the wine came in tall bottles of rough red.

'I *know* this must be slumming for you two,' said Sue and paused to flash her LMH grin at the African boy at the next table. 'But I like it—which is what matters. And I like the décor.'

Condon said, 'Nonsense,' very seriously and looked around him with the curiosity of an English tourist in the Sainte Chapelle. When Sue was like this it only made him play up to her. 'All those dinners in the House of Commons are making you a snob, Sue.'

'I haven't been there for at least a month.'

'What about the Sultan of Oman last week? Weren't you invited?'

'All right, you win. But I like this, don't you?'

'It's all right for a change,' I said and put on my most City face. 'In fact it's rather quaint. Now shall we try the Napoletana or would that be too risky?'

Ten minutes later Sue said, 'I'm sorry, I'm getting fed up with this chit-chat. You're either playing games with me, or you're like condemned men gossiping on the tumbril. Why don't you tell me what's going on? All I know is that Thomas came back this afternoon, turned up at the flat looking as if he'd had the sack, and said he was going away again at once.' She broke off and sawed at her pizza, pink with well-bred embarrassment.

Condon said, 'My dear Sue, it's my fault. If I weren't here Thomas would be able to talk to you more freely.'

'That's ridiculous,' said Sue. 'You work together. If you can't trust each other, who can you ever trust?'

The wine was beginning to steady me. I knew it would help, and I poured another glass and called for more.

There's an important difference between red and white. The white takes you out of yourself beyond the reach of everyone around you. You hear everything, see everything, but have no wish to participate, and the next day you have a headache. But the red, if you drink enough of it, adds confidence to the awareness. You become more self-conscious, more with it. You don't give a damn, life is good, you discover that you are a doer of deeds. I was drinking red, enough of it, and I knew Sue and Condon were watching me from across the table. I didn't give a damn. Condon was not a drinking man, I knew, and Sue was a prude. She was looking worried and tense.

I said, 'Relax, friends. Have I ever told you two about never flying in a plane that's been serviced in Cairo?'

Sue said, 'I think you've had enough. You look *ghastly*.' She pushed her plate away from her and started swigging the wine as though to catch up with me.

'It's the flying,' I said. 'Always up then down. It's beginning to catch up with me.'

'I don't believe it's just the flying. There's something else. Something's wrong in Cairo. I'm not a fool. I get to hear about things.'

Why shouldn't she know? Why not see if she let something else out of the bag, a corollary to the cable.

'All right,' I said, and listened to the blood throbbing through my head. 'Everyone else in London must be talking about it by now. What's happened is that I've been sold a pup by someone who we've discovered is working for the Russians.'

Sue said, 'I see,' as punctuation for my pause, and Condon looked mildly embarrassed.

I said, 'I got Guy to break up the issue before I discovered she was a plant. That's the bit I still haven't told Magnus. Guy's said that's his problem. Some problem!'

173

'*She?*' asked Sue. 'So it's a *she*.' She gave a little crowing sound and inspected my face. Not a friendly inspection. 'So that's why you look so ghastly.' Condon moved his expression from embarrassment to apprehension and through to surprise. 'Why hadn't you told me?' she went on. 'I might have warned you off.'

'I didn't have a chance,' I said, and grinned back at her, feeling close to her for the first time in weeks. 'Anyhow, I'd have put down any warnings to jealousy.'

'I knew some of it from the Office,' said Sue and I knew she'd understood. 'That's why I took a risk and sent my cable. But what happens now?' I decided not to pick it up and Condon answered.

'Thomas goes back and pretends nothing has happened. We try and pick up the pieces from this end. We don't understand how it works out. The problem is that we can't ask the Egyptians what's really going on. They have their own problems of urgency. So all we have to work on is an equation where one girl is a rogue factor.' He had made it sound very simple. It had taken us three hours to work out a rescue plan and was probably going to cost us both our careers.

Sue said, 'Because the Russians are involved doesn't mean you give up?'

'Of course not. We put in Thomas and then watch to see what they do next.'

'Sitting duck,' I said. The wine had run out for the second time.

'And Magnus?' Sue asked.

Condon said, 'That's something I shall have to cope with.' Sue's face went into neutral. He said, 'I don't want to be stuffy, but we really shouldn't be talking about this here.' Perhaps he also meant that he hadn't yet worked out how and when he was going to tell Magnus the truth.

'You're the boss,' I scoffed and realised I was drunk. They sat there side by side across the dirty tablecloth like JPs on the Bench. The wine wasn't working properly. I was feeling sorry for myself. The waitress brushed past the table and I tapped her on the rump and ordered cassata and brandy for three in what was supposed to be flawless Italian. Sue winced and Condon made quick brushing motions with his left hand. I said I gathered my friends would just have coffee. As for me, I needed building up.

Sue said, 'Really, Thomas!' which was a mistake because I got angry with her and told her to get off my back; that this was what I worked for, to be able to drink brandy whenever I felt like it.

'Why do you think I spend my life in planes and strange hotels?' The speech was the one I'd been working on for ages. 'Why keep rushing around like this? Working with people I despise—yes, so does Condon, though he kids himself he doesn't. Doing things I detest. Running a system I disown. Why do you think I'm looking ghastly and feeling worse and asking you to drive me to the airport for the thirty-third time this year? Why begrudge me my little extravagance? I'm going to be sacked pretty soon, don't worry, and Condon's just thrown his job away for my sake. Why not let me go to Carrier's, or Prunier's or the Mirabelle if I want to?'

It was getting ridiculous and the diction wasn't too clear, I suppose. They both had the same stupid expression on their faces. Tense. Shifty. Then I realised what it was —they were both trying not to laugh.

Condon said, 'I think Sue remembered I was paying the bill—she was being tactful.' Sue shook her head.

'I was thinking you'll need building up, darling, if she's a real Russian girl.'

175

Then she stopped smiling at me and forgiving me: she pronounced very straight, 'You're not being fair to yourself. You see, my love, you leave out the *real* reason why you are doing all this. I used to wonder too, when I met you, but I think I know the answer by now. It's all a game, isn't it? And you can't help being fascinated by the rules? It's rather the same with Guy, too, though he doesn't bang on about it in restaurants. You see, you almost—not quite—you *almost* enjoy the nonsense. You have the same attitude about England—you say you can't stand us and yet you are fascinated. In fact, you *like* us. You came from America and you *chose* us. And you'll get along nicely with us and the job, until and unless you ever get hooked by something you can respect. Guy too —yes, I mean it Guy. Something real. Something *worthwhile.*'

She ducked back behind her coffee cup and away from my stare. Condon said nothing, studiously. God knows what he was thinking. I sat there swirling the sinful brandy in the glass, and thought it over with somewhat less than perfect concentration. Sue didn't usually carry on like this. Perhaps she was right. True, I didn't complain seriously. It was as good a job as any other. Perhaps it was as good a life as any. Any other I'd get. Anyway, I was the most unserious man in London. But yet I wished sometimes I could feel committed to something. Or someone. Anything or anyone at all.

'Time for the airport,' announced Condon, and Sue asked, 'Shall we pour him into the car?'

The Cairo skyline had changed again, like a chorus girl coming out for the big production number. The six hundred mosques were still there, of course, but the view from the revolving restaurant on Cairo Tower was coming in for competition and I don't mean from the Post Office in London. The women were smarter than I remembered. The city was as cosmopolitan as ever and getting sadder with every day, like a famous beauty in decline. The air-conditioning in Shepheards was lethal after the filthy blanket of lead in the streets and I lay on my bed for a long time, damp and chill; either I didn't know what to do or I knew it and couldn't face up to the knowledge. The cold air began to bite at my lungs and I got up to open the door on to the balcony and stood there, naked, high above the city, listening to the growling of the traffic far below, jagged with shrill horns.

The air was fetid, it was Africa and Arabia, millennia of death in the sun. I wondered whether I was beginning to enjoy it at last. Danger signal! It was time to leave. I began to sweat again and went back into the twentieth century and the air-conditioning that dries up the juices of the body.

The 'phone jangled.

Toby said, 'Sorry I didn't fetch you at the airport,' in a way that showed he didn't mean it. I told myself to remember that the man probably hated my guts for the way I'd stolen his girl. With another griping effort I reminded myself that he needn't know a thing unless Moscow Narodny was in the habit of reporting back to the British Embassy. So maybe he just hated my guts full stop.

'You sound tired,' I said carefully.

He hummed and hawed so I got fed up and said, 'Come and have a drink and you can tell me what's on.' I was going to chalk up Cairo's biggest expense account of all time. Lord Magnus owed me a break. So Toby could help me, poor sap.

He was burned very red above his biscuit-colour linen suit and insisted on talking about the new beach resort out beyond El Alamein. 'Fantastic!' he kept saying. *'Fantastic!'* as though any serious diplomat gave a damn for swimming face down in the mud with a ping-pong ball to keep the water out. After five minutes I realised it wasn't the bathing but the company he was talking about. He was anxious to tell me he'd been one of a party —a foursome. Sex was rearing its ugly head. 'Two sisters,' he volunteered. 'Twins! Came to stay with the Thomsons and don't want to go home. Fantastic!'

I said, 'You've gone off Mara then?' chancing my arm and keeping an eye on his right uppercut just in case he knew and was as old-fashioned as I feared. He didn't seem to worry.

'Haven't seen her for ages,' he said, without a trace of concern. 'Always reckoned she was a bit out of my line. Didn't you?'

It was too good to be true. 'What line is that?' I asked, nastily, but he didn't care any more.

'Sounds silly,' said Toby, 'but I always thought she had rather an eye for you.'

I was absurdly gratified and noted it with shame. 'Never saw it myself.'

'No? Well, maybe I'm wrong. But she always kept talking about you.'

'I'm sorry,' I said, not enjoying it any more. 'That must have been a bore.' He scarcely heard me.

I said, 'Toby,' and pushed another Scotch at him. 'Toby, what about business? How goes?'

He took a mouthful, made a face and waved at the barman. It seemed he needed more soda. I repeated 'How goes?' gently, the way Lord Magnus used to speak to Sir Felix when he was starting to get old.

'No idea,' said Toby. 'Thought it was your pigeon.' He drank too much for a bachelor diplomat. I must mention it to Sue. It must be the squash at the Club—and the riding—that kept his paunch in order.

'I've just flown in. Remember?'

He looked puzzled and honest at the same time, which is a typical English expression. 'It's all the same as far as I know. They haven't said a thing. But we expected that—you told me so when you were here the other day. They are probably waiting to decide the best date to announce it—you know, anniversary of the glorious revolution, birth of the President's mother, or whatever. HE was saying in conference only this morning that he was waiting for the chance to buttonhole the Minister.'

I said, 'You don't mean everyone in Chancery is chatting about it?'

'Well, not exactly. There aren't so many of us these days, you see, and most of us don't have too much to do.'

'You know Larochelle?'

He said, 'Yes, of course. The World Bank man.'

'When did he leave town?'

'I didn't know he'd gone. He was here the day before yesterday.'

'He's not here now. I've checked.'

'He seemed to be very rushed. I saw him at a reception

in the Finance Ministry and he was supposed to have had a long session with the Deputy Foreign Minister. That's what I heard at a cocktail party last night. Oh, and the usual World Bank team of economists and engineers have been pulse-taking over at the Central Bank and the Ministry. But you know all that of course.'

'That tallies,' I said, as though I knew. I didn't. God knows why Joe should have to start running round in circles at this stage. It was time I gave up. Let it go. 'Have another drink.'

I said it out loud. Toby said, 'No, really, I've had enough——' and hesitated long enough to be asked to stay to lunch.

'What about the twins?' I asked as we aimed for the restaurant. 'Bring them along as well.' Toby chortled happily. I was feeling tired again.

She 'phoned me in the late afternoon when I was lying across my bed trying to sleep off the lunch and failing. The bell was harsh, sharp as a hacksaw on my shinbone. It hit my nerves so I jumped and probably groaned and waited for my heart to steady but it rang again, insisting. I said, 'Yes?' and she said, 'Darling, how wonderful!'

I asked, 'Is that you, Mara?' cautious as a housewife who's been burgled three times. She shot back, mock-petulant, 'You seem to have forgotten me already.' Her voice didn't sound at all hostile. It wasn't true, I hadn't forgotten her. 'It's not true, Mara,' I said, because my body knew the voice even if my brain didn't want to.

I was mumbling, 'This is wonderful. Where are you?' It wouldn't sound so phoney on the wire.

She said, 'Downstairs. I'll come up,' and rang off.

I slammed down the receiver and then said 'Oh Christ!' out loud. The banker's training told. I put away the bottle of Scotch and went to wash my teeth. Then I left the door ajar and went and pretended to read the *Economist*. I didn't know what to do next.

She came in through the door like a commando in plimsolls. She was shorter than I remembered and appallingly beautiful. I didn't get up but held up my arms and said 'Come here,' as though I was hailing a cab, and she smiled at me and said 'Just a minute,' and looped the 'Do Not Disturb' sign on the door handle and closed it with a discreet click.

Then she went suddenly shy. She tossed her handbag on the dressing table and said 'Hullo,' like in Fredericks Place, and pretended to float around, flicking through the papers on my table, prodding the corner of the black suitcase where it was starting to fray. I still didn't know what to do. But she was leaving it to me to make up my mind.

I said, 'Stranger, I thought you were out of town.'

'You didn't look very far.'

'I've only just got in.' My voice was not quite my own. She smiled, almost nervous. 'I know. I asked.'

'Open the balcony door,' I said. 'It's too cold in here.' She was wearing blue again, pale and slight. Her body moved gently under the smooth linen. She opened the door.

'Where have you been?'

'Here and there. Nowhere important.'

'I worried about leaving you like that in Kyrenia.'

'I thought you were tired of me.'

I said, 'Come here,' without authority, but she came all the same and sat on the bed, knees primly together, and looked down on me with a smile of something I couldn't place. It was hard to grasp, she looked as though she was happy and shy and confident all at the same time.

Oh Christ. Sweet Christ, she thought it was still all right.

'I missed you,' I said, which was true in a way. It ought

to be moments like these when the training counts.

'You were the one who went away.'

'You knew I'd come back.'

She said, 'Yes. I knew.' She said it quietly, so intimately that I felt ashamed and humiliated. She was wearing a gold chain around her neck; it was for its own sake, there was no cross or pendant to draw the eye to her breasts. I caught the force of her perfume and remembered it and my body betrayed me. I got up and pretended to push the door wider, out on to the Cairo air. I would be stronger on my feet, and I still didn't know what to do.

She said, 'It's all right, then?' so I wondered for a moment whether she meant the Nile issue but her eyes corrected me in time, there was something so frail and lost in them that I went to her despite myself, despite all that she'd done to me.

Her body tensed, violently, in my arms when I held her and she kissed me fiercely, greedily. Then she relaxed again and Cyprus was recaptured for us both. She was drawing patterns on my neck, down the shirt, then under, laughing at me, playing with her mouth against mine, her breath and her body warm and sweet.

'Did you think I'd gone back to Toby?' she whispered; then, 'What have you been doing, my darling, all these days and nights?'

I thought, 'One of these days I'll tell you' and listened to the buttons surrendering on my shirt. 'This is ridiculous,' I began to say, as my shirt hit the carpet, she was the one who was overdressed. 'Let's walk before we run?' she murmured, complete with question-mark, and her tongue slipped over my ear. Her hands reached for my belt and I gave up and pulled her to me.

THIRTY-SEVEN

The guide in Aswan looked like Akim Tamiroff, I decided. Short and plump and bald and sweating. The rest of us were hot, too, which wasn't surprising since it must have been over 110, but it was the guide who was giving out water like a sponge. He made vain efforts to stem the flood by scrubbing at his brow with a damp handkerchief. It was ridiculous because he ought to have been used to the climate by now, he had been taking official visitors to the High Dam for five years and more. Now the Dam was finished he had gone beyond boredom but not beyond the heat. Promotion had meanwhile passed him by.

He stood us on the dam wall, the three of us under a rough plank roof, and harangued us about installed megawatt capacity and that sort of thing. Multiply 110 MW by twelve units and you get 1200 MW. Mara shook her head and he said, 'Of course, I make allowance for the required reserve capacity.' It would teach him not to skimp on the briefing. Mara gazed at the section diagrams as though they meant something to her and asked clever questions about the seepage. The guide mopped furiously at his face and offered pious reassurances.

The Czech diplomat who was with us asked, 'How many Russians still here?' and made a little note of the misleading answer. There was only a handful of workers to be seen, tidying the granite facing blocks on the sheer slope of the wall. 'How much they are paid?' asked the Czech, 'the workers, not the Russians,' and made another note. Lake Nasser stretched away behind us, deep into the desert and into the Sudan. The Nubians had been moved to Kashmelgirba years ago and were always said to be dying like flies in the raw Ethiopian air. There were three machine-gun emplacements on the approach road and sentries slouched in the shade below. The landscape of Upper Egypt stretched round us, perfect, ochre hills against a steel blue sky. Abu Simbel was hours away, far down the Lake. The Czech began to take photographs and the guide nearly died of horror. The guards began to shout, then subsided in the shade. I could feel the sun burning a brand into my neck.

Mara was on her very best behaviour. She asked to see the power station. The guide said, 'Yes, but first we talk about irrigation.' He looked at me with the weary expectancy of the PR man who has stopped caring one way or the other. It was my cue. This was why I had been brought all these hundreds of miles upstream with a group of officials. The trip had been promised months before by the High Dam Authority and I'd kept putting it off, but now that I needed to fill in time it was as good a way as any of doing nothing for another twenty-four hours. Anyhow, I could take Mara with me for the ride. It was a way of keeping an eye on her.

The irrigation projects were all that Cairo had promised, no doubt of it, but my heart wasn't in it. After five minutes of acreages and metres of water pressure I was ready to call it a day and so was the Czech diplomat. He was a thin harassed man with spectacles he kept wiping on a silk handkerchief; he said he was with the trade delegation. We stepped delicately around another anti-aircraft gun post, dodging the blank stare and hollow cheeks of the *fellahin* behind the sandbags. The Czech tapped the guide on the shoulder: 'This dam,' he pronounced, concentrating on his syntax. 'It is easy to blow up, no? From the air, with bombs?' It was far too innocent a question for a trade

184

delegation. I turned to grin at Mara but she was frowning, distracted, looking across at a group of men who had just got out of a Land Rover in front of a storage depot piled with steel cables and old planks.

'What is it?' I asked, and she swung round quickly, as though I'd startled her. She shrugged and hesitated, then said, 'It's nothing.' I said, 'Just a moment, do you see a familiar face?' She frowned again and replied, 'That's what I thought. But it can't be.'

I said, 'It is, you know, it's your German admirer—what's his name?'

'Dietrich,' she informed me, as though I didn't know.

'What the hell is he doing here?'

She shrugged again. 'Same as us, I expect. Sightseeing. Selling something. He seems to know the engineer.'

'Let's ask him.'

'Don't do that——' she said hurriedly, and stopped short.

'Why not?'

She said, 'It's better to pretend we haven't seen him. Don't let's get mixed up with him again. Please.' No doubt about it, her voice reflected fear.

'To hell with that. I want to know why he's following me around.'

'He's not following you,' said Mara, but I was already leading the way across the track. Ever since Cyprus I had been trying to work out Dietrich's role in this play-acting. Here was a chance to see if he remembered his lines.

Dietrich was wearing a yellow hard-hat and a stained bush shirt. He had long trousers streaked with dirt and looked as if he was taking a course in heavy electrical engineering. I didn't like his face any better than I had the last time I'd seen him in the lobby of the Semiramis. He was talking to an Egyptian with a heavy brown moustache.

I said, 'Mr Dietrich, isn't it?' Mara had caught up with

185

me. The guide was promising the Czech that the dam wall would stand even the shock of an Israeli A-bomb.

Dietrich looked mildly puzzled until he saw Mara, which was natural enough, I calculated. He opened his mouth in greeting to her and let me see he had remembered my face. 'Yes. Forgive me,' he said. 'The American banker ... ?'

'English,' said Mara. 'Mr Kane.'

'English,' said Dietrich. 'Mr Kane.' We bowed briefly to each other across five feet of Nubian dirt. No one tried to introduce the Egyptian who stood there listening to us.

'We wondered if you were on business or holiday,' said Mara in English. She sounded tense, apprehensive.

Dietrich raised his hands high in the air and puckered his features and made waving motions. 'Unfortunately,' he began, 'it is always work with me. Hard bloody work, yes, that is so.' His English was confident but less fluent than his French on the tape recording.

'What business brings you up here then?' I asked, casual as a tourist. It was ridiculous but I wanted to know how she had fixed the tape-recording. And the evidence from his room. Perhaps—somehow—it wasn't faked after all. Perhaps, for that matter, they were both genuine, I wasn't their dupe.

He grinned shyly at me. 'There is always business if you take the trouble to make the journey. You know that better than I do—if you permit me to say it.'

Mara intervened, too quickly. 'Mr Kane pretends he needs to see Aswan because of his work, but *I* think he's really on holiday.'

Dietrich smiled again, which didn't suit him at all and looked me boldly in the eye. He said to Mara, 'Perhaps the gentleman's business is not so brisk as it was,' and laughed abruptly, harshly. It hadn't been said as a joke. The Egyptian smiled as though he understood, which was impossible.

186

The Land Rover driver started his engine and Mara said quickly, 'We mustn't keep you,' and took me firmly by the arm. Dietrich stiffened briefly, his heels together, and we bowed again. Then Mara and I walked back to our guide and didn't turn round even to watch the Land Rover drive away.

The Czech was saying, 'But I have read that this is possible. It is a danger, you think not?' The sun was strafing us relentlessly and there was no shelter for miles.

Mara said, 'If the dam wall broke, the whole of Egypt would be washed into the sea.'

'You've heard that story as well?'

'The streets of Cairo would be under water in twelve hours.'

'Three hours,' I said.

'Nonsense,' said Mara. 'Twelve.'

The guide said nothing. The diplomat made another note. Dietrich's Land Rover had vanished.

THIRTY-EIGHT

They gave us the use of a room in the New Cataract and we stood on the balcony and looked out over the palm tree at Elephant Island and talked about Dietrich. 'Perhaps he thinks his deal is still on,' she said. It was getting too complicated for me. I had to explain Dietrich's arrival to myself and at the same time remember to give her another explanation, the explanation I would be expected to offer since I was not supposed to know she was with the Russians. I gave up.

'Forget him,' I told her and went to shower. Strangely

enough I really did forget him as the water sluiced down my chest and back and I felt my leg hairs prickle under the cold stream.

Perhaps I heard the knock on the door, far away behind the roar of the spray, and imagined, if not heard, her answer it. The shower worked, the cool shaded imperceptibly into ice-cold at the touch of the taps and I was shivering as I pulled aside the curtain and slipped a towel round my waist.

It took me several seconds to take in the view in the bedroom. I stood there dripping water on the beige carpet and forgot to close the door behind me. It was like a still from a B-movie.

Mara was sitting on one of the beds, looking very composed, almost prim. She nodded to me. Her hands were folded on her canvas skirt. She had company.

There was a soldier, for one thing, standing unevenly with his back to the door. He was pockmarked and very swarthy and he was pointing a piece of ironmongery in my general direction. He wasn't looking at me, though, but across the room towards the window, so I followed his eyes and discovered a slim, khaki-clad Egyptian.

He was young but old enough, slouched against the dressing table and smiling as though he were Omar Sharif's brother. He didn't move. Nor did I. The soldier was too close to me.

I began to move into the room and the carbine followed close behind.

The officer—he looked like a Captain—smiled again and fiddled with a cigarette, which gave him a misleading off-duty appearance. The three of us waited for him. He was the star. It was his cue.

The cigarette spilled a flake of tobacco and he frowned briefly.

188

'Forgive me,' he said. 'Forgive this intrusion.' He had a faint American accent.

I found my tongue. 'What the bloody hell are you playing at?' I opened. It sounded far too weak and I made it worse by gesturing at the carbine and trying to hitch the towel tighter at the same time. Water ran down my legs into the carpet.

'Forgive me,' he said again. 'A few enquiries.'

'By whom?'

'The security police,' he said quietly.

'Now just a minute . . .'

'You *are* Mr Kane, the man from the London bank?'

Mara spoke from the bed. 'Thomas, get dressed,' she said. 'If this gentleman will permit.' Her voice told me nothing. I started to say that this must be a stupid mistake, then stopped myself. Perhaps it wasn't.

I said, 'May I?' The Captain said, 'Of course.' But he sent the soldier into the bathroom with me. At least I wasn't wearing Marks and Spencer underpants, I thought. I nearly said as much to Mara when I re-emerged in shirt and slacks but her face told me it wasn't a day for wise-cracks.

'Please explain,' I ordered in what I hoped was an authoritative voice. Clothes were a big help. I began to prepare for a 'phone call to the Embassy in Cairo.

The Captain was still smiling and it was a kind smile. I couldn't doubt it. He said, 'It's very simple, I fear. I have orders to arrest you. Both of you.'

I said, 'Ridiculous.'

I said it twice more. It's not a particularly effective word, I suppose. Mara was a mile away.

He said, 'I promise you I am very serious. I have instructions to escort you to Cairo.'

'What,' I asked, 'what is the offence? Or can't you say?'

'You are both to be arrested. We have evidence that you are agents of the Zionists.'

My mind went into a four wheel drift and I only came out of it with an immense effort.

'Both of us? Israeli agents?'

'That is correct.'

'What utter bloody rubbish!' I said this as though I meant it and my voice was getting loud. 'How on earth ...?' I began, and words failed me. The bloody Egyptians had done it again! They deserved everything coming to them. I'd had enough! I was getting out of the place for good and a plague on every one of them. And why the hell didn't Mara chime in? She was sitting there like a penitent before the confessional. If we didn't stage a genuine denial they'd have us for God knows what ridiculous concoctions.

At that moment my brain took a lurch and my heart began to pound. Mara's silence was the clue I'd missed.

Of course, that was it!

It fell into place like a Japanese box puzzle. Of course she didn't want to say anything—she thought I didn't know. She didn't want to have her cover broken in my presence. *That* was why she looked so grim. Well, to hell with that—I'd had enough of her, too, her and her games.

The Captain was saying how they'd been watching us for a long time. 'We have all the evidence we require. You will be interrogated when we ...'

I brushed him aside impatiently. 'You idiots,' I said, and I think my voice was shaking with urgency, not nerves. 'She's not working for the Israelis—she's working for the Russians! It's the *Russians*, man, don't you understand?'

Mara was looking at me with the face of Joan confronting the bench of Bishops. Her mouth was tight; her eyes were hooded. She had gone very pale. She stared at me.

I repeated, 'It's the Russians. The Moscow Narodny

Bank. Go on and ask them if you don't want to believe me.'
After a moment I added, for her benefit, 'I've known for
months. She didn't know I knew.'

The Captain's smile spilled wider and wider. He didn't
bother to contradict me. I said again, 'The Moscow
Narodny is a Russian bank. It's controlled by the Soviet
authorities. She is working for the Russians.' I kept on
plugging the silence with useless words. 'Look, you don't
have to believe me. Go and ask the Russians. Telephone
them, go on! Tell your friends in the Soviet Embassy who
you've picked up. *They'll* put you straight.'

He didn't even bother to answer.

Mara said, so softly I barely caught the words, 'Was it
you, then ... ?' and her voice fell away like an echo on the
tide. She closed her eyes and clenched them tight like a
child who is thinking very hard. Half a minute went past
and none of us said anything. We were all watching her,
waiting.

She opened her eyes and looked straight at me, as she
had in the Gezira Club that first afternoon.

'*Al tid'ag chabibi*, it's no good,' she said, calmly and
clearly. 'There's no point in denying it. They've got us
both.'

She flashed a grin at the Captain. He laughed aloud, his
cup flowing over. 'Thank you!' he said. 'I hope it will all
be easier for us, now that we understand each other.' She
nodded. He was saying, 'Believe me, a confession would be
so much simpler for all of us.'

I said, 'Just a minute...' I couldn't take it in. I couldn't
believe the evidence of my ears and eyes. That bloody girl
was still playing some game, and why the hell had she
addressed me in *Hebrew*. Oh no, she wasn't going to pin
that crap on me.

'Mara, you've gone off your head!' I exploded.

'Tommy, be sensible. Let's try to be dignified about it. It's no good denying it ...'

'Why not, for Christ's sake? What the hell are you talking about?'

'Because they know it all. We're not ashamed to be working for Israel, are we? There's nothing more to say. Nothing more!'

I said bitterly, 'So there's nothing more to say is there?' then caught myself.

It was a message, I suppose. If she could still give me a message, she couldn't be entirely off her head.

I said, 'It's nonsense. You must telephone the British Ambassador at once,' but I was talking for the record only, if anyone was bothering to keep one.

The officer was saying, 'Of course, Mr Kane, we shall inform the Embassy in due course.'

Then I shut up.

They made us pack our bag and walk downstairs. We could see the Czech sitting at the first floor bar bent over his notebook. He didn't see us. Or pretended he didn't. There was someone in the lobby. Dietrich, carefully reading a newspaper at the far end. He made no sign of recognition either. I began to worry about witnesses.

The Egyptians at the front desk must have noticed us leave but they all deserved Oscars for the way they too pretended to see nothing. Mara said, 'Goodbye,' to the door porter, who looked straight through us, and *'Shukran'*, to the soldier who opened the door of a battered, long-wheel-base jeep. The officer took the seat behind us and borrowed the carbine from the guard.

'You will not try any funny business?' he asked, and I marked him down as another Egyptian hoodlum who would far rather be in the States with his cousins who had left for Southern California.

Mara said, 'Of course not,' with dignity, and I said, 'The sooner we get this sorted out the better,' which was my prize understatement of the year.

We drove back up the highway, past the apartment blocks originally built for the Russian engineers, then speeding up the hill past the gardens with the date palms and the houses under the Old Dam. Over the wall the new road cut into the hill and over the ridge to the airport.

'Are we going to Cairo at once?' Mara asked the Captain. She hadn't looked directly at me since the hotel.

'The Army is sending a plane.' He was smoking Kents from a UAA packet. 'You're important, you see. Important visitors. Many, many people want to talk to you.'

'How long have you been cooking up this ridiculous story?'

'We have been watching you, Mr Kane, since you arrived. You came with very good references so we had to be careful. We were very anxious to welcome you and your mission. But then you made contact with Miss Tal ...'

I said, 'Wait a minute,' but he went on with the confidence of a man whose riddle has been solved.

'We had been interested in Miss Tal for a long time, so we had to work out why you were operating together.'

'We weren't operating together,' I said, and glimpsed with horror the number of times I would have to go through this before they let me go. 'I don't know anything about her. Go on—ask her.'

'Please Tommy, it's no good,' Mara pleaded, and this time she looked full at me. Her eyes were blank as a china doll.

'This is mad!' I cried. 'Crazy. It's all lies.'

I knew I was repeating myself but what else could I do? I said, 'Look, I can prove who I am, you know that. You must know I've been arranging an issue for your government—a big one, a lot of money.'

He was very patient. 'You must please not think we are stupid, Mr Kane,' he said. 'That was your mistake, a common one among your countrymen, if I may say so. We know what you pretended to be doing. And we have no quarrel with your bank in London. We have done them a service—we have discovered how you are betraying them.'

'*Betraying* them? *Me?*'

'Yes, you have been trying to defeat the policy of your directors.'

'That's utter nonsense.'

'Mr Kane, we have copies of all your cables. A fortnight ago you advised your alleged principals in London not to proceed with the loan. There are those of us who will take a dim view of why you chose to send such a cable.'

I thought, 'My God,' and looked down into the abyss.

He said, 'You don't deny it, I'm glad to see.'

I said, 'You will have to call the Ambassador. This will need a lot of explaining. There are Ministers who will have to be told.'

'They already know. That is why I had to let you come up to Aswan. We were waiting for agreement from the highest level.'

'I'm sorry to have kept you hanging around,' I said.

'Don't mention it,' said our captor.

THIRTY-NINE

He was as decent a security man as you could ever hope to meet. It was almost a pleasure to be picked up by him. He didn't even lose his cool when they told him they didn't have a plane waiting for us. There was some squabbling in Arabic but beneath their bilharzia-lethargy they were all scared stiff of him and they took him away to use the radio. He apologised to us and requisitioned two glasses of a sickly purple drink. It was the first food we'd had since breakfast on the plane, back in the Stone Age of the morning.

They took us through the barn that masquerades as the Aswan passenger lounge, except that these days Aswan has so high a security priority that only officials and the military are allowed to use this airport, the tourists are off-loaded at one of the desert airstrips miles away. Three Poles were sitting pale and pasty on the bench together, looking like refugees from one of the rouble-piastre package tours. The soldier had his gun again but had stopped pointing it at anyone, so no one paid us much attention and this time it could have been genuine. We went through the check-in office, past the old UAA posters and the mural of Abu Simbel, into a room with a sign on the door that said 'Private' in Arabic. Through another room and we were in a corridor. There was a sentry scuffling up and down and a trio of closed plywood doors and a window through which there was a glimpse of the side of the apron. I could see the blast walls behind which the MiGs were scattered in twos and threes—I'd noticed them from the air when our Air Force plane touched down that morning.

The airport man stopped at the fourth door and motioned us in. The soldier followed and the guide went away again. The soldier took up a vaguely threatening stance against the door and the barrel of the gun jerked to cover us. Like in the movies, I thought. Life imitating art, as usual. The room was quite empty, heavy with dust and larger than a storeroom. The skeleton of a filing cabinet stood in the corner. There was nowhere to sit. We went and leaned on the window sill: the glass was streaked with rough blue blackout paint.

She said, 'Will he let us talk?'

'I doubt it.'

'He can't stop us. And he won't understand.' For a girl who'd been going round for an hour looking as if she was in a trance she sounded remarkably lucid.

The soldier gazed at us with utter incomprehension, like an aboriginal at Woomera. I smiled once at him, reassuring and hypocritical, and decided she was right.

She hissed at me, 'We haven't much time. They'll be back in a few minutes. I heard them.'

'Time for what?'

'To get out of here, of course. What do you think?'

I said, 'Just a second. You've got a lot of explaining to do. You've just dropped me in the shit from a very great height and I'm beginning to get angry.' Yes, and scared too, I realised. I was sweating miserably.

It would have sounded more impressive if we hadn't been instinctively trying to keep the conversation casual and quiet—a handsome European couple chatting about the weather during a moment's pause in a busy day in Upper Egypt.

I added, 'To start with, you can tell me why in the name of Mary and Martha you gave me all that Israeli comrade bullshit.'

'I'll tell you later. It was the only thing to do.'

'It was, was it?' It didn't worry her that she'd dropped me like a cold-blooded whore.

'Look now,' I said, 'I can believe you're deep in something. But don't try and pull me in with you. I've had enough of your tricks.'

'Darling,' she said, so I wanted to catch her by the throat

196

and slam her head against the wall. 'Darling, don't be like that. Please! Please! This is desperate.'

'Desperate for you maybe.' I would not look at her. I refused. She gripped my arm but still I refused. She let me go and I felt her turn aside.

'I warn you, Tom,' she said and her voice was suddenly something I had never heard before. 'You're in it with me now and I'll take you with me all the way—just as far as that may have to be.'

I believed her. I knew what she meant. She said it as though she were the pro and I were a very silly young amateur. I began to think positive and calm down.

There was a pause. The guard was still staring at us. He must have thought we were cool customers, if he thought at all.

I said, 'I gather it's true you're with the Israelis not the Narodny.'

'That sort of thing.'

'So you're in trouble.'

'Real trouble.'

'Why drag me in on this?'

'Because two of us have a chance of getting out of this. By myself I don't have a chance.'

'You still haven't got a chance.'

'Yes I have. If we're very clever. And very quick.'

'Look, count me out,' I said. 'I'm in the clear and you know it. I'm going to sit it out with the nice Captain. It may take some time but they're bound to clear me in the end.'

'What about me?'

'Mara,' I said, and I wondered why I still didn't detest her. 'If you are what he says you are, then it's an occupational hazard.'

'Don't waste time,' she said. 'Are you with me? Now?'

'Not yet.' I don't know why I said that. I had meant to say a simple no.

'Tom, I need you. I'm sorry for everything. But now I *need* you.'

I said, 'I'm no good at the violent stuff. I'm a banker—a real one. I'll sit this out.'

'You know what they'll do next?'

'God knows.'

'They'll start by doing things to me. As soon as we get to Cairo. You too, I expect. But don't worry, the Ambassador will tell them to apologise if ever he gets to see you. But they'll have to make me talk—to tell them about the whole network. You know what that means? In Cairo?'

She started to tell me, in the same calm tennis-club voice, what she expected them to do to her. She had a very clear view of her future and she described it casually but in expert detail. When she got half-way through the anatomy lesson I stopped listening and did some more hard thinking.

Then I sighed, so that the soldier must have thought my feet were getting tired, and I said, 'Perhaps we'd better get out of here.'

She replied, very quietly, 'My love, thank you.'

'Then how do we get out? Can't we wait till Cairo?'

'No, it's a miracle they haven't put us in chains. We'll be finished once they get us on this plane they're waiting for.'

'So get me out of here.'

I suppose I thought she was Modesty Blaise with a Bren gun up her skirt and a hacksaw in her hair.

She said, 'It's not going to be easy.'

'Or possible?'

'It has to be. You understand me?'

I nodded. 'Window?'

'No good. There are bars on the other side, you can just see them through the paint.'

'Then what?'

'We've got to get the guard.'

'How?'

'Just distract him.'

I looked at him and he looked at me. If this was all I had to do it was easy. I looked back at Mara, and for a split second I allowed myself to think how I was going to get my own back for Shepheards, for London, for the Islamic collecting, for Cyprus under false pretences.

'You don't mind if I hit you?' I asked her. She hesitated, then said, 'Go ahead.'

'Now *look!*' I said and pushed away from the sill. 'I'm fed up with this bloody nonsense.' My voice cracked convincingly. 'I won't have it,' I said and began to shout, but not too loud. 'You two-timing bitch, you double-crossing whore!'

The rest of the words were an inarticulate shout. She swung round as well and was snarling back at me, a pulse beating in her temple. The guard sprang to the alert and was staring at us anxiously.

I shouted a bit more, she started to shout back and I suddenly let her have it, a smack across the left cheek and jaw that stung the palm of my hand, resounding like a pistol shot in the little room, and sent her sprawling across the floor on her back. She kept her head and came rolling back on to her feet, going for me like a wildcat, striking furiously at my face. I gave her one more slap, more carefully, then pushed her away with a play-actor's grunt of effort. Come on, you cretin, I thought, get a move on, you're the guard aren't you—and at last, at long last, I felt the rifle butt thud sickeningly against my ribs.

I doubled up on the floor and it wasn't for make believe,

he'd hit me over the heart and my breath jammed against my lungs. I forced myself to look up and knew as I did it that I was expecting the worst. An exploding barrel and silence? A steel hammer to crush my skull? Yes, seriously, I was expecting, for the first and last time in my short, sweet life, to be dead. He was standing over me, the barrel was wavering around my left ear, and I was watching him standing there, bewildered, frightened, wondering whether to pull the trigger.

That was when Mara hit him from the side.

It would have been beautiful to see in slow motion. Her foot hit his forearm in a low, hard, driving kick which paralysed him and must have terrified him for the instant it took for her arm to sweep up and crack across his Adam's apple. The carbine hit the stone floor after she had hit him again, I'd swear it, but I wasn't sure, she was on him now with both hands, one to jerk forward the head by the thick black hair, the other to smash it back on to the paving with a crack that made me think of murder.

'Are you OK?' she said.

I nodded numbly.

'Take the gun then. Quick.'

'No, you. I don't understand the things.'

She grabbed it, cradled it in her elbow, practised and swift. She gave me a quick grin. I was still struggling for breath.

'What I could do with an Uzi,' she gasped. 'But this will do.'

She ordered, 'You go first,' and I made for the door.

I didn't know what I was going to do. I doubt if she did either. Perhaps we were both living on borrowed time.

But I went down that corridor like a man set free from the world and all its cares. Christ! I was happy, for those few yards. Past one door. Quiet but fast. Then the next.

Still silence. And the third.

Then I froze. The door at the end of the corridor was opening. My brain over-revved, then steadied, hopeless, like the motorist the moment before the collision.

He came in the door too fast. It was his fault. I insist— it was his fault. He had the door almost closed behind him —not quite—when I saw him and he saw me.

It was Dietrich.

Without the hard-hat.

His face did something very strange when he saw me. I didn't understand it. Then he came towards me at a rush, as though to drag me down.

I thought I could do it. I went forward fast and hit him. I hit him with my right hand as hard as I could, and meant to reach his jaw. I landed on the cheekbone, just as he shouted at me and Mara shouted again, behind me.

I felt—no, I heard—my hand crack, and the pain ricocheted up the arm, slammed against the elbow and rushed on stabbing into the shoulder and the neck. I nearly fainted. I could feel that the finger had snapped and I must have stood there in the corridor, swaying and gasping, holding my hand in front of me like a dead bird, and looking at Dietrich, who was flat on his back against the wall.

Mara shouted again, or rather she screamed furiously at me, and I looked up and saw the door was wide open and the Captain was standing there against the light. He had a pistol levelled straight at me. The doorway was crowded with soldiers and guns.

Very slowly, I turned and looked behind me. Mara was standing ten yards away with the carbine directly levelled at my chest. It wasn't me she was aiming for, it was the Captain, and I was right bang in her line of fire.

As I watched she let her hands drop; then she tossed the

gun on to the cement, where it clattered and was still.

'Oh Tom,' she said. 'I was going to shoot you. I would have! Really, I was going to.'

'Why did you stop?' I mumbled, and the pain from my hand burned on again and brought the sweat cold to my brow.

She didn't answer. Dietrich was trying to get up and falling back, cursing, on the floor. At least, I'd done my best for England. I had done my best, poor sod.

They put us out on the tarmac, round the corner from the main terminal building, against the near blast wall. Three soldiers guarded us with levelled guns. Their predecessor's body had been carried away. This time we were handcuffed together. The Captain had lost his poise at last and was running back and forth shouting urgently at the airline staff, dark patches of sweat spreading on his uniform.

It dawned on me slowly; now we were three. Dietrich was with us, handcuffed to Mara. Half his face was swollen like a rotting peach and he looked sick and old.

He saw me looking at him and shook his head, very delicately, so as not to damage the mechanism.

'Mr Kane,' he said. 'You are a hopeless bloody fool. You have done for us all.'

'What?'

Mara said, 'Tom, it wasn't your fault, but you made a terrible mistake.'

I said, 'What do you mean—what's this *us* business?'

'Dietrich was coming to look for us.'

I couldn't take it in. She managed a wry smile, and said, 'You didn't know it but Dietrich is one of us. He came to try to rescue us.'

'I thought he was one of them,' I said, stupid and miserable. 'I mean I thought he was a Russian. One of your

202

Russians. What d'you mean, he was rescuing us?'

'He was working for my people. Tom, dear, he's with me. Didn't you realise it? It was all a charade. He doesn't have anything to do with selling weapons. There isn't any arms deal. It was all a plot to frighten you away.'

'Yes, I know all that.'

She stared at me. 'You mean, the arms deal...'

'Is all nonsense. And the tape-recording and the evidence from his bloody bedroom, yes, I know.'

Mara was still gazing at me thoughtfully. I allowed myself a brief spasm of satisfaction. At least they wouldn't think they had conned me to the very end.

'Then what about me?' grunted the German, savagely. 'Why you hit me when I came to find you?'

I said helplessly, 'I thought you were Moscow Narodny. Anyhow, why were you here on the Dam?'

'He was keeping an eye on me,' said Mara. 'We knew the Egyptians were getting suspicious of me but I couldn't pull out till you had finally given up. It's Dietrich's job, he's been based here for years. He reports to me when I'm in town.'

I said, 'All right. I'm sorry. I'm an idiot and you deserved it. No, I don't mean that...'

I was trying to work it out in my mind. At the same time I was keeping an eye open for the Captain's return, sparing a thought for our three trigger-happy guards and calculating how much harder I had made it for Sir Wilfred to talk me out of the Captain's clutches.

Mara must have been psychic. She said, 'They'll never believe you now, darling, you've convinced them for all time.'

'So what happens now?'

'They take us to Cairo.'

'And there?'

Dietrich said, with anger and bitterness thick as phlegm in his throat, 'They'll probably hang us all in the Citadel.'

FORTY

The Captain came back and told us the plane was on the way. It had been diverted to collect some other passengers. The sun moved down in the sky and the shadow of the blast wall moved up to the back of our knees. They gave us another drink and my swelling hand began to ache again, heavily and emphatically, like a hammer pounding up from the broken finger. Dietrich called out in Arabic to the guards and one of them went and brought me a rough cotton sling. A Russian mechanic, blond and crew-cut, came out to tinker with the MiG behind the wall and gazed at us with blank curiosity as he passed.

I had it worked out by now. She must be working for the Israelis as well as the Russians. Or perhaps she had left the Russians? I said, 'When did you leave the Moscow Narodny?' and without any hesitation she said, 'I haven't, I still work for them. I'm a banker like you, my dear.'

Which made sense. As Lord Magnus had guessed, the Russians would be delighted if they could use their own banking charms to block so big a deal between Egypt and the West. It made sense for the Israelis, too. Perhaps she was Jewish. Of course, she *must* be Jewish; strange that I had never seen it before and now it stood out clearly in every feature. So she could serve two masters and play me for a sucker twice in every round. I doubted what Dietrich had said about a public hanging. I thought the Egyptians were cleverer than that—at least as far as I was concerned. Mara and her German would be good propaganda but I would be an embarrassment. If I were the Captain, I decided, I'd be preparing a nasty motor crash and the sad decease of a promising young English banker, a good friend of the Republic. Flowers from the President, if I was lucky, and the Ambassador would attend the funeral.

'Stop brooding,' snapped Mara.

I stopped.

'We've got to get out of here now, somehow,' she said, and for the first time I heard her ready to give in.

'It's impossible.'

'I know.'

We were right. A plane came swinging unsteadily from the far horizon and the Captain marched across the tarmac to join us. He looked as cheerful as a man who's won the national lottery. The silhouette of the new arrival —it looked like one of the Ilyushin 14s—dipped and was lost against the dark of the desert, then bounced on the tarmac and rolled unsteadily towards us. We watched—I suppose the adverb would be 'sullenly'. It stopped twenty yards in front of us and the props shuddered and whinnied to a halt.

'Just a few minutes,' said the Captain, who seemed to think we were anxious to get away. They had pushed a rough set of steps against the open doorway and a couple of young Soviet officers emerged from the buildings across the way and moved towards the plane. A reception committee.

There was a movement inside the aircraft and two middle-aged men appeared and looked out at us. They came down the stairs, blinking in the late afternoon sunlight. They were Russians and wore grey uniforms and one of them had the certain number of stripes and crowns which put him very high up.

'He's a colonel,' muttered Dietrich, as though he was trying not to move his lips. 'No regiment. Probably KGB. They've been doing a series of inspections out here.'

The two Russians had reached terra firma and the younger ones were saluting in the sloppy but deferential Russian way.

I said to Mara, 'Friends of yours?' meaning it as my contribution to an anthology of gallows humour. But she didn't take it the way it was intended. Instead I felt every nerve in her body snap into action and her hand jerked against the metal bracelet that held us together.

'Tom!' she said. 'Thank you. I wasn't thinking. It's just possible...'

The group of men had turned and was coming towards us. They hadn't looked at us; at least they may have noticed but gave us none of their attention. They were about to pass ten yards in front of the three of us.

Mara's voice reached out, piercing the crispness of the desert air. She was speaking a language I didn't understand, but there were only a few words and she repeated them so I got the drift.

She said, 'Tovarishch polkovnik,' and then I heard, 'Gruppa Chaika, gruppa Chaika.'

The Egyptian Captain swung round on her. His face was flushed with embarrassment and he said, 'Silence at once! What is this?'

She ignored him; she ignored all of us except the older of the Russians who had turned towards her, listening.

She repeated, 'Gruppa Chaika, slushaite, Chaika!'

The Russian poised, peered at us. He thought.

Then he swivelled abruptly on his heel and—yes, he strode towards us. His voice was deep and harsh and unsympathetic, and he threw a torrent of Russian at her, speaking as fast as I would speak any language I knew if

I did not want an Egyptian to understand me.

Mara answered him with the same urgent syllables. She was fast and cool and businesslike, and he was listening intently to what she said.

He swung round again, back to his companion, and there was a mutter of Slavic sibilants. The Captain had lost the initiative. Mara's hand gripped mine tight; her face was taut and more beautiful than I had ever seen it. Dietrich was following the exchange with his eyes; I couldn't tell whether he understood.

The Russian turned to the Captain and spoke to him in laboured Arabic. They had some trouble in communicating. The Captain asked a question that ended with a double questionmark and a gaping jaw, and gave in. Mara was still holding my hand.

The Captain said, 'There is a slight problem. We must return to the building for a few minutes.'

He looked sick as a dog, and frightened too.

FORTY-ONE

Dietrich and I were put back into the room with blue paint on the window. This time there were three guards and a plate of crumbling biscuits. We slumped on the floor. I nursed my broken hand, which was still pounding with pain.

Mara had been taken away. She was away for a long time; half an hour maybe. When she came back she came over to me and said, 'Show me your hand.' It was swollen and mottled with purple bruises, hideous and useless.

'You need a doctor soon,' said Dietrich, 'or you will be

207

crippled.' He didn't sound too sad, which was under-
standable when you looked at the left-hand side of his
face. He said, 'Shall I make you—how do you say, a split?
No, a splint?'

I gritted my teeth. 'No thanks. No splint.'

Mara didn't pretend to be all that interested. She came
over to the wall and slid on to her heels, balancing herself with her back against the scabby plaster. The guards
fixed our chains again. They looked like three brothers;
it was impossible to guess what they made of us.

She sat there for a minute saying nothing and Dietrich
did the same. The soldiers were stinking like dancers at
curtain-call. They got on my nerves and my hand was
hitting me harder and harder so I was ready to give up
the act.

I said, 'They didn't rape you, then?'

'Who?'

'The Russian officers.'

'No, of course not.'

Dietrich grunted like a peasant paying tax and said,
'They're KGB men. I've seen them in Hurghada.'

'One of them is a Colonel from Riga.'

It was the beginning of a limerick. 'I don't see how it
makes any different to us,' I said. 'I mean, to you.'

Dietrich laughed savagely. 'You're with us now, Mr
Kane,' he said. 'You've been with us since you helped her
kill the guard.'

'She didn't kill him.'

'Just cracked his skull,' said Mara, absentmindedly.
She had changed again. Some of the vitality had come
back. Her face had lost the hopeless, angry silence she
had had since the hotel. She sat there as composed as
a Zen master, looking as though, whatever came next on
the programme, it wouldn't be a complete surprise.

I asked, 'What happens now?'

Dietrich said, 'Shut up, she can't talk here. They're probably listening.'

'No they're not,' said Mara blithely. 'The room must be clear, it's just a spare office. And the guards still don't understand.'

'Then the Captain will be somewhere in earshot.'

'No,' said Mara. 'He's being kept busy by the Colonel.'

I said heavily, 'Will one of you please tell me what's going on?'

Mara said, 'Not now, darling, I can't.'

'Then give me a clue.'

Dietrich said, 'She can't, didn't you hear her?'

They were still trying to treat me as one of the team, and a stupid junior, too. I resented it fiercely. I'd done my bit, I'd smashed a couple of knuckles so I'd probably be left-handed for life, and they expected me to sit here in the funeral parlour and do as I was told. It was their privilege. It was their birthright, not mine. Very definitely not mine. I had no intention of joining them in a repeat of the last stand of Masada.

But Mara didn't look like a suicide-case any longer; she was crisp as a new tennis ball from the fridge. Her skin was glowing, warm with excitement; I could feel it.

Mara said, 'Tom, please ... Be patient. We shall have to wait here.'

'Why, for Christ's sake?'

'The Russians have been asking questions. It was all because of your idea. We're gaining time. It may be enough time.'

I said, 'It was what you said to him. It sounded like "*Chaika*" all the time. Wasn't that it?'

Dietrich said, with a spurt of anger, 'Don't let yourself believe her. They can take us off to Cairo at any moment.

She's just trying to cheer you up.'

No, there was more to it than that. I looked back at Mara. She nodded.

'Yes, it's true,' she said. 'The Captain can overrule the Russians if he has the courage. Or the Russians can decide to let us go to Cairo. They don't have any real authority. They can only give advice. So don't be too hopeful—you'll need your Ambassador yet.'

'Or Toby?'

'We'll need even Toby.'

OK. So we waited. The minutes went by in the heat and stink of the little room, and I timed them against the throbbing beat of the beast in my right hand.

It must have been an hour later. We'd been sitting on the concrete, silent, and not a word passed between us all that time. Dietrich was slumped forward, gazing morosely at the floor between his legs; his flesh was heavy, in rolls, and the unbruised part of his face looked white and tired. Miserable too. But he didn't bother us. Mara had been sitting cross-legged, her back as straight as though she were a Victorian schoolgirl with a book balanced on her head. Her hand was on my arm—the bad one—and from time to time her fingers claimed and released the muscle as though to reassure me. But her attention was far away. It was as though she was attempting an effort of will. She didn't notice me trying to attract her attention, so I had to say it out loud. She came back to us abruptly.

'What did you say?'

'Can we do something about this hand of mine? It's going to fall off.'

'You poor man,' said Mara, and her voice was warm though her eyes merely glanced at the darkening swelling and the twisted knucklebone. 'Can you wait a little longer?'

'What are you waiting for?'

'I don't yet know.'

'Yes, you do. You're expecting something.'

The guards had been lulled by our silence, and by the heat, moving only to slap at the flies. Dietrich had not yet looked up at us. It was hard to tell whether the sky outside the blue-smeared windows was dark yet, but the dusk must have come down by now. There had been no sign of the Captain.

'I don't know, Tom,' she repeated. 'It's impossible for me to know. I've told them everything, it's up to them— and something must be going on because they've left us alone all this time.'

I still couldn't work it out. 'Up to who? Told everything to whom?'

Dietrich intervened. He scowled and lifted his head briefly from his examination of the floor. 'She means her KGB comrades,' he said. 'She's relying on those Russian bastards. So don't get too cheerful, Mr Kane.' His head slumped from his shoulders again.

Yes, I thought, but what can they do about us? Why *should* they do anything, for that matter? Or was this an after-care scheme for Moscow Narodny bank clerks? And what did Dietrich have to do with the Moscow Narodny? If he was so cool on the Russians?

I said, 'I suppose they're trying the Embassy in Cairo. The Soviet Embassy.'

Mara said, 'Just be patient, Tom, please.'

'But if they're going to talk to the Embassy for us, why do they leave us here when there's a plane waiting to take off?'

Dietrich snapped, 'Please, you shut up now Mr Kane. You say too much. We will not understand. Because she cannot tell us. So shut up.'

Mara hadn't moved. The night moved up a notch. I was one day—or one century—older.

FORTY-TWO

I must have fallen asleep, there against the rough plaster of the wall, because when I came to my senses, with a moment of panic, then confusion, then understanding, my head was half-resting on Mara's shoulder so that my neck was stiff and my shoulders ached. Mara was awake, still tense, poised, erect. On the other side of her, Dietrich was half-lying against the wall, breathing heavily through his mouth. His right arm with the manacle which attached him to Mara was stretched awkwardly across towards her like a machine-gunned corpse, and their hands lay in crude contrast on the concrete floor. The guards were awake and watched us without expression or reaction. But they were watching.

It might have been the throbbing of my hand that had woken me. I cradled it to my chest and turned my head to see that Mara was awake. She hadn't noticed me. She had the same expression on her face; still waiting, willing, expecting—what?

Then I understood. No, she was listening.

That was it. Her head was crooked slightly towards the window, pitched over and beyond Dietrich's grunting.

I listened too, painfully. And then I heard something.

It was a distant mutter, no, a ripple, a fan-beat, carried across the desert air; very faint, alien, machine-made.

I tugged on the cuff and when she looked down on me, querying, I tried to show her with an inclination of my head and a roll of my eye towards the ceiling. She gave me a questioning look but then seemed to understand.

She cocked her head again. The blood began to pound through my veins, suddenly, which was ridiculous, it could have been a heavy Leyland truck up at the Dam. I listened again, heard nothing this time, remembered to look at the guards and slumped back again against the wall, as though to show them I was bored.

There was a slight jerk at my left wrist. I strained my ears—the right one was the keener and I tried to angle it towards the window. I heard the sound again, it was getting louder. There was a double note, a heavier grumbling and the same flutter, like the movement of the high wind in a palm plantation.

I was very awake now, my brain racing hopelessly, uselessly, ahead of the evidence of my senses. I could feel that Mara was as tense as a coiled watch spring. Her left arm moved, imperceptibly, on the floor; she was tugging gently at Dietrich's wrist. He stirred, settled again and stirred a second time. The chain was tight, I saw, and his arm tried to drag it back.

The noise was loud in my ears. Surely they must have all heard it by now. It was like a wind across a wide valley.

One of the guards suddenly reacted. His eyes jerked upwards, the whites thickened and he listened.

Abruptly he stood up, staring irresolutely in the centre of the room. His two companions stirred themselves and gazed at him, and then they heard it too. Dietrich grunted and woke, muttering. There was a sudden hail of shouting, high-pitched and warning outside, and a clatter of boots running helter-skelter across the tarmac. Five seconds more: the high-pitched wail of a siren.

The noise was frighteningly near, just outside us, and I still didn't know what could be happening. An engine started with a wild scream of the starter and there was another flurry of Arabic, answered from farther away and repeated louder.

Then all was swept aside in a thunder of sound and a torrent of confusion. The wind became a roar, they were machines, deafening machines, and they were very close overhead. There was a ponderous, sustained revving of a great aircraft, a thudding burst, as of a cannon, and the abrupt chatter, just overhead, of a machine-gun raking the roof. I pressed myself instinctively into the wall.

Mara gripped my hand. The ground heaved beneath us. The window collapsed in a shower of glass and lay on the floor at our feet. Suddenly we were shouting, the three of us on our feet. One of the guards was sitting still, holding his forehead delicately with one hand and blood was seeping through his fingers.

'What was that?'

She strained up at me and shouted, 'Bombs!' and pulled me down away from the gaping window.

It was pitch-black outside, punctuated by red flashes of bullets and a desperately erratic searchlight. There was the pencil stabbing of the light, the stars, a half-moon, and still the hideous din. A jeep drove past very fast and still the noise was beating against our ears.

The guards were shouting at each other, yelping and snarling. One of them was waving his gun in our direction. The second was pointing towards the door. They probably wanted to shoot us right away and get the hell out of the place. The third one was still holding his forehead and blood was slipping down like sweat and massing at his eyebrows.

Dietrich was gesticulating at the corporal type, who looked blankly back at him. Dietrich was shaking the chains, miming the turning of a key. The guard took the point and rejected it out of hand. He raised his gun to prove it, his eyes panicky. Dietrich froze, we all did, then the door opened and this time we could hear the din funnelled down the corridor. A sound of panic and apprehension. I expected the Captain. It was the Russian—the younger one.

Mara snapped something in Russian and he shouted back. He gestured abruptly at the guards and they fell back. Dietrich waved the chains again, dragging at Mara's arm, but was ignored. Mara had stepped between the two of us and was leaning forward to listen to the Russian. He was shouting urgently into her ear and she shouted back at him once, then a second time, and shrugged her shoulders as though rejecting something. He seemed angry, not just flustered, but whatever it was it gave him a splendid urgency. He was speaking again, a torrent of gutturals, and Mara stopped arguing, she was listening with an intensity, a rapacity, I had never seen before on a woman's face. She nodded; nodded again rapidly.

He drew a cumbersome revolver from whatever the Soviet Army calls a Sam Browne and twitched it experimentally so that I was looking down the sights from the wrong side. He was speaking to the guards in what must have passed for Arabic. They stood still which seemed to be what was required. Then he gave another flick of the barrel, from me to the door and back again, and I guessed we were going for a walk.

I led the way. The other two trailed behind me; I supposed the Russian was at their backs. The corridor was shadowy and littered with glass which crunched under our feet. Two of the doors had been blown down.

When the door opened at the end of the corridor the noise came crashing in at us. A brace of mechanics were squatting on the floor behind the desk, teaching each other to feed the cartridges into an ancient Luger. They were concentrating so hard I'd swear they never saw us. Over the counter, in the barn of a lounge, there was a hullaballoo of shouting and a deafening clatter of gun-fire. It seemed to be coming from directly over our heads, on the roof. An Egyptian officer dashed the length of the room in pyjamas with a flying jacket trailing over his shoulder. The windows were jagged with broken glass. There were bodies on the floor—no, not bodies, I realised, but everybody was lying on the ground behind heavy sofas or jammed against the doorways.

I paused and looked around. Mara said urgently, 'Go straight through the far door. Get ready to do as I say.' Her voice convinced me. We trailed across the room, arms still linked by the chain; a frieze, a dance of death, I thought, and repressed the image hastily. We were almost running and the Russian hadn't stopped us. The noise, I reckoned, had slackened only it was impossible to be sure so long as the gunner up aloft had any shells left. I nearly trod on the Pole I'd seen earlier. He was lying on the floor holding his ear to the dirt.

I reached the door and stopped. There was smoke out-side but no flame. The beat of the engines had passed overhead. A machine-gun was chattering across the tarmac and suddenly a spurt of flame beyond the main hangar showed me two men running across an oil-shadowed arena. Then I heard a crunch—a thump, a weight drop-ped from a great height—a mile or so away.

Dietrich shouted, quite clearly, 'They're going for the Dam,' then Mara cried, 'Go on—through the door.' I pushed it with my shoulder and it opened with a clang of an iron bar like the emergency exit in an American cinema. We were on the sheltered side of the airfield. There was still the racket behind us and overhead, but it was dark again and my pupils struggled to adjust fast enough.

I'd slowed to a halt as the door clanged shut behind us.

Mara said, 'You see the Land Rover?'

I said, 'Where?' and saw it as I spoke, over in the shadow of the main building, next to an iron fence.

She ordered, 'Get in. Fast.'

I must have hesitated. She shouted, 'Get moving, you idiot, quick, we've only got a minute,' and led us both at a crazy lope across the yard.

She ran, dragging me along savagely and I knew we didn't have a chance. I waited for the Russian or Egyptian bullet in my back. Nothing happened. I slowed and looked back. I could see no one—no Soviet officer, not even a shadow against the bulk of the building.

Dietrich must have realised it already, he stopped at the door of the Land Rover, shaking his wrist furiously and cursing in German. She said, 'Never mind, get in— we've got to get out of here.'

'Where's the key?'

'He said it was in the ignition.'

They pushed me up and I slid across the benchseat, cradling my hand from the levers and knobs. Mara came next. Then Dietrich, wriggling under the wheel. We were all still chained together, and I wondered which of them could handle the gears. It was quiet, sheltered, inside the cabin. We were all three panting, more with the tension than the speed.

'Where now?' said Dietrich. He seemed to know where the keys and levers were and I saw his hand move automatically from the ignition to the headlight switch and then freeze abruptly.

Mara said, 'Across the tarmac is the best, if we can risk it. There's supposed to be a gate in the wire about 300 metres from the last guardhouse. If we miss it there's wire-cutters in the back.'

'And then?'

'Three miles north, up the bank of the Lake. Take the second track. If you see anyone, drive straight through them.'

I said, 'Do we all dress up as Russian colonels?'

Mara snapped, 'Shut up,' so I did.

FORTY-THREE

The engine caught at once and Dietrich fought the wheel around and back again with one arm and his knee. She was trying to coordinate his right arm with her left but it wasn't easy. We were lurching from side to side so I gave up trying to get rid of the chain and jammed myself with my elbow against the plunging of the Land Rover.

Then we were out of the glare, accelerating away across the silver black of the concrete. The hero on the passenger roof was still firing away. The smoke had begun to clear, but the sole searchlight had been shot out. Something went bang in the night at the far end of the runway. Mara shouted, 'We're using delayed action bombs.'

I thought, 'We?'

'Don't follow the tarmac,' Mara cried at Dietrich. 'They'll be trying to get the planes up,' and she was right, a jet came roaring towards us like a banshee trailing smoke, but we were safe, out in the hard-packed sand, bowling across the desert like old newsreels of the Eighth Army chasing Rommel into the sea.

Dietrich found the gate. There was no sign of a guard. We hit the right track, stuttered into a sandhole, then came through, over a ridge, and saw the water down beneath us. It was going like a dream. They argued once about where to turn into the sand and off the track but he was the one who gave in. The three of us were leaning forward over the wheel like stock car drivers. The wind through the window was cool, chilling the sweat; exhilarating, free.

The moon was higher now, and as the airfield receded the desert took shape around us. We tilted steeply towards the water and I remembered what Dietrich had said. I leaned to look for the Dam wall. I couldn't see it, but the water looked still, undisturbed. I said, 'Is the Dam wall still safe?' and no one answered.

Dietrich was having trouble with the wheel, we began to slither down into thick sand and he asked, 'Where now?' as though still angry for the day and blaming her. Mara ordered, 'Take it down to the water,' and she was right: as we drifted to a halt and the engine died a shadow rose from the ground and thrust a gun into the open window.

A voice, light and young, asked a single word. Mara replied in a language that sounded like Arabic but wasn't. It seemed to work. The gun vanished, a second shadow was at my ear, and the doors were open. We pulled in opposite directions, Dietrich won and we slipped out into the night.

The shadows were slight and thin and wore loose dun-coloured clothing. I couldn't have hoped to see them ten yards away. Their faces were very dark and when one of them turned towards me unsmiling, I saw the eyes starting out of the sockets and realised his face was deliberately blacked. I could also see it wasn't a man but a boy, cradling a sub-machine gun. It was the Israeli Army. He talked quickly in a hushed mutter with Mara and the second one joined them.

They seemed to settle something and she turned to us where we stood tethered, and said, 'We're late. Hurry! We must run,' and started dragging us in a half-run, half-shuffle through the sand. The one boy led the way; he was clasping his gun as though it were a tennis racket. The second boy had lingered at the Land Rover. After a few yards he caught up with us and said, in English, 'Stop. I cut you.' He was holding a pliers as big as a crowbar and with a grunting effort he snapped two links, one to Mara's right, one to her left. We were free and the chains clanked, jangling, as we laboured on.

Over the ridge, down into the soft deep dale, and the water vanished to our left and we could see we were protected from view. The dunes were rising all around us. 'Stop!' one of the boys called. We halted, panting, sweating. There was a lantern and a pistol at the boys' feet; it was done very quickly. A flare in the pistol, a quick glance at a watch, and the green star plummeting into the blackness of the sky.

The star burst and the glare was hideous, terrifying. We stood there on the sand, our faces ghastly as we gazed up, terrified at this all-revealing brilliance. Some Egyptian MiGs must have made it into the air by now, I thought. How could they miss us? And the blaze hovered so slowly, it seemed, as though suspended from a balloon.

But the helicopter was on us instantly; we were late, it must have been waiting for the signal. The fluttering came in fast over the desert, the put-putting loud overhead; the wind whipped the sand off the dunes and the chopper came down, brilliant under the flare, the Star of David defiant on the tail. It touched down on to the ridge above us, it couldn't come down below, and the five of us hurled ourselves up the slope, slipping up to our knees, hearts pounding, chains swinging, gasping for breath. It was too bright, it was madness; the sand was luminous green and the flare drifted lower and still brighter. It was like daylight in the south of Spain; I could see the doorway open, two men crouched on the sand, two more stood, guns levelled down at us, in the hatch.

There were thirty yards, then twenty, and Mara and I were leading. Dietrich was struggling behind. One of the men shouted at us anxiously. I could see the pilot's head twisted back at us, gauging our progress. The rotor was sweeping gently around, leisurely as a ceiling fan in Delhi.

I was on the last slope when the flare drifted down to the horizon and flamed for the last time. The glare beamed straight, devastating, on our faces.

I heard a voice shouting suddenly, frantically, over the motors, and looked up in time to see an older soldier standing up in the doorway. His hand was pointing down at us—no, not at Mara and me, over our heads, to Dietrich. He was screaming something—which of course I couldn't understand—and I saw his eyes staring grotesque in his head.

Then it was done. His Uzi came up, across at us, and the blast sent us sprawling, grinding our bellies and faces instinctively down into the sand.

The shots could have been heard in Cairo; our ears stung with the shock and the soldier was still shouting incoherently, hysterically, but his gun had dropped to the sand. I could also have reached out and taken it, we were so close.

Mara was lying on her back now, looking down the slope of the dune. The two boy soldiers were crouched over the bundle that had been Dietrich.

'He must have been cut in half,' Mara said without emotion.

There was no requiem. The pilot was already shouting

at us. The night had gone dark again. They left his body in the sand and called us up into the hatch. The man who had the gun was standing quite still, aghast, doing nothing. Mara shouted at him impatiently, in Hebrew, as though she would soon lose control. Another boy pushed him roughly aside and leaned down to pull us up into the womb of the machine.

I gave him my right hand, without thinking, and he seized it, gripped and hauled me up, but by the time I had steel under my feet the fractured bones had rasped and smashed and before I could scream with the pain I had passed out like the heroine in a Victorian swoon.

So I missed the take-off, the hedge-hopping across the horizon and the Phantom air support, screaming out from behind the moon to shadow us back to the airbase in Sinai. When I came round Mara was squatting on the floor supporting my head on her knees and slapping my face with the energy of an Italian pizza chef; we were high over the desert and the boys were laughing at Mara and she was holding me and laughing too, as though all the bad things were far in the past and never a need to think of them again.

They'd put a sling on my arm and tied it to my chest so I couldn't move it properly. And I lay there, at peace, as we lurched loudly across the night sky.

I said, 'Dietrich's dead?'

She said, 'Yes.'

'What were you shouting at the man with the gun?'

She said, '*Meshuga, haragta et hanatsig shelanu b'kahir!*'

'What does that mean?'

She grinned. 'It means—let me see—"You crazy fool, you've just killed our man in Cairo!"'

FORTY-FOUR

I said, 'You have some explaining to do,' and Mara
replied, 'Have I?' smiling up at me. So I insisted, 'Yes, you
have,' and waited patiently, like a child for a bedtime
story, although at that precise moment we were no longer
in bed.

She sighed, ran her hands through my hair, smiled
secretly to herself, looked up at me again.

'Where do I start?'

They had brought us to Jerusalem and taken Mara
away for a day and a night. A surgeon had packed my
hand in plaster and given me my worst moment of the
year when he asked if I seriously expected to hold a teacup
again. Israeli humour: I was in fact going to be all right.
They had also given me an open line to London. Lord
Magnus was in the country, so I spoke to Condon, who
rang Sue, who told the Near East Desk, who presumably
sent a cable to the Cairo Embassy. It seemed to be in
order, all of it.

Mara came back to me the next morning. She wore the
sort of white linen dress which you don't expect to see in
the egalitarian streets of Israel and her skin was burnished
and rich, her hair loose and hanging heavy so she kept
pushing it away with the back of her arm. The Army
had given me a flat up in a quiet part of Rehavia overlooking the Valley of the Cross, with a view of the University and the Museum buildings. At least, I thought it was
just for me until the Yemeni maid asked where to put a
carton of new clothes that had arrived in Mara's name.
'Mara Tal,' the label said. No address. There was a discreet police guard outside the entrance to the apartments

223

but they seemed to be on my side for a change. A curtain of old pine trees sheltered us from the road, and their scent in the warm air reminded me of Cape Cod holidays.

I said, 'You can start by telling me why I'm here in the Promised Land—when I'm supposed to be handing $125 million to the enemy over the Canal.'

'I thought you'd prefer to know how we got you out.'

'That too.' And make it simple, I thought.

Mara lay flat on her back on the tiled floor as though to concentrate better. The position also managed to show her off to advantage. Her legs were brown and bare and her sandals were a cat's-cradle of white-thong leather.

'Well, darling,' she began—and I never knew whether she meant it or had picked it up from some drama school —'It was the Russians who got us out.'

I waited and she began to exercise her ankle muscles, flexing them in circles three inches above the ground.

'You remember when I went to talk with the Colonel?'

I nodded, 'Yes.'

'Dietrich was right. Colonel Belyaev was KGB. I told him enough so that he had to get us out. We couldn't risk being taken to Cairo and he knew it. He was the only one who could help.'

'And he told the Israelis? Whose crazy idea was that?'

'I had to get word to Jerusalem—it was my only hope. That was the first reason why I got them to arrest you as well. I thought you'd have a better chance of getting a warning out to my people. You might have been able to tell Dietrich. He knew how to send an urgent message.'

'But I messed that up.'

'Not really. Dietrich was taking a fantastic risk. He'd come up to Aswan because he heard a rumour the Egyptians were on to me. He saw us at the hotel with the Captain and realised what had happened and thought he could bluff his way at the airport. He must have realised you wouldn't know who he really was.'

'But why did he do all this? Why take such a stupid risk?'

She hesitated. 'It's—it's part of his contract. If anything happened to me, we would pass his files to the West German Government...'

'His files?' I repeated, beginning to understand. Mara was sitting up now, unsmiling.

'Yes, his files. Let me tell you a bit about Klaus Dietrich.' Her voice was flat now, as she recited: 'Dietrich joined the Nazi Party as early as 1936, when he was still a student in Munich. When the war came, he joined the SS, where he was on the staff of the SS Hauptamt. He ended the war as Standartenfuhrer and assistant head of Amtsgruppe Wirtschaftliche Unternehmungen—you know what I mean? It controlled the economic enterprises of the SS and administered the concentration camps. Dietrich didn't soil his hands with workaday brutalities in the camps. He was an administrator, an expert, you understand, in the efficient allocation of labour resources. The British captured him in 1945, but he disappeared before trial.' She stopped, looked up at me with something like contempt. 'We found him in 1954, in Frankfurt, where he headed his own firm as economic consultant and commodities broker. He specialised in cotton, travelled often to Egypt. We knew all about him, he knew enough about us to be more than willing to co-operate. I kept an eye on him in Cairo. He was useful. He had to be. A swine.' It was an old-fashioned word. She shrugged. 'Now he's dead. That was an accident, a mistake. You see, the man who shot him from the helicopter happened to be one of Dietrich's personal playthings, back in 1944. The man suddenly recognised Dietrich and lost control, he had a gun, that's all. I'm not in mourning.'

'Neither am I,' I said, but she refused to look at me. I had never felt her as remote from me as then. There was a long pause. I could hear sparrows chattering in the pine trees.

I wrenched myself out of the heavy silence in the room with another question.

'I still don't understand what you said to the Colonel.'

She paused again. 'It's all to do with the way I've been working for the bank at the same time.'

I said, 'That sounds too vague. What was that word you kept shouting at him on the tarmac. "*Chaika*" or something like that.'

She rolled over and sat up as though she had decided it would have to be said earlier, not later.

'I'm involved in some—let's say, some negotiations— between Jerusalem and the Kremlin. They're quite important and very secret. I'm sorry I can't say more than this. We were lucky the KGB had one of their senior men down in Upper Egypt—a man sufficiently senior to know the codeword and enough besides to realize he had to get me out.'

'Why didn't he leave it to the Soviet Embassy?'

'It's all too complicated. We don't work through the Ambassador, you must realise. And the Ambassador's relationship with the Egyptians is terribly delicate. I would have been the biggest catch the Secret Police had had for years. Obviously it could have been highly embarrassing to the Soviet Government. Think of what propaganda might have come out of a trial at the present moment. And Dietrich too—they'd been trying to track him as well.'

'So whose idea was it?'

'Colonel Belyaev agreed to pass word to Jerusalem.

226

Fast. I don't know how, they have their channels for this sort of thing.'

'Did he know what the Israelis were going to do?'

'No, that was what annoyed them. He and I had been talking of letting us escape to a quiet pick-up in the desert. He specifically said there mustn't be any operation that would damage or discredit the Russian military advisers.'

'But then your people came down like wolves on the fold.' Only their cohorts weren't gleaming, I thought; it was the scruffiest army in the business.

'They decided they had to lay on a distraction. Which they did—even faster than I expected. Of course, they weren't seriously going for the High Dam.'

'You mean you could if you wanted to?'

She grinned. 'It's built pretty thick. But you know what Egyptian cement is like.'

I said, 'It all went fine. The American observer was very impressed—you must tell them. Except he wants to know more.'

Mara said, 'Look...' and stopped. She changed her mind, sprang up, took my hand.

'Come on out,' she invited, 'I'll show you the real Jerusalem.'

'I haven't got any decent clothes—I left them all in Shepheards.'

'That's something else we've been arranging. I've got some things here for you, and that nice girl in London—what's her name, Sue? Don't look so startled!—she said she'll tell Toby to send them on.'

I said, 'Thank you.'

'Now come on out.'

We walked into the bright sunshine, through the quiet Rehavia streets into the broad hurry of King George. Past the massive ugliness of the Supersol block, a building any lover of Jerusalem could cheerfully blow up, beyond the valley, lay the Old City, its wall and domes clear against the blue sky. We went into the little park opposite the Tirat Batsheva Hotel and sat down. I still felt a bit shaky, although Mara was clearly in good enough form to set out for a thirty-mile full-pack route march.

I said, 'I still don't see how you planned this. Who *are* you working for, for Christ's sake, Israel or the Soviets?'

'The two of them,' she said simply, as if that were the most natural thing in the world. 'I spend most of my time with the Narodny.'

She must have seen the expression on my face because she went on quickly, 'It's true, Tom. I'm a banker just like you. Why don't you want to believe it?'

'For a banker you asked some pretty innocent questions. In Beirut and in London.'

'Oh dear, don't you see how careful I had to be. You were talking technicalities and of course I had to stop myself looking as though I knew what it meant. And you and Joe Larochelle were pretty close-mouthed. I was able to persuade you to talk only by pretending I couldn't understand much!'

'Don't boast,' I said. 'You're just lucky to be built the way you are.' A man would have had to be a eunuch to refuse her anything. She made a face at me, then leaned across and buried her face in my shoulder. She said,

'Because I have this connection with the Israelis you mustn't think I'm a full-time operative with *Shin Beth*. That's nonsense. There aren't so many full-time agents any more. It's the part-timers who do the work.'

'Who were your bosses this time?' I asked. I couldn't understand why I wasn't angry at the memory of how she'd led me on.

'On the Nile issue? Both of them! It makes sense. The Soviet Government wanted to stop the West making a comeback into Egypt. The Israelis obviously will try to delay anything that looks like improving Egypt's economic strength—at least, so long as there's a war going on. And the Moscow Narodny is happy to carry out instructions from Moscow, because we like matching our wits against our colleagues in the West.' She laughed. 'And you know who our shareholders are!'

'Yes, I do. But which of those three were you *really* working for? There must be one fundamental loyalty.'

'Not at all. I'm a good Soviet citizen, truly I am. And I'm a Jew by birth and emotion. I can work for both. They both know it and understand it. The two countries are still far closer than you people realise—the Russian-Arab thing doesn't compare, even now. Remember, it was the Soviet Union which was the second government to recognise Israel. Think of the number of Cabinet Ministers here in Jerusalem who are Russian in background. It's bound to influence a certain relationship between us. I'm just one of the go-betweens and they can allow me to be just that because they make sure my loyalties never clash. And because there are these very important negotiations going on—I'm sorry, I really can't say anything more. And you see, this is something I can do because I am who I am.'

I said, 'It's all still beyond my pigeon brain. Why do

you have to make it so bloody complicated?'

She wrinkled her nose. 'That's the way it is. Loyalty is one of the most complex and highly qualified of the emotions. Or at least, it is this century. If you want to keep things simple in this part of the world you join Al Fatah or the Greater Israel maniacs.'

'This doesn't make it any easier for innocents like me,' I said. 'You've concentrated on one thing ever since you met me—the meeting was all planned, I suppose.'

She got up and stood on the path in front of me, looking down on me.

'My dear, I'm afraid so. I'd been waiting for you for weeks. I had a file on you right down to the colour of your socks and the neuroses of your girl friend. That was why I made sure I met Toby, the poor man.'

She was smiling broadly, brazen now, and at last I felt a spasm of anger : it might have been a final brief acknowledgment of my own stupidity; or resentment of her beauty and her poise; and despair, too, for her utter inaccessibility, because I knew then we would soon have to part.

'It may be funny to you,' I exclaimed, 'but don't deny you played me for a sucker all along the line. You deceived me with everything you said and did. You played on all my stupid weaknesses. You were a real bitch...'

She cut in sharply and there was a cold note in her voice which she tried to conceal beneath an accent of mockery. 'Shame on me! Have I offended your sense of fair play? Did I break the rules? Are the English still like that? Do you have any idea what was at stake for us? I *had* to do it—you know that. You have no right to complain. Or do you think you have?'

'For Christ's sake. You use me like Mata Hari and lead me on from the beginning and nearly get me killed and then ask if I'm bloody well complaining.'

'Don't be a hypocrite. You've done the same yourself. You'd do the same without thinking twice. And for what? For a business deal! You were pathetically grateful when I agreed to play the whore with Dietrich. Don't deny it!'

'It's not that you "agreed". It was you who suggested it. And that's another of your bloody lies, that and the tape recording. All right, so we all sail close to the wind on occasions, but I've never gone at it with your sort of natural talent.'

'You're all the same,' said Mara bitterly and swung around and away. Her voice was quiet again, but angrier for that. 'You put us all on a pedestal. You expect us to play by different rules from the rest of you. What's so special about being double-crossed by a girl you've slept with? You're an odd sort of virgin to cry foul. And again, what stakes were you playing for—money, success, a pat on the back from Daddy Magnus in London?' Her voice was contemptuous now.

I let her go on. She was edging up against the truth. I suppose I wasn't exactly scrupulous in my private life. I was no kid to start crying 'foul' when the ball game got rough. But that bit about Daddy Magnus hurt.

'There's a limit to what we should do to other people,' I muttered. 'I reckon you crossed it. I reckon you know it and won't admit it.'

'You idiot!' shouted Mara, at last really angry. 'Who the hell do you think you are to patronise me! I'm as aware of my actions as you are. You're being a hurt little boy male, and I hate it. You slept with me, so you're thinking what an honour you've done me, and now you decide I'm unworthy of you. It's a charming way of saying goodbye. All right, go on, I won't be shedding any tears over you, believe me.'

My own anger had drained like water from a colander. I wasn't ready for the end. Not yet.

I said, without looking at her, 'Was it as bad as that?' She stopped.

I let her work it through. She was very still. I still didn't look at her.

'No,' she said and her eyes searched me out and she came, quickly, across to the bench and leaned very close against me. 'I'm sorry,' she whispered. 'I'm sorry I cheated you. I'm sorry I seduced you! But don't you remember how I tried to wait until the work was done?'

'I never noticed.'

'Yes, you did. You were very impatient. But I made all those excuses not to go with you in Cairo because—don't you understand? I wanted you to have me and I wanted it to be straight. Just us! Nothing to do with our jobs or the Nile or anything.'

'You were kidding yourself.'

'Yes, maybe I was. But it was important to me. I told you I'd tell you when I was ready, so when we went to Cyprus I could go without bad faith because I knew you'd done everything necessary to break up the deal. I wasn't being a bitch—I was a girl, going to a man.'

'I'm sorry I was so stupid,' I said. The trouble was, I still found it hard to pinpoint this switch from integrity to deceit and back again. 'What are you up to now, for instance? Is it good faith or bad—here, now?'

She frowned as though she could not or would not follow me. 'I always knew that in the end I was being honest with you. Couldn't you tell that in Cyprus? That it was straight and honest?'

I said, 'Yes,' ungrudging, remembering.

'I could never have done to you what you did to me when you got back from London ...'

'What did I do?' I asked.

'You carried on as before, although you'd discovered what I was. You tried to pretend nothing had happened.'

'You knew?'

'Dear Tom, you're pretty transparent to me,' said Mara. 'I knew something was wrong.'

I must have looked dubious.

'You don't make love to a man you know and not notice he's got questions on his mind, especially when they're about you.'

I grimaced, mainly for effect and because she was looking smug, then asked, 'You always use your instinct in your work? Even in banking?'

'Yes of course. Look, there is one question we haven't answered—*who* betrayed me? How did the Egyptians get enough evidence to arrest us?'

I hadn't thought of it. 'Could it have been the Russians?' I asked helplessly.

'Why should they? I'm more use to them than I could be an embarrassment.'

'What about Toby? In a fit of jealousy?'

'What? Of you?' She laughed, which irritated me. 'No, he won't do. He doesn't have the image. It's against the code.'

She said, 'I wondered if it was you.'

I was genuinely startled. I almost got to my feet. I told her, 'Don't be crazy! And get myself into that mess in in Aswan?'

Pass over her unspoken point, that I was capable of it but Toby wasn't.

'Am I still under suspicion? Is that why I'm being guarded so carefully by your friends?'

'No, darling, you're in the clear. It was so obvious you were taken by surprise in Aswan. You were way out of

233

your depth, and anyone could see it.'

'Thank you,' I said. 'So I bungled on, which was lucky for you.' She seemed to have forgotten all about my hand.

'No, it couldn't have been you,' Mara was saying. 'You couldn't do it either.' She paused, then added, very quietly, 'Not yet.'

'What does that mean?'

She shook her head, refusing to answer.

There was no need. I knew what she meant. I hadn't needed to put the question. 'One day you will,' she had wanted to say, and it needed a categorical denial I couldn't for the life of me make. 'I'm sorry,' she repeated and her eyes were hard. I looked away. 'You see, Tom, some of us are serious. *Au fond.* You must watch out for us. And you mustn't pity us, or scorn us, or look down on us. That's the way they'll corrupt you, the people in your world, the people you have chosen to work for: not with their money and their racehorses and their first-class travel. *But with their contempt for the ones who care.*'

Later—when we were still in Jerusalem because she'd said let's go to Eilat for the weekend and I'd said no, it was too much like Egypt—we were holed up in the flat drinking Gold Star beer, trying to ignore *Kol Israel* and catching up on the days we'd lost in Cyprus. My right hand was a loss to both of us but we managed to compensate. She was very skilful when she was trying, and she certainly was trying.

I said, not for the first time, 'And you never slept with Dietrich?'

'God, no. I've told you, my love, it was all a trap and you fell for it beautifully, tape-recording and all. Dietrich preferred poor Arab boys, if that makes you feel better.'

'You took a hell of a risk.'

'Oh, no. You were so excited about my going to Diet-

234

rich's room that you weren't going to ask any searching questions about my noble sacrifice.'

'I meant the whole thing was a risk. Your cover was paper-thin. You don't know a thing about Islamic art, do you?'

'That was my bad luck,' she said. 'Sotheby's, of all places! I couldn't have guessed that you people would know everything about the subject. It was good enough for the Embassy before you arrived. And I do know a little about it—enough to steer clear of the difficult questions.'

'Not enough to hold a conversation in Cyprus.'

She nodded, smiling. 'I wondered what I'd done wrong. Dealing is a con-game anyway. Anyone can say "hum" and "ha" if they're shown something beautiful. It seemed to be enough for working in Egypt—they're so keen to sell their surpluses that they welcomed me and never realised I didn't get very far with my negotiations.'

'Well, you won't be going back to Cairo.'

'Nor will you.'

She had a point there. I hadn't thought of it.

I said, 'You had a good run for your money.'

'Three years.'

It must have been a good time to operate in that part of the world. 'Always in the region?'

'Cairo, Tel Aviv, Beirut, Cyprus a lot. Up to Teheran.'

'Over the Caspian,' I said, 'if you got homesick.'

'If it was urgent. But it had to go wrong one day.'

'I hope the Moscow Narodny sees it like that.'

'They're being philosophical. And there's plenty of work for me in Europe. Serious work. The sort you do.'

'Surely not.'

'Oh, yes.' She saw the expression on my face and began to laugh. 'You still don't believe me! Come on, come and

235

join us and see for yourself—we do your sort of thing, you know, only we do it better!'

'Is that an offer?'

'You know it is...'

And that, I reckon, was the nearest the Moscow Narodny has ever come to recruiting a Thorne Reinhard man. We spent the rest of the day discussing the terms. They were all that a man could ask.

I said no.

She flew back to Moscow two days later. I went with her as far as Vienna and she kissed me goodbye in the transit lounge when they called the London flight. She had two hours to wait for Aeroflot so I bought her the *Wall Street Journal* and the *FT* and added *Connaissance des Arts* to help her set up a better cover next time.

Her eyes were wide and white and young and I could have sworn they were full of tears, but I couldn't stop and see, they were calling my flight for the last time.

<figure>⦿⦿⦿⦿⦿⦿⦿⦿⦿</figure> FORTY-SIX <figure>⦿⦿⦿⦿⦿⦿⦿⦿⦿</figure>

It was late summer in London and the *FT* Index had gone over the top again. The trees in St George's Square were as high as the Pyramids and twice as dusty and Sue was wearing Levis and looking more beautiful than any English girl has a right to when you consider what their mothers look like. Camden Passage was crowded with American tourists buying junk from anarchists in corduroy jackets. The poster shop had been raided by the police for obscenity and had won its case.

The flat was clean and cool and surprisingly quiet and

Sue let me sleep away the afternoon. She woke me because of *Philadelphia Story* at the NFT, which is worth a seventh visit except for the scene where Katharine Hepburn talks French which somehow spoils the effect. Afterwards we ate hunks of cheese and spiked them with malt whisky, neat, in the Mexican glasses, and I slept the night through and woke two hours early because my body hadn't noticed it was back from the Middle East.

The orange juice was cold and came from Haifa and Sue made the coffee twice as black as usual before she went off to the Office, looking innocent again in a grey dress with a white collar. The dry cleaner had found my suit at last, which was just what my morale needed—a dove-blue featherweight, too bright for Fredericks Place and to hell with them; a white shirt to show off the Aswan tan; a silk sling for my Aswan hand.

They had been having problems in the front hall in my absence: the lift had expired, this time probably for good. There had been a nasty takeover battle while I was away: the House had won, and New Court were furious. Some of the allegations put about by the losers had been too sharp for comfort and a couple of Labour backbenchers were saying silly things about the role of merchant banks and the duties of the Bank of England. Monica was on holiday and had sent me a postcard from Sidi Bou Said, down the railway from Carthage. Good luck to her. They had given me a temp with a cleavage and an aura of California Poppy who had spent three days reading Norah Lofts in paperback at her typewriter and asked me who I was when I tried to go through to my room. I sent her to Xerox the *Bank of Egypt Bulletin*.

Outside in the corridor I bumped into KK, who looked as if he'd willingly shake my hand—the bad one. 'Looking very fit,' he managed to say. We smiled insincerely

237

at each other. 'You must be very relieved everything worked out in the end,' he added. It was a strange way to refer to the goings-on at Aswan.

Condon was standing in Lord Magnus's anteroom, deep in conversation with Miss Spielter. He looked like a man just off a jet: rough, tired and overfed. His briefcase was sitting on the desk wearing a baggage stub which might have proved it.

I said, 'Have you been travelling too?' and, 'Where was it this time?' and caught a worried expression on Miss Spielter's face. Neither of them seemed to want to talk. I thought, Hell, I know the deal was botched but they might at least pretend they're glad I'm not strung up on a gibbet in Cairo.

Condon managed to ask, 'How's your hand?' and Miss Spielter remarked, 'I'm sure Jerusalem is frightfully hot just now,' which showed she knew what had been going on. So I left it at that. If the big chop was coming, they wouldn't be the ones to tell me. 'When do I tell all?' I asked Miss Spielter. Condon and she agreed I would be lunching upstairs. I went to write to Joe Larochelle. Perhaps McNamara had a job for me.

The House seemed half deserted. A handful of directors wandered into the dining room and chatted about yachts on the Aegean and the awkward business with the Bank.

They had one of the bright new boys from New York over for the vacation so they gave him the usual treatment—'Martini, sherry or tomato juice?'—but their hearts weren't in it. You're supposed to say sherry. The Yankee boy played too safe, said tomato juice and was written off. Even the disembodied hands behind the silver salvers had changed colour for the month of August.

Lord Magnus was remarkably, alarmingly benign. He came in with Condon, his arm round his shoulder, deep

238

in mutter and confabulation, and when they looked up and saw me it was clear they had been talking about me. At least the court-martial had my friends on the bench. But then, if I remembered, it was my friends whom I had let down. They called me to sit with them. KK took the seat on my right and I asked him to cut my lamb roast for me. Lord Magnus reminisced about Cabinet Ministers he had known who had broken bones in the course of their duties. They still hadn't bothered to ask me how I had done it.

I thought I'd better tell them, and did so in three minutes flat. 'Who was Dietrich?' asked Lord Magnus vaguely and Condon interrupted, 'He was associated with the girl. You remember, sir, he was shot shortly after Thomas had hit him.' Magnus raised an eyebrow, dropped the subject. 'And where is the girl?' The question seemed to be aimed at Condon but I chimed in.

'She's gone back to Moscow. She claims she's gone back to straight banking. The only thing I'm sure of is that she won't be staying in the Middle East.'

'Ah!' said Lord Magnus, with manifest pleasure. 'So we settled that little game for them.'

His gratification seemed rather strange. I said, 'She offered me a job.'

'Jolly good! Did you take it?'

I peered at Magnus. He wasn't smiling.

'I said I already had one.' I wondered whether it was true. Lord Magnus was in no hurry to tell me.

Condon said, as though he'd been poring over the files, 'There's one thing I still can't understand. Why is everyone so *patient* with the woman? She tries to murder Thomas and he can't wait to make excuses for her. The Narodny is meekly taking her back in Moscow. And you'd think the Russians would be flaming mad with her—just think of the session the Soviet Ambassador's had with the President, he's had to call in a Deputy Foreign Minister from Moscow specially to cool the Egyptians down—but no! They're shrugging like Frenchmen and trying to turn it all into a girl-guide jape.'

'She's involved in something that arises out of her double connection with the two sides,' I volunteered. 'Some sort of wider-range negotiations. She wouldn't tell me what.'

Lord Magnus cleared his throat vigorously to tell us he wanted to make a contribution. 'It is eminently simple,' he declared, and his expression was part complacency, that he could still inform his young men about the ways of the world, part surprise that we hadn't managed to inform ourselves more fully. 'There is only one important subject at issue between Tel Aviv and Moscow. The same one for twenty years. I'm speaking, of course, of the negotiations for the release of the Russian Jews. About three million of them. Some Israelis claim more. The Tal girl has been involved in these talks for a couple of years —or so my friends assure me.'

'Are you sure?'

'Of course I am sure.'

Condon said, 'The Chairman could be right.' Lord Magnus glared at him and he said hastily, 'Yes, of course that's it. The Soviet Jews are one of the priorities of all Israeli policy. With three million new immigrants—or even a portion of them—they could populate all the desert and go some way to compensating for their small size. It's the Russian secret weapon in the Middle East and all the Arab Governments know it. The Rumanians have let the Jews go to Israel. The Poles have kicked most of them out. Most Western Jews aren't interested in living in Israel, so there's only been a steady but small stream of immigrants recently. But if the Russians said yes in a big way it would be a flood.'

'The Russians have in fact quietly been releasing some of these people,' said Lord Magnus, with the same air of authority. 'Naturally, no one broadcasts the numbers too loudly for fear the door might be closed tight again. That's what your lady friend has been working at.'

I quibbled: 'Yes, that's all very well, but what on earth does one Jewish girl have to do with all this? She's just a banker. Or so I believe.'

I still believed her, I suppose. I suppose I'd forgiven her long ago. I knew I was being a sentimental fool, but for once I preferred it that way.

Lord Magnus was saying, as though to humour me, 'You spent a lot of time together?' He was looking smug.

I nodded.

'And she never told you who her uncle is?'

I shook my head.

Lord Magnus told me.

Who her uncle was.

After a minute, when I'd taken it in, I said, 'I give up.' The other directors were gossiping at the far end of the table, and KK had made his excuses and left. 'I give up! I've finished up bungling everything I tried to do. I've been played as a sucker, I admit it. I can never go back to the Middle East. I must be the laughing stock of the City. Even New York will know by now.'

'You could always join the Moscow Narodny,' said Condon.

I wondered why he was laughing. Then Lord Magnus began to chortle, his chins bouncing on his collar.

'I'm glad you find it so funny,' I said bitterly. 'It was all my fault, I always said an Egyptian issue was madness. Then when I tried to pull out of it you—yes, you Sir

—you made me go back and kept on about how important it was we should get into the developing world. I always knew it wouldn't work. Yet now you can all sit back in London and enjoy the joke...'

Lord Magnus had straightened his face again but the effort had told. Condon was grinning like an Indian babu.

My Chairman said, 'Guy, this must mean you haven't told him yet?'

Condon said, 'I thought you would want to, Sir.'

I said, 'Tell me *what*?'

They were still grinning at each other. I repeated the question, louder.

'My dear boy,' said Lord Magnus at last, and he would have embraced me if he hadn't been an Englishman. 'You don't understand. All is well! The Nile issue has been fixed and will be floated. It will be a great success for the House and you are the hero of the hour.'

I said, 'Just a minute...'

Condon said, 'It's true. I've just come back from Cairo for the second time in a week. Joe and I had a devil of a job to persuade them you didn't have a Jewish grandmother but they are so delighted that the money is still available despite all the Israelis' efforts they decided to let you go. They've even swallowed the loss of Mara.'

'That doesn't mean I'll be going back to Cairo?' I put in, hastily.

'No. You stay in the clear for the time being.'

I said, 'Tell me again. It's on? But how?'

Lord Magnus was getting bored so he called for the hramsa which was sent down specially every week from the Highlands. It's an obscure cheese made from wild garlic—a grim reminder that in a week or so the grouse would be arriving, smelling and scraggy, from his friends on the moors.

Condon was saying, with the patience that had got him his job and his £12,000 a year, 'We always knew there was something wrong with the Mara girl. How? Oh, the Chairman said she didn't look quite at home in Sotheby's. It was a hunch, both of us agreed. But we couldn't warn you, remember, because we needed to see what she was aiming for.'

'Thank you,' I murmured, waiting for more revelations. Another banker's hunch and I'd missed out on this one too. And been left to play the decoy duck.

He went on, 'We tried to trace her from the Israeli side through our friends in Tel Aviv but immediately got the sort of panicky denial which warned us something fishy was going on. Then you came back with your story about the arms deal and Dietrich and the tape recording and it began to look much too pat. But we still didn't know what was really going on so we decided to let you carry on.'

'And then you were damn' faint-hearted,' said Lord Magnus. I didn't have an answer to that one and braced myself for the rest of it—this was where I would discover whether he knew what I had done to kill the issue.

Condon had scarcely faltered. 'You were getting more and more depressed, Tom,' (he was giving me his warning stare, so I sat tight) 'and after you discovered the girl was a fraud you came back to tell the Chairman that you saw no point in going on. Right?'

I took my cue and nodded and he went smoothly on.

'The Chairman and I decided you were unduly pessimistic. We thought we could pull the cat out of the bag provided you could keep the girl out of the way and not let her smell a rat.'

'Which you did very well,' conceded Lord Magnus, poker-faced. I wondered whether Condon's mixed metaphors weren't giving his game away.

Condon rushed on. 'Joe Larochelle held the Cairo end tight and I did a quick round of the underwriters because we felt they needed a personal reassurance...' He gave me another of his stares.

I got the message. He had calmly ignored the message from me in Cairo, and had held the fort on his own. More than that, he had let me carry on, even when I went back into Egypt, under the impression I'd been on the dole. So why wasn't I furious with him? Because I had to admit he had protected me from my idiocies all the way through.

'We had a bit of trouble with the Foreign Office. They got very jittery about you.'

I said, 'Why didn't you tell me all this?'

'Because, my boy, you were much too useful to us playing it as an innocent,' said Lord Magnus brusquely. 'You'd only let the Egyptians get confused if you started to unravel it yourself. Remember, we couldn't be sure the Egyptians would stand firm all the way—the Minister was in a very shaky position. Most important of all, we didn't know what the Israelis—or the Russians—would do if they thought we were getting away with it. If they discovered they were losing they might have tried God knows what fiendish tricks! We weren't safe till the Egyptians had signed.'

Condon said, 'And even then we didn't want the faintest hint of trouble. We just couldn't risk any questions. It would make the issue price impossible. As it worked out, the Russians and the Israelis are both too embarrassed to want the truth to get out. Especially as neither of them wants to hear what the girl has been up to.'

'Mind you, she was always a dangerous creature,' said Lord Magnus reflectively. 'Just as well she got herself arrested.'

'I hope you didn't worry,' I said, getting as close to sarcasm as any Chairman will allow. 'They arrested me too. She made sure I was in it up to my neck. I might have been shot or tortured. And I nearly got killed when the Israelis arived.'

'Rubbish,' said Lord Magnus. 'You ought to have sat tight. I could always have got you released. Might have been a spot of discomfort but you certainly weren't in personal danger...'

'And what about Mara?'

Lord Magnus waved me down impatiently. 'She'd been playing a dangerous game. And what's worse, she'd been getting in our way too often. Anyhow the Russians wouldn't have given her up—she's too valuable, she was worth a couple of squadrons of MiGs. Her uncle would have bought her back. She's professional to her finger-tips.'

I didn't listen to the rest of it. I only caught the first two indignant sentences. I said, 'What do you mean? Mara told me in Jerusalem that she didn't know why she'd been arrested. How did the Egyptians cotton on to her? She was wondering who betrayed her. Yes, *who did*?'

' "Betrayed?" That's a dramatic word,' said Lord Magnus with distaste and a cold Ministerial stare. Condon was suddenly vastly uninterested, which wasn't in character. He isn't an incurious person. I thought about that, and toyed with my cheese knife, and then it came to me.

I said slowly, 'So she was right. She'd guessed.'

'She guessed precisely what?'

'That it was us.' I could see they knew exactly what I meant. But still, they paused.

Then, 'Yes, it *was* us, we did it,' snapped Condon. 'We told Joe what to tell them.' He started to explain, but gave up with a gesture which could have been helplessness but was more likely disgust.

I said, 'She guessed that we might have done it but she wasn't sure. She thought *I* had done it. In fact, she said I *would* have been able to do it—later. One day.' I looked across at Guy. 'When I'm like the rest of you. That's what she said.'

Lord Magnus heaved himself away from the table. 'I'm sorry about your hand,' he said. 'No, no coffee,' he added, which was strange because he always enjoyed the Colombian mocca from the filter machine.

He hesitated again. 'But never mind. Everybody's all right. Everybody's happy.' He propelled his bulk towards the door and paused to glower at the Lear drawing as though he was wondering whether he really liked it or not. 'Griegson's are going to be pretty sick about all this,' he growled with satisfaction as he went out.

Condon said, when Magnus had disappeared, 'I'm sorry! I'd have preferred you not to know. I won't say we really had to do it.'

'That's just as well,' I replied, feeling relief, anger, and the bitter aftertaste of too much knowledge.

He paused a long moment. 'Well ... Perhaps it was,' he said, and paused again as though waiting for me to press him, as though he wanted me to insist.

Suddenly I really began to understand. I turned to Condon, and said, 'You made it sound very easy just now when you told us how you charged about and reassured the underwriters. But no details?'

He shook his head. 'No details! Please. It would be a bore. For both of us. But try to realise how much it helped me for them to think you had actually smashed the issue. That was why I couldn't risk reassuring you. Sorry about that!'

I let him lead me towards the door. The other directors had long since taken their coffee and left, but the staff would not emerge from beyond the serving hatch until the last of us had gone. I stopped and said, 'Surely it wasn't just the underwriters who were your problem. It was Cairo. How could the Egyptians take you seriously, since they knew I had tried to scupper the issue? It needed more than Larochelle's charm surely.'

Condon grinned abruptly, though there was no humour in it. 'Yes, it needed rather more than charm.'

I went on, 'It needed proof—hard proof—that the House was on their side even if I appeared to have joined the Zionists.'

Condon said, 'Not proof, just a gesture,' and walked away down the hall.

'Like the girl,' I called after him.

He didn't turn round. 'She was in our way.' I heard him saying it quite clearly. He said it again—'She was in our way'—then rounded the corner.

I never knew whether he believed it. We never mentioned it again. And I don't think I ever got round to thanking him for the way he saved the Nile issue. And my professional neck.

That evening I remembered to thank Sue for the cable. She said, 'Don't mention it,' which was what her aunts had taught her to say, but when I produced her present from Jerusalem—a Hellenistic figurine—she began to say things her aunts had only dreamed of. I said, 'I needed a reminder from outside. The system was starting to get the better of my judgment.'

Later, she sat in her wingback chair flicking through one of the coffee table books her admirers were always giving her before she called it off. She said, so anyone but me would have thought it came out of the blue, 'What was she like?'

I asked, 'What was who like?'

'What was *she* like?'

'I don't know.'

'Don't be difficult.'

'No, I really don't know. I never had a chance to know.' I struggled to explain that Mara had gone out of my life so cleanly, like a body sliding under the sea, and I didn't understand why. Sue listened, carefully. 'She was—she was incomplete. For me. I mean, I knew her very well in some ways and yet I knew nothing about the rest of her; the real person.'

'Love her?'

'I'm not even sure I liked her.' There was a silence.

'Glad to be back?'

She was looking very small and slight in her big dark chair. Her accent didn't grate on me as it once did. I suppose she couldn't help it. The accent, I mean.

I said, 'Very glad.' And for a moment 1 knew I meant it.

But they tried to send me away again the day after next. Miss Spielter called me in and gave me her troubled-waters expression as I went into the Parlour. Lord Magnus was seated at a clean desk in a sea of discarded newspapers. There was a sheet of paper in front of him, liberally dashed with green ink. He was putting down the telephone as I went in.

'Ah!' he said. 'Thomas, I want you to go to Johannesburg.'

I groaned, so that he heard it. 'Not the West Vaal business again?'

'No, no. Something else. Very big. Very urgent.'

I took a deep breath.

For the first time in my life I said No. I couldn't face it, West Vaal or anything. The night flight is a killer and the alternative, the SAA Boeing round the perimeter of the continent, takes a lifetime. I said, 'Give me a break,' which sounded like TV drama. I added, 'I've got a broken hand,' and waved it at him. 'I can't sign my name let alone a cheque. I can scarcely do my buttons up. I'm tired. I need a holiday.' Which didn't mean eating *boerewors* at a *braaivleis* in Jo'burg.

So Condon went instead. He went that night, on the VC-10 through Nairobi, and when Sue and I left him at Heathrow we didn't know how soon I'd be down there with him. But that's another story...

There was a postcard on my desk in Fredericks Place the next morning. A gaudy façade of the Hermitage. Postmarked Leningrad. On the back it said:

Так не забудь, голубчик, место всегда твоё. Привет, Мара

There's one card Monica couldn't read. But then neither could I. What the hell was Mara up to this time? She knows I can't speak Russian. And God knows what the message says. And who on earth do I dare ask to translate it for me?